ALEX ROBINS

THE CITY OF MIST AND TEARS

MOTHERS OF SORROW BOOK 1

Cover Illustration by Andrew Maleski
Cover Layout by miblart
Maps and Interior Design by Alex Robins

ISBN 978-2-9588450-3-2 (paperback)
ISBN 978-2-9588450-4-9 (ebook)

Published by Bradypus Publishing
49380 Bellevigne en Layon
Dépôt Légal : décembre 2024

www.warofthetwelve.com

To all of those who read

The War of the Twelve

This one's for you

The City of Keselgraad

Hark, hark! the dogs do bark,

Beggars are coming to town

Some in rags, some in jags,

And some in velvet gowns.

PART ONE

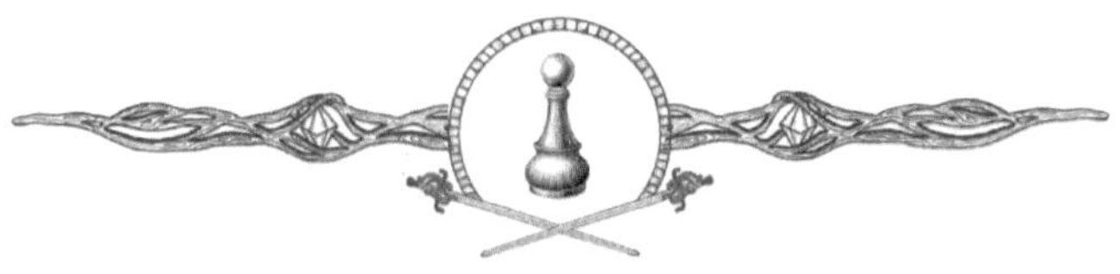

ONE
A CAGE OF LIES

"It has happened before, and it will happen again. Round and round in a never-ending circle; until the light fades and the stars fall from the sky. It would be madness to deny such inevitability. It would be madness to attempt to break the chains that bind us to this fate."

First Technologist Arniel Sin, The Time Before

IT ALL STARTED with the apple.

Roe first caught sight of it as he was weaving his way through the tightly packed market stalls, shadowing a potential mark. It drew his gaze like a glittering jewel, a splash of bright red against the muddy hues of brown and grey. Roe sensed a wetness on the tip of his tongue. He imagined what it would feel like to bite deep into that crimson-tinted flesh. To feel those sweet, sticky juices dribble down his throat.

Swallowing a mouthful of saliva, Roe abandoned his victim to the bustling crowds and took a tentative step towards the ramshackle stall.

"What are you doing?"

He felt spindly fingers wrap around his arm and turned to see Ant staring at him in panic. The young boy's eyes were bulging so far from their sockets that Roe half-expected them to pop out of his friend's grubby face and spatter all over his battered leather shoes.

"It's an *apple*, Ant. And not one of the maggot-infested, half-rotten husks that sometimes find their way down here from the upper levels. It's … red and *ripe*. Mother's Grace, I've never seen anything so perfect."

"Aye, I'm not blind. Nor am I an idiot. I recognise that stall. It's one of Pearlton's."

"That crusty old dandy? He wears more makeup than half the poxes! Strutting around the Slums like he owns the place, trying to convince anyone who'll listen that he shares blood ties with one of the Noble Houses. He's harmless."

Ant sniffed and released his grip. The crowd around them was thinning as the light dimmed, and late afternoon became dusk.

"He's anything but. Under that perfumed veneer and all those frilly cuffs hides a cold-hearted bastard. He'd have never survived down here otherwise. Slit plenty of throats in his time, I'd wager. Or had them slit, so as not to dirty those dainty little hands."

"That doesn't sound so bad," Roe replied absently, brushing a lock of curly black hair from his face. He looked beyond the jumble of stalls towards the towering city wall that loomed over the market like a gargantuan cliff face. "We could wait until dark. Avoid the patrols. If we managed to get up onto the roof of one of those houses there, we'd only have eight or nine feet to climb up to the ramparts, then all we'd need to do is—"

"*We?* You have got to be joking. There's no way I'm taking part in any of this." Ant gestured skywards with a skinny arm. "Sun's nearly gone. That means Krabbon will be expecting us back soon. With *tribute*. You know what'll happen if we return empty-handed. The birchwood kiss. Do you really want to eat standing up for a week?"

"Suit yourself. It'll be harder without a lure, but I can make it work."

"You're mad," Ant murmured, shaking his head. "All this for an apple. Why do you always have to be so reckless?"

"Why do you always have to be such a coward?"

"It's not cowardice. It's plain good sense. I—" he stopped. "I'm not going to lose any more of my sanity arguing with you. Do as you please. As for me, the chapel of the Mother will be opening for evening mass. I'll try my luck there. Just … just be careful, will you?"

"Of course." Roe pointed to the mouth of a nearby alleyway. "That's where you'll find me if you change your mind."

"I won't. And you can expect me to laugh each and every time Krabbon's stick hits your scrawny buttocks."

Roe flashed an easy smile that split his broad face. "My arse will be raw, but my lips will have tasted paradise."

Ant sighed and turned away. Roe watched his friend leave for a moment, then entered the dingy alley, found a spot between two mouldering sacks of refuse, and settled down to wait. He rubbed the worst of the dirt off his flat nose, tilted his head back, and stared up at the colossal, man-made mountain that was the city of Keselgraad.

Over half-a-mile high from the tip of the jewelled steeple of the Church of the Mother to the mud-clogged streets of the Slums, Keselgraad resembled an impossibly large termite hill; its grimy, weathered walls bristling with balconies, gantries, spires, and towers. Narrow alleyways wormed through its various levels, forming a labyrinthian network that culminated in a spiralling central staircase and wrought-iron elevator so prohibitively expensive that it was only ever used by members of the Noble Houses or their proxies.

There was money to be made taking messages up and down those vertiginous stairs; missives and deliveries sent from the sweltering workshops and forges of the lower levels to the bakeries, inns, slaughterhouses, and shops above. From there, the staircase climbed ever higher, past fields of wheat and orchards of fruit, twisting like a corkscrew, round and round until it reached the fortified mansions of the Noble Quarters.

Roe had never seen those lofty peaks, but he had heard the rumours. There were said to be buildings the size of warehouses used only for theatre and dancing. Gas lamps that functioned day and night, bathing the wide avenues in perpetual light. Unsalted meat and fresh vegetables, unrationed. Brightly coloured robes and dresses, worn once or twice and then discarded. And, perhaps most importantly, access to the Church of the Mother, the capstone that held the entire city together; an architectural masterpiece of sculpted columns, stained-glass windows, and marble floors. It was the Church and the shining amethysts of its steeple that kept them all safe from harm.

It was the Church that protected them from the Mists.

Roe suppressed a shudder. Thinking of the Mists always sent a shiver down his spine. He pushed the nightmarish images from his mind, exhaled slowly to calm his beating heart, and peered out from his hiding spot. The sun had disappeared behind the colossal city wall that encircled the lower levels of Keselgraad in its cold embrace, abandoning the marketplace to the encroaching darkness. Shadows writhed among the rickety stalls, twisting the tattered awnings into sinister shapes.

"Mother keep me," Roe whispered. Perhaps Ant was right. Perhaps he was being a *tad* too reckless.

A rusty pot clanged onto the cobbles behind him, making him squeak in panic. He spun on his heel, his dark brown eyes straining to pierce the gloom at the far end of the alley.

"Who ... who's there?" he challenged, fighting to keep the fear from his voice. "St ... stay back. Don't come any closer! I ... I have a knife!"

"No, you don't."

Ant dropped down from the window ledge, a wide grin stretching his dirty cheeks.

"That must have been the most pathetic thing I've seen all day."

"Ant! I knew you'd come back to help me."

"Actually, I was hoping to talk you out of it. Krabbon was furious to learn you were out after curfew. That vein on his forehead was throbbing so much that I thought it was going to burst."

"Maybe I should save him a piece of the apple."

"Roe ..."

"A small piece, mind you. We're the ones who'll be doing all the work."

"I'm not going to be able to dissuade you from this, am I?"

Roe sucked his lower lip, wondering how he could explain to his friend what he felt. "It's ..." he began. "It's not just about the apple. It's about what it represents. It's about … experiencing another life – a *better* life – even if it's only for the slimmest of moments. When I bite down on that piece of fruit, I'm going to close my eyes and imagine myself in one of those verdant green parks far above our heads. Sitting on a marble bench, looking out over the Mists, my ears filled with birdsong and the bubbling of the crystalline fountains. I won't be down here in the Slums with holes in my boots and Krabbon's foul breath on my back. I'll have escaped. Escaped this terrible place. That's what'll make it worth it. Even if it's only for a single breath."

Ant's grin slipped. "Aye," he answered with a touch of sadness. "I understand. Tell me what you want me to do."

Roe cleared his throat. "The stall will be guarded, I'm sure of it. No way will Pearlton leave it unprotected. You'll have to cause a distraction."

"Oh, I'm good at that. Which one do you want? The abandoned orphan? The drunken rich boy? The seductive gigolo?"

"I don't care."

"Right." Ant straightened his tattered tunic and patted down his greasy hair. "Lead on."

They crept out of the alley into the soft stillness of the market, past tarpaulin-covered boxes and large chests wrapped in corroded chains. A trio of rats scampered across their path, the leader holding a chunk of mouldy rye bread in its jaws. Old wooden posts creaked. Pearlton's stall was less than fifteen feet away, a squat black square near the base of the city wall.

Roe frowned. "Where are they?"

"Hmmm?"

"The guards. The patrols. It looks empty."

"Must have gone for a piss," Ant smirked. "Lucky for us. And that perfumed pamperer hasn't even chained the place up."

"I don't know. Something doesn't feel right."

"Mists, you're the one who pulled me into this, remember? You can't be getting cold feet now!"

Roe could feel a dryness in his mouth. His tongue was heavy and swollen against his cheek. "I'll … I'll go and scout it out. You stay here."

He edged forwards, his head whipping left and right like a snake, his eyes roaming the rows of silent stalls. He was so intent on searching the shadows for the missing watchmen that he failed to see the crumpled burlap sack blocking his path and leaking liquid onto the cobbles. Roe cursed as his shoes landed in the small glistening puddle with a soft squelch. He looked down to see that the leather was spattered with something red. Blood.

He stretched out a trembling hand and lifted a corner of the sack. Pearlton's dead face stared back at him with glazed eyes, pasty-white cheeks stark in the twilight, and his thin lips pulled tight in a final rictus. His throat had been expertly cut; a line of bright crimson from which trickled a dozen gory rivulets, dribbling down his wrinkled neck to stain his frilly ruff.

Like pearlescent drops of water on the skin of an apple.

"Unfortunate."

The voice was slightly muffled, calm and monotone.

Roe rose in time to see a tall figure emerge from behind the stall. It wore waxed linen robes, a flat wide-brimmed leather hat and long gloves that reached from fingertip to elbow. The face was completely covered by an ivory-coloured mask shaped like a bird, with circular, glass-filled eyelets and a viciously hooked beak.

A warden. A custodian of Keselgraad, charged with protecting the city from threats both without and within. They were the only ones who could leave the sanctity of the Mother's light and venture forth into the Mists. The only ones who had any knowledge of what lay beyond the walls. The wardens were one of the richest and most power-ful guilds in all of Keselgraad, answering only to the Keeper of the Peace himself. So, what was one of them doing down here in the dirt and muck of the Slums?

The man cocked his head, a gesture made all the more avian by his beaked mask. "You were not meant to see this."

Roe scrambled backwards, dragging his rump through the pool of blood. The warden stalked after him, slow and methodical.

"I cannot let you live, I'm afraid. It will lead to rumours. And rumours lead to questions. *Unwanted* questions." He drew a dagger from his belt, its tapering blade needle-thin. "You will not feel any pain. I am very good at what I do."

A shape bounded out of the darkness and slammed into the arm holding the weapon. Both figures tumbled to the ground in a maelstrom of flailing limbs. Ant was first to emerge, his face flushed red.

"RUN!" he screamed just as a gloved hand snaked out and tried to grab him. He dodged away, catching himself on the edge of a nearby stall. His cry of pain cut through Roe's panicked mind.

"The wall!" he shouted to Ant, springing to his feet. "Get to the wall!"

The warden was rising, his ivory mask askew, his

wide-brimmed hat scuffed and dented. He jerked the hooked beak back into place.

"Troublesome."

He bent to pick up his dagger, its silvery surface gleaming in the twilight. Behind him, Ant and Roe had reached the base of the wall.

"There!"

A two-wheeled rickshaw loaded with crates had been left next to one of the many buildings pressed up against the stone facade. Roe used the spokes and stacked boxes to reach the tiled roof then held out a sweaty hand to drag Ant up there with him.

"Why isn't he following us?" the boy asked, risking a glance back over his shoulder.

"I'm not sure, maybe—"

Roe heard the unmistakable twang of a string releasing and threw himself flat. Something buzzed angrily overhead and ricocheted off the roof, inches from his face.

"Crossbow," Ant gasped. "We're finished."

"He has to reload. Up onto the ramparts. Quickly!"

Roe studied the massive slabs of worn granite that made up the wall. Keselgraad's protective barrier was supposedly the oldest structure in the city, its venerable sides cracked and marked from centuries of enduring vigilance. Pockmarks dotted its surface like miniature craters. Crumbling mortar revealed finger-wide gaps. Handholds too small for a fully grown man, perhaps, but for two boys …

He began to climb, trying to push all other thoughts from his mind.

Damn the Mists, what an idiot he had been. All of this for an apple.

A second bolt thunked into a moss-covered chunk of stone near his hand, sending up a shower of razor-sharp shards. One cut through the flesh of his right cheek. Blood dribbled down his face into his mouth. He could taste its salty tang on his tongue.

With a cry of desperation, Roe quickened his pace, covering the last few feet in a matter of moments before hauling himself up onto the ramparts. He lay there, panting, the slick paving digging into his back, the hive-shaped monstrosity that was Keselgraad rising above him like a claw reaching from the earth to grasp at the stars.

Ant collapsed beside him in a trembling bundle of sweat and fear, his breath escaping from his body in short, rattling gasps. "I … I don't think he's following us."

Roe waited for the pounding in his chest to slow before replying. "I scraped the skin off my knuckles trying to fit my hand into some of those holds. He'll have to find another way up." He struggled into a sitting position, wrapping his arms around his knees, and looked out beyond the wall, feeling a familiar tingling in his spine as he did so. "Mother's Grace," he breathed. "Have you ever been this close?"

"Close to what?"

"The Mists."

The top of the wall was lacking any sort of defensive structure. No parapets or crenellations. No towers, bulwarks, arrow slits, or machicolations. All would be useless against the enemy that it had been built to keep out.

The Mists.

They filled Roe's vision; a rolling, boiling sea of milky-white, as if the clouds had fallen from the heavens to smother the lands below. They stretched as far as the distant horizon, dense and opaque, completely obscuring whatever might lie beneath their pallid veil.

The wind buffeted the rippling surface, creating waves and currents, tugging at loose tendrils to send them writhing upwards like smoke from a cooking fire. Roe knew that he could walk the entire length of the wall without seeing any change. The Mists encircled Keselgraad in their crushing embrace.

And their touch was death.

"There is a sort of beauty to them, don't you think?" Ant asked softly, his gaze following the hypnotic swirls. "They look so … peaceful."

"Dangerous, you mean," Roe corrected. The air was chill and damp on top of the wall. Goosebumps prickled along his bare forearms. "Come on. Let's find a place to climb back down."

"Have you ever seen anyone taken by the Mists?"

"What? No, but Krabbon told us of a—"

"I'm not talking about rumours and hearsay; I'm talking about witnessing something with your own two eyes."

"I …"

"Exactly." Ant half-nodded. He rose to his feet and took a step towards the edge of the paved walkway. "Maybe it's just falsehoods spread by the wardens to keep us all imprisoned here in the Slums. A cage. A cage of lies."

Another step.

"Ant, we can't stay here …"

"Wait. Listen. What if that's all it is? A deception? We scaled the outside of the wall easily enough so what's to stop us from climbing down the other side? Away from the stinging kiss of Krabbon's stick and that piss-soaked pile of straw we call a bed. Together, we could—"

The stone had been worn smooth by erosion. Made slippery and wet by its proximity to the Mists. Ant's shoe skidded, his ankle cracked, and suddenly he was tumbling off the edge of the walkway.

Roe leapt after him with a shout, catching hold of his friend's wrist just as it was about to disappear from sight.

"Mother keep me!" he cried as fresh agony exploded along his lower back. "Ant. ANT!"

"P … pull me back up!"

"I can't do it by myself, Ant. You're too heavy. Help me! Look for a handhold."

"My ankle. My Mist-spawned ankle. It's twisted or broken or something. The pain … it's … it's as if my whole leg is on fire!"

Roe felt his grip loosening, weakened by his own sweat and moisture from the Mists. He risked a glance over the edge and saw Ant dangling from his arm, his eyes filled with tears.

"I'm sorry," the boy moaned. "I'm sorry, all right? I should never have doubted anything. Don't leave me! Please!"

Roe cursed and pulled as hard as he dared, feeling his spine tremble from the effort. "It's no use. You have to find a way to push yourself up. Hurry! I don't know how much longer I can hold you!"

Ant wailed back at him, his feet scrabbling uselessly against the wall. A tentacular strand brushed against his thigh; a slow, languid motion. A caress.

Ant screamed.

More semi-transparent tendrils wrapped around the

boy's legs, spiralling around and around the naked flesh, creeping steadily upwards like vines. The skin beneath began to bubble and redden. It appeared to stretch, becoming smooth and shiny.

Like an apple.

Then, with a sickening tearing sound, it ruptured, revealing a ruin of bloody muscle and pulsing veins. Yellowish tendons wriggled helplessly. Pockets of glistening fat steamed and popped.

Ant had fallen silent, his mouth still cranked open in a silent cry of terror, his slowly dissolving cheeks wet with tears. The Mists wormed up his dying body to pour over his lips and down into his throat.

Roe watched in horror, unable to avert his gaze, as his friend was turned into an unrecognisable mess of red meat, twitching and jittering as his dying muscles spasmed one last time.

But the Mists were not yet sated. An inquisitive thread slithered unhurriedly up the remains of Ant's left arm. Towards the top of the wall.

Towards Roe.

He stared at it in morbid fascination.

Let go.

His fingers refused to obey. The Mists were inches from his skin, leaving a trail of slimy red in their wake.

Let go!

His thumb trembled, then his forefinger, until finally, his grip loosened enough for Ant's dead hand to slip through the gap.

The corpse fell without a sound, swallowed by the boiling sea of white and grey.

Roe howled in frustration and grief.

And, far above, the amethysts of the Church of the Mother twinkled like frozen tears.

TWO
MYSTERIES AND MIRRORS

"We grieve for those who are lost, but we also grieve for ourselves. For we are condemned to follow in their footsteps. That is our unescapable reality. The more we fight it, the more difficult it will become. And only by accepting that fact will we find the strength to live out these final precious moments in peace and dignity."

First Technologist Arniel Sin, *The Time Before*

JETHRO SPRITT HAD been dead for days.

His wasted body lay forlornly on an old straw mattress, his lifeless eyes fixed on the ceiling. A small dribble of vomit had trickled from his half-open mouth and congealed on the sheet beside his head. The nauseating stench of rot permeated every corner of the poky living space; a vile concoction of bile, faeces, and slowly decaying flesh.

"Mother keep me," Captain Aldin Pine grumbled, his voice slightly muffled by the damp cloth he had wrapped around his nose and mouth. The chunk of old rye bread and half-cup of mead that he had had for breakfast churned in his stomach, and he swallowed with a grimace.

"Neighbours found him," Selene remarked, her lithe form a dark silhouette in the open doorway. She was staring at him mischievously, her green eyes sparkling under a tangle of curly copper locks that matched the metallic sheen of her watchman's breastplate.

"Uh-huh."

"Or rather, they *smelt* him. Walls here are so thin that the air pretty much slips right through. Would you like a bucket?"

Pine glared. "Stop trying to be clever. Get your arse in here and process the scene."

"*Process the scene*? Really? Poor man's just choked on an olive pit or something, Captain."

"And I suppose you can tell that from where you're standing?"

"Well …"

"Inside, Watchman."

Selene rolled her eyes and stepped into the dingy interior. She wrinkled her freckled nose slightly, much to Pine's satisfaction. "Mists."

"Not so smarmy, now, are we?"

She wasn't listening. Her gaze swept over the cramped room, pausing as it alighted on its meagre contents: a large chest full of clothes, a shoddily constructed mushroom-shaped table and stool, a lopsided shelf sagging under the weight of a haunch of salted pork, and a pair of leather boots in the corner by the door.

"No mud on the boots," she murmured, half to herself. "It was raining all day, yesterday. The road outside would have been covered in muck."

"He could have cleaned them."

"With what? His fingers?" She bent down and brushed her hand against the soles. "They're not even damp. There's no fireplace here; the leather would have taken a while to dry."

Pine nodded. "Good. What else?"

"The candle," she said, pointing at the table. "It's burnt down to a stub. That piece of wax is the most expensive thing here; he would never have let it run down on purpose. Which means that he was either already dead or far too weak to snuff it out."

"Aye. Why did you say it was the most expensive thing here?"

"Pretty sure it's beeswax." Selene held her auburn curls back from her face and leant close to sniff the candle. "No smell of old meat. No flies or pieces of straw. It's not tallow, Captain. Mother keep me, how did Spritt get his hands on a proper candle? Even you can't afford one of these!"

"If he didn't buy it, then it was either stolen or a gift. We'll interview the chandlers, see if any of their stock's gone missing recently."

Selene's eyebrows scrunched together, and her lips formed a familiar pout. The one she always made when she wasn't happy. Pine watched her silently. There were two types of people who signed up for the Keselgraad Watch. Those who genuinely cared about keeping the city and its citizens safe … and those who ended up there by default: the drifters, the loners; men looking to either escape their past or avoid their future. Selene was most definitely one of the former, a product of the upper levels, the daughter of a distant cousin to a member of House Eckelston. She was well-mannered, educated, and, if her letter of recommendation was to be believed, with a reputation as shiny and clean as her gleaming breastplate.

Pine had no idea what had spurred the young woman's decision to leave the comfort of the Noble Quarter's gaslit streets and rolling green parks for the grimy, refuse-strewn alleys of the lower levels, and he probably never would. Every watchman had his own bag of secrets, some fuller than others. There was an unspoken rule to leave those drawstrings firmly knotted.

Perhaps Selene's presence here was just a fad. A bet between bored socialites. A way for the daughter of a Noble to slip into the shoes of a lower-class citizen and experience life in the Slums for a time before returning to her marble mansions and gilded theatres. Pine didn't care. In the six months since her arrival, Selene had become a better watchman than most of the others: surly veterans who spent more time in the local taverns than patrolling the streets. It was … refreshing.

Pine studied her now, watching her run her hands over the dead man's body, searching for hidden pockets sewn into his tunic. He looked down at his own palms, the flesh marred by hundreds of tiny white flecks; a myriad of old scars that peppered his skin like snow. The same scars that dotted his face, from the roots of his greying hair down to his stubbly chin. He rubbed absently at one of the marks as if the simple gesture would make it disappear.

Every watchman has his own bag of secrets.

Fate and fortune.

"Captain?"

He glanced up to see Selene staring at him expectantly. "Hmm?"

"Mists, have you not been listening to anything I've been saying?"

"I was gathering my thoughts."

"I hear that's something old people do a lot."

Pine took a deep breath, then immediately regretted it as his lungs filled with the smell of decay. He coughed and flicked his thumb at the pallid corpse.

"The body, Watchman."

"Nothing on him. No other visible wounds or bruises."

"Did you check his nails?"

"Dirty and chipped, but not broken. No blood." She reached up to finger the silver chain of her necklace. "No sign of aggression, Captain. Poor man must have just sat down for his evening meal and choked to death on a morsel of salted ham."

Pine smiled. "Right. So, where's the food?"

"What?"

"The table's empty, Watchman. Where's the food he choked on?"

"Maybe he …"

"Cleared everything away while suffocating on his own vomit?"

The pout became more pronounced. Selene didn't like to be wrong.

"I suppose you've come to another conclusion?"

"You have an excellent eye," Pine said, coming to stand beside her. "Far better than mine. But there's one thing where I still have a slight edge over you, and that's experience. Look at his mouth."

She squinted. "There's some redness. A rash, maybe."

"I've seen that before. Must have been seven or eight years ago, before I made captain. A butcher called the Watch when he found his wife dead in their bed one morning. The coroner cut her open and discovered that she was all black and rotten inside. Turns out her husband had been slipping poison into her food."

"Poison? Are you trying to tell me that Spritt was *poisoned*?"

Pine shrugged. "I'll get the rickshaw to come and take the body back to the Stables. It pays to be thorough."

He coughed again. The churning in his stomach had become a tempestuous sea. He could taste something hot and acidic in the back of his throat. "Come on. I don't think we'll find anything else here. If we leave now, we should have enough time to make it down to the jeweller's district and back before nightfall."

"Why in all the Mists do we need to climb all the way down there?"

"You missed the marks on his hands. They're acid burns. Spritt must have worked with metal. Engraving, etching, lithography. It's a rare profession. Shouldn't be too hard to find his atelier."

Pine stepped back outside, cursing as the tip of his scabbard caught on the doorframe. The pommel dug into his side, just under the breastplate. He tugged at his belt. The straight-edged officer's blade had saved his life more than once, but he still hated it. Just like he hated the curved cuirass that somehow still chafed his shoulders even after having worn the thing for ten long years.

"Air's good today," Selene remarked from somewhere behind his left shoulder. "You can almost see the wheat fields."

On the opposite side of the street, a row of decrepit single-storey buildings leant against one another like drunken friends, their moss-covered roofs and fissured walls a grim portent of imminent collapse. There were hundreds of similar filthy, run-down houses scattered all over Keselgraad, especially on this level, too close to the workshops to avoid the oily black smoke that belched from their chimneys day and night.

Above, the city continued its vertical climb. The next two tiers were clearly visible; more spartan dwellings perched along their outer rim, some boasting terraces or balconies that jutted out from their weathered facades, others with chipped wooden shutters or tiny glassless windows. Shabby tunics flapped from a couple of washing lines strung between gaps in the houses, ash and soot seeping into the fabric as they dried.

And beyond, just under the shroud of slate-grey clouds, a splash of colour, a scintillating curtain of golden yellow that rippled ever so slightly. Thousands of stalks of wheat, arguably more valuable than anything Spritt or his fellow jewellers would ever make. The lifeblood of Keselgraad. The fields of the agricultural levels and the glittering steeple of the Church of the Mother were the only reasons that the city's inhabitants still lived while so many others had perished.

"Looks ready to harvest," Pine remarked as he removed his mask. The ebb and flow of the flaxen stems was strangely relaxing. He felt the nausea gripping his throat and stomach begin to release its stifling hold.

"Damned if I know," Selene snapped, pulling the door shut with a clang. "I'm no farmer."

"Not much of a conversationalist, either."

Her head shot round, a barbed retort on her lips, then her expression softened. "I'm sorry, you're right. Bad night."

"Everything all ri—"

"Just some things I'm having to work through."

Pine knew not to press any further. "Central staircase should be a hundred feet or so to the left." He turned just as a bright white flash appeared on the edge of his vision. Light shining off one of the large mirrors placed at strategic points all along the level to redirect the sunlight.

"Hmmm," he muttered.

"You've got that squiggly line on your forehead," Selene remarked. "You're thinking."

"I am. I'm hoping I might have just found a witness."

"Mother keep me, really? Who?"

"Someone so ubiquitous that we often forget they even exist. Follow me."

He set off down the street, mud squelching under his leather boots as he settled into the leisurely pace he had perfected over his many years patrolling the neighbourhoods of Keselgraad. The cobbled road soon joined a half-dozen others to form a small courtyard, at the centre of which stood a stone plinth topped by an oval-shaped mirror roughly seven feet wide. Its copper frame was attached to a series of gears and levers that allowed the reflective glass to be rotated along different axes. A man wearing a thick leather apron and gloves was kneeling beside one of the brass cogs, his hammer rising and falling as he pounded the metal.

"The mirrormen," Pine said with no small amount of satisfaction. "Our city's unsung heroes. Did you know that there are more mirrormen than lamplighters now? Half of Keselgraad would be plunged into darkness without them there to tame the sun's rays."

Selene raised a sceptical eyebrow. "Lounging around all

day, greasing the occasional axle? Doesn't sound very heroic to me."

"Exactly!" Pine exclaimed. "*All day*. With a near-perfect view of the surrounding streets."

"Including Spritt's house," Selene admitted begrudgingly. "Not bad, Captain. Not bad at all."

Pine twirled his wrist and bent as low as his breastplate would allow, then cupped his hand to his mouth and called up to the mirrorman who was still focusing on his work.

"You up there! A moment of your time? We have a few questions …"

The banging continued unabated, echoing off the ramshackle houses that bordered the square.

Pine tried again. "KESELGRAAD CITY WATCH!"

The mirrorman leapt to his feet with a yelp, twisted round, and loosed his hammer straight at Pine. The improvised missile whistled through the air and thunked into his bronze breastplate with enough force to dent the metal. Pine reeled backwards and would have fallen if Selene had not been there to steady him.

"Mists," he snarled as the mirrorman bolted off down one of the side streets. "I hate being right. After him!"

And drawing their swords, the two watchmen set off in pursuit.

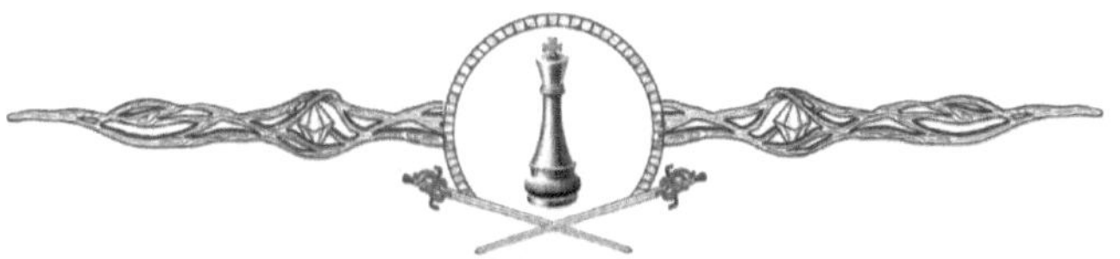

THREE
THE KEEPERS OF KESELGRAAD

"The Uprising? Worst thing that ever happened to us. All that pain and death just so we could replace one unhinged despot by an entire gang of 'em! And yeah, the King bled us dry, but at least he was upfront about it. This new Council is all smoke and mirrors. They pat us on the head with one hand while stabbing us in the back with the other."

Fletch, Barkeep of the Dripping Bucket, 823rd Year of the Mother

L ORD MATELLAS THANE twisted his head and gave a soft tut of disapproval. The servant had used far too much starch to stiffen the raised collar of his dress shirt and now the corners dug painfully into his neck like the fangs of a serpent whenever he moved. Damned man took no pride in his work. Thane would need to find a suitable punishment. Two lashes of the whip, perhaps, just enough to restore some sense of discipline.

He selected a burgundy waistcoat with engraved silver buttons and a long overcoat of midnight blue, examining his lean frame in the mirror as he readjusted the cuffs. Stony eyes stared back at him from the depths of a patrician face that was all hard edges, from its bony cheeks to its square-cut jaw. The close-cropped grey hair and the faint wrinkles that pulled at the corners of his thin lips betrayed his age, yet his gaze had lost nothing of its intensity. Firm and uncompromising.

Thane gave his reflection a curt nod, picked up a metal pin from the dressing table, and attached it to his left lapel. The pin was his badge of office: a diamond-shaped shield embossed with the heraldry of Keselgraad. The Keeper of the Peace. Protector of the City. Commander of the Watch.

He left the sanctity of his bedroom and made his way down the curved marble staircase to the main hall where a servant was waiting for him, holding his cane and gloves. Thane took them without a second glance and snapped his fingers to let the man know he was ready to leave. The front door was made of heavy oak reinforced with strips of iron and required significant time and effort to be dragged open.

Thane tapped his booted foot impatiently. Too long. Far too long. Had his entire household become prone to indolence? A misstep he would correct at the earliest opportunity.

The gap finally became wide enough to allow him passage. He stepped through with a scowl into the early morning air. The sky had not yet lost its pinkish hue. The rising sun was hidden somewhere behind the imposing spire of the Church of the Mother, its auroral light enveloping the myriad twinkling amethysts in a soft caress. The Church was the heart and soul of the city's faith; the only building to grace the topmost level. It sat proud and alone, forming the needle-sharp peak of the monstrous mountain that was Keselgraad.

Thane's mansion was situated just below, as close as possible to the summit. It was an honour shared among the Noble Houses that formed the Keepers Council, placing them above all others save for the Mother herself. Each estate was located on one of the cardinal axes, equidistant from the central shaft with its spiralling stairs and elevator. The complex mechanisms that enabled the lift to function were housed in a long, rectangular structure further down the street; the creaking of its pulleys and the metallic thuds of its counterweights producing a near-constant background hum that most would find distracting. Thane, who had lived in the shadow of the Church of the Mother for over fifty years, no longer heard it.

A couple of lamplighters sauntered into view, chatting amicably to each other. They both caught sight of Thane almost simultaneously, their smiles falling from their faces in the blink of an eye. He watched them pass by, their heads bowed.

You fear me. Yet, I am your saviour. If only you knew. If only you knew all I do to keep you alive.

The older lamplighter reached the gaslight and used his hooked pole to open the small glass window that contained the flame and the lever that would cut off the fuel supply. Thane studied him as he expertly manoeuvred the curved end into place and gave a sharp tug. The flickering light sputtered and died.

That is what will happen if I fail. Keselgraad will be snuffed out.

Extinguished.

As if in response to his sombre thoughts, the four bells of the Church of the Mother began to toll, summoning him to morning mass. Only a hundred feet or so separated his mansion from the wide flight of steps that led up to the highest level, now slowly filling with Keselgraad's social elite as they emerged from the elevator or staggered from the central stairwell, their chests heaving and faces beetroot red.

Thane steeled himself as he strode to meet them. Sycophants. Leeches. A host of snivelling, conniving bloodsuckers, no better than the cheats and thieves that populated the lower levels. All believing themselves more deserving of his attention than the others. He despised them. No spine. No ambition. Bickering over petty responsibilities. If it were up to him, he would gift every single one to the Mists.

Suddenly, he was among them, assailed by floral perfumes and garish garments.

"My Lord," the closest courtesan crooned, her ample bosom threatening to spill from her tightly laced corset. "What a pleasure it is to have you join us."

"Indeed," he replied through clenched teeth, searching for an escape route.

"We have still not heard back from the City Watch, my Lord," the woman continued. Her powdered wig was slightly askew, uncovering a few locks of greasy black hair.

"I'm sure Captain Pine is fully committed to—"

"There are criminals running amok, my Lord. *Criminals!* How can we sleep safe in our beds when—"

"Of course," Thane agreed, spying a gap between two portly Nobles. He darted away, taking the steps two at a time, his cane and boots tapping the marble like the rhythmic beating of a drum. The surprised twittering of the petitioners faded away as he reached the top.

A small patch of grass was all that separated him from the majestic entrance to the Church of the Mother. Previous Council members glared down at him from carved pedestals, many of his own ancestors among them, clutching scrolls, swords, and sceptres in their lifeless hands. The immense double doors were framed by a series of arches, each inscribed with part of the Mother's prayer. And above the porch, surrounded by more statues depicting men and women with their hands raised in supplication, sparkled a window in the form of a rose in full bloom; the reds and purples of its stained glass mimicking the jewelled amethysts set into the roof of the spire that pierced the dawn sky overhead.

It was said that the Church of the Mother was the very first edifice that the city's founders had begun to build and the very last they had finished. A thousand labourers toiled for untold years in the hope of creating the perfect expression of the Mother's beauty and the perfect residence for those who dedicated their lives to her service: the nuns of the Mater Sorores.

Even the patch of grass beneath Thane's feet was a sign of the Church's prosperity. Keselgraad was a finite space with no room for expansion. As such, every inch of land had to be exploited efficiently. Every structure had a predetermined purpose. Places such as the small park on the thirty-fourth level existed for a reason: the bark, sap, wood, and fruit from its trees were harvested. Fish swam in its trio of freshwater ponds. Its flowers were used for perfumes and salves. The immaculately cut stretch of vibrant green, however, was arguably the only site in the entire city that served no specific function. A blatant reminder to all who walked upon it that the Mater Sorores were not bound by the rules of the Council.

Thane hated the very sight of it. He dug his heels in as best he could as he crossed over, leaving great gouges in the earth that would need to be tended to. The doors of the

Church swung open at his approach, each held by a nun, their hair and faces partially obscured by white wimples.

"The Mother welcomes you."

Thane didn't reply, his long strides carrying him swiftly down the nave to the frontmost pew and the cushioned seat that was reserved for the Keeper of the Peace. The altar had already been decorated for morning mass with golden chalices and jewelled candles displayed on a velvet cloth. Beyond, dominating the far wall, a magnificent stained-glass window depicted the smiling form of the Mother. The goddess was portrayed descending from the heavens towards her congregation, her pale arms stretched wide to envelop them all in her loving embrace. Her long blonde hair flowed around her like gossamer while her eyes were a brilliant cerulean blue.

The window was perfectly positioned to catch the morning sun, its rays infusing the glass with a soft, ethereal light that only heightened the Mother's otherworldly divinity. Thane was not an especially religious man, but even he could not deny feeling a sense of reverent wonder whenever he gazed upon the goddess's benevolent face.

The pews around him began to fill as the lesser Noble Houses found their allocated seats. Lady Hellington, Keeper of the Coin, a petite woman with silvery hair and half-moon glasses, sank into her spot next to Thane, while across the aisle Lord Jeckle, Keeper of the Anvil, and Lord Potsworn, Keeper of the Fields, had arrived together and were conversing in subdued tones, bent so closely that their noses were almost touching.

Moments later, the bells ceased to toll. The doors swung shut with an ominous thud, heralding the imminent start of the morning mass. A strong voice rang out, echoing off the nave's rounded columns.

"The Mother welcomes you."

Sister Superior Nayelle, Keeper of the Faith, stood before the stained-glass window bathed in light, her palms raised in a gesture of peace. The current head of the Church was very different from the goddess she worshipped. Squat, broad-shouldered, and big-boned, her black tunic and crimson scapular were stretched tightly over her plump form. Her wimple hid most of her greying hair and rotund face, revealing only a flat pug nose and wide green eyes that gave her a permanently anxious expression, like a fish caught in the hypnotic beam of an angler's lantern.

"By her Grace, we endure," her congregation answered. Nayelle gave a satisfied nod and launched into one of the many hymns praising the Mother's name and was soon joined by the dulcet harmonies of the nuns lining the choir stalls. The acoustics were perfect, amplifying the sound and reflecting it back to create a perpetual canon. Thane could feel the wood of the pew thrumming under his cushioned seat. He closed his eyes and allowed the music to wash over him, helping him to forget for the slightest of moments the terrible secret he was forced to carry within him day after day.

The psalm swelled to a powerful crescendo before fading into a spiralling series of soft repetitions. Thane lifted his head and saw that Nayelle was gazing straight at him, a strange smile on her lips.

"May the Mother keep you," she said. Thane had the distinct impression that she was speaking only to him.

"May the Mother keep you," she repeated. "May she

shoulder your burdens. May her strength be our strength. Her will our will." Her voice became grave. "For the devil is never far from our fair city. He hides within the Mists. Always watching. Always waiting. He searches for a way inside. A crack through which to slither. All it takes is a moment's weakness. A single second of doubt. Any lack of belief is an open invitation for him to rip us apart."

The silence was thick and heavy. Lady Hellington produced a handkerchief from the sleeve of her dress and dabbed at her brow. Thane forced himself to keep a straight face. His wardens had spent decades scouting the land around Keselgraad, protected from the corruptive properties of the Mists by their masks and sealed clothing. Nothing prowled that barren wasteland. Living or dead. The devil was pure fabrication, a bedtime story invented to prevent the Nobles from straying too far from the thrall of the Mater Sorores.

The tell-tale clinking of the donation box only further proved his point. He shook his head in disbelief and fished a few coins from the money pouch secreted in a pocket of his greatcoat. Nayelle had replaced her wimple with a crimson mitre and was leading the choir in another deafening hymn to the glory of the Mother. A nun touched Thane briefly on the shoulder. It was time. He rose and offered his arm to Lady Hellington, who accepted gratefully. They knelt on the steps before the altar, soon joined by Lord Jeckle and Lord Potsworn.

"Thane," Jeckle hissed furiously. "You arrogant bastard. I know what you did. How dare you—"

"Let us partake in the blessing of the Mother," Sister Superior Nayelle boomed, a beatific smile plastered on her face. She lifted one of the golden cups with both hands and proffered it to Thane who took the slightest of sips. Red wine. Dry and acidic. He grimaced.

"May the blood of the Mother become your blood," Nayelle intoned, offering the cup to the other members of the Council before setting it down and grasping a large platter piled high with wafers. Thane took one and bit down hesitantly.

"May the flesh of the Mother become your flesh."

Thane resisted the urge to cough. *If I'm not careful, the flesh of the Mother will choke me to death,* he thought, attempting to produce enough saliva to swallow the salty dry biscuit.

"Mother keep you," Nayelle said to Lady Hellington, leaning close and placing a kiss on the woman's wrinkled forehead. She came to stand before Thane and repeated the gesture. Her lips lingered near his ear.

"Keeper of the Peace," she whispered. "We must talk. After the service. In the cloister."

He nodded to indicate he had heard, then returned to his seat. It was obvious what she wanted to discuss. He just needed to think of the best way to profit from the situation.

For the next half-hour, he pondered while the lesser Noble families lined up like docile cattle to receive the Mother's blessing. Then, at last, the great bells began to ring again, and the congregation filed out of the Church to continue their monotonous, meaningless lives. Thane crossed the aisle and pushed open an inconspicuous door half-hidden behind a statue of Lord Keselgraad, the city's founding father.

The cloister was traditionally reserved for the nuns of the sisterhood, its covered walkways and central herb garden providing a place for recollection and contemplation. Thane relished the near-silence after the resonating din of morning mass. He leant against one of the columned arches as the bells faded, to be replaced by the low buzz of the bees humming between the floral herbs.

"Keeper of the Peace."

Sister Nayelle had crept up on him, once more clad in her wimple, her soft slippers making little sound on the smooth paving. Thane could see the fear glistening in the depths of her doe eyes.

"It's happened again, hasn't it?" Thane enquired.

"Yes."

She drew forth two shards of transparent glass from the folds of her robes. Her hands were shaking uncontrollably.

"Look," she whimpered. "Just look!"

"The amethysts," Thane stated. "They've lost their colour."

A single tear rolled down Nayelle's cheek. "The barrier. It's failing. And without the Mother's protection …"

Her next words were distorted by a wracking sob.

"… the Mists will swallow us all."

FOUR
DEAD END

"The day the Mists arrived, the entirety of our defensive forces became obsolete. Thousands of hardened, battle-trained soldiers suddenly found themselves out on the streets. A few were able to incorporate the City Watch, but most were forced to pursue more ... unscrupulous endeavours. There is always a place for a skilled fighter and a sharp blade down in the murky underbelly of the Slums."

Lord Matellas Thane, 814th Year of the Mother

"CITY WATCH!" PINE bellowed, his feet thundering along the cobbles, the ramshackle shacks and slowly collapsing houses flashing by in a blur.

"I think he knows who we are," Selene panted. "That's why he's running away."

Pine opened his mouth to reply just as the mirrorman put on a burst of speed and skidded around a stack of rotting crates into a side alley. The residential levels of Keselgraad, riddled with narrow passages and cul-de-sacs, were by far the worst place for a manhunt. Some of the oldest buildings in the city were found here, with each new resident attempting to shore up crumbling walls and reinforce termite-infested rafters to delay the inevitable.

Stone, of course, was in plentiful supply, a near-endless reserve from the Mines below the Slums, as was the clay or slate for roof tiles. Wood, however, was a problem; closely rationed by the Keeper of the Fields and attributed according to an archaic system that functioned on a mixture of merit, importance, and the occasional bribe. In all cases, the middle and lower classes got the short end of both the proverbial and actual stick.

A person risking a chase through one of the residential districts would inevitably have to deal with streets clogged with rubble, overflowing gutters, and piles of decomposing refuse. It was a dangerous obstacle course that Pine had become accustomed to navigating during his ten years as a watchman. Unfortunately, it seemed that the mirrorman was equally adept.

Pine swerved round another corner, nearly decapitating a grimy-faced washerwoman with his flailing sword. He barked an apology.

"Keep up!" Selene yelled as she overtook him. She appeared only mildly out of breath.

"Mists take you," he growled in reply. He used to be able to run for hours. When had he become so *old*?

Pine wiped the sweat from his brow and pelted after the others, his lungs heaving. The mirrorman was leading them further and further away from the central staircase. The alleyway was becoming steadily narrower; soon the tiled roofs overhead would be so close together that they would block out what little light had found its way down here. Pine followed a bend in the road and nearly ran into the back of Selene who had halted her relentless pursuit.

And for good reason.

The alleyway was a dead end. The mirrorman was pressed against a pile of fallen masonry that completely blocked the way ahead.

"Wrong … turn?" Pine puffed, his breathing short and ragged. "By the Mother, I haven't exerted myself like that in months. Shall—"

"Captain?" Selene called.

"Don't interrupt. Shall we try this again?"

"*Captain.*"

Selene tugged on his arm. He turned as three dark, hulking figures emerged from the penumbra behind him. Pine had seen men like this before, mostly locked behind the rusting iron bars of the Stables' prison. Men who spoke with their fists rather than their mouths. In fact, it was quite possible that some of them couldn't speak at all. Bandits, brawlers, and bruisers.

"Morning, citizens," Pine said calmly, his officer's sword still held nice and tight in his right hand. "I thank you for your concern, but we are in no need of assistance."

One of the men loped forwards. He had a long, equine face riddled with pockmarks and a piercing through his left nostril. "That's my brother," he replied with a jerk of his head.

"We just want to ask him a few questions," Selene said. Her voice was not quite as steady as Pine's, but it was close.

"Don't like watchmen." Pockmark produced a chipped blade from his belt. "They sent my pa to the Mists."

Pine licked his lips. His eyes flickered to the other two men. One was as thin as a rake and held a cudgel studded with rusty nails. His companion was big and burly, fat and muscle fighting for dominance of his massive frame. He was unarmed, but the two spade-like hands that dangled from his hairy arms looked dangerous enough.

"I'm sorry to hear that."

"Think it might be time for you to join him."

Pockmark lunged. Pine whipped his sword up and parried clumsily. Metal screeched on metal. Selene charged Pockmark's companions, the Mother's name on her lips.

Damn girl is going to get herself killed, Pine fumed, leaning back to avoid a cut to the face. He went on the offensive, releasing a flurry of blows that made up in speed for what they lacked in skill. Pockmark dodged and deflected calmly, then twisted his grip and opened a red furrow in the skin of Pine's cheek.

"Another scar for you, Watchman."

Pine brushed his fingers against the wound. They came away bloody.

"You're good," he admitted begrudgingly. Over the other man's shoulder, he could see Selene trading blows with the cudgel-wielding ruffian.

"My pa taught me," Pockmark replied with a flourish of flashing steel.

"Wait … that's a watchman's sword, isn't it? Your father was part of the Watch?"

"Aye. Worked tirelessly to protect the men and women of this city. For the right price."

Pine scowled. Bribery and corruption. Problems that had always been endemic to Keselgraad, but in recent years, they had grown steadily worse. Why adhere to the strict rationing of food and supplies when it was so much easier to take them from others? And while it was true that the population was shrinking, the same could be said of the number of watchmen; spread more and more thinly until, eventually, they would become invisible.

"We serve all of Keselgraad equally," he said. "Not only those with the coin to pay for it."

"Then, you are fools," Pockmark countered, punctuating his words with a downward thrust that grazed Pine's boot. The Watch captain tried to dodge away, but his opponent was faster, punishing him with a ringing clang to the breastplate.

Selene screamed. A crimson rose blossomed on the sleeve of her tunic.

We're losing, Pine thought. He glanced down at his sword, at the diamond-shaped shield etched into the crossguard. The first and only reward for joining the City Watch. He remembered the wrinkled old quartermaster who had given it to him and then taught him how to use it. What was it he had always said? Surprise and luck win more battles than strategy and skill.

Pine smiled at the memory and looked deeply into his assailant's eyes.

And dropped his sword.

Pockmark couldn't help himself. His eyes followed the movement, his nostrils flaring in surprise.

Pine stepped in, bunched his hand into a fist, and hammered it as hard as he could into his opponent's nose. Cartilage cracked. Bone shattered. A dozen dagger-like splinters were driven deep into Pockmark's brain. A wheezing moan hissed from the remains of his ruined face before he collapsed onto the cobbles beside the fallen sword, his feet kicking and jerking.

"Erkle!" the lanky man with the cudgel yelled. "What have they—"

Selene rammed her sword deep into the man's belly. A foul-smelling mix of acidic bile and thick viscera spilt from within, running down the length of her blade to spatter over her hand and tunic. She pulled her weapon free, allowing the man to sink to the ground, then turned to face the last of their assailants, her chest heaving.

The barrel-chested bruiser studied both watchmen carefully, his porcine eyes squinting under his overhanging brow. Pine bent to retrieve his own blade, and for a moment, the three of them stood there, blood pooling at their feet. After what felt like an age, the hairy behemoth gave a non-committal grunt and stomped away.

"Please."

The mirrorman hadn't moved since the beginning of the skirmish, pressed so tightly against a pile of crumbling masonry it was as if he thought it would open up and swallow him whole. The peaked cap had fallen from his head, and Pine saw that their fugitive was barely out of puberty, his dirty face and wispy beard making him appear older than he really was.

"Mother's Grace. Why did you run?"

"I … I canna go to the clink, Mister. Me sister got 'er 'and trapped in the loom down at the weaver's. They won't give 'er no rations no more! She needs me!"

Pine blinked slowly. "You're … you're not a mirrorman, are you, son?"

"Don't know nuffin' 'bout no mirrors, Mister. It's just—"

"The copper," Selene interrupted, wiping her sword clean on her tunic and sheathing it carefully. "You weren't repairing anything. You were stealing the copper. In broad daylight."

"It was me brother's idea, Miss. No one bothers the mirrormen, do they? Found meself one of 'em caps and an 'ammer. Made me look all important, like."

Pine felt the adrenaline pumping through his veins begin to fade. His legs ached. His cheek stung. Something hurt under the padding of his breastplate.

"What were you thinking?" he asked wearily. "The mirrors are welded to the frames. You can't just pry the metal off."

"Defacement of public property," Selene stated, stony-faced. "Theft of city materials. Assaulting soldiers of the Watch. All punishable by death."

"The Mists?" The boy's eyes grew wide and pleading. "No! Please, no! I watched 'em take me pa. I 'eard 'is screams. I … I 'ear 'em still. I beg you."

"You should have thought of that before you led us headlong into an ambush."

The scars on Pine's hands were itching terribly. Familiar images left their prison deep in his mind and swirled to the surface. An explosion of purplish light. Plumes of billowing smoke. His skull thrummed. "Watchman—" he began.

"You have the right to a trial," Selene was saying. "You may also choose to petition one of the Noble Houses to represent you."

"Watchman!"

"WHAT?" she shouted, turning on him in a wave of fury, her eyes burning with a fire that matched her burnished auburn hair. "He tried to kill us!"

"His *brother* tried to kill us," Pine corrected gently,

indicating the mangled corpse lying still and silent on the cobbles. "And he is dead. Justice has been served."

"But—"

"Enough." He bent down on one knee so that he was level with the boy's panicked face. "You know of the furnaces on the second level, son? The smelter master, Lindon, owes me a favour or two. You get your scrawny arse down there tomorrow morning and seek him out. Tell him I sent you. He'll find you something to do. I warn you, it'll be back-breaking work. Pumping the bellows or offloading the ore. But you'll get your rations."

"Th … thank you."

"Hah! Wait until you've been working there a week. You won't be thanking me then." Pine grasped him firmly by the shoulder. "Oh, and if I or any of my men catch you trying to steal from the city of Keselgraad again, I'll gift you to the Mists myself. Do we understand each other?"

"A … Aye, Mister. Mother keep you."

He darted between the two watchmen and fled.

"You'll never see him again," Selene said pointedly, probing the patch of blood on her tunic.

"That's the difference between you and me. You only see the worst in people. I try to see the best."

Her shoulders rose and fell in a disinterested shrug. "Not my problem. I'm looking forward to watching you try to explain all of this to Lord Thane, though."

"We pursued a lead that didn't work out."

"That's sure to satisfy him. Especially when he hears about the three dead bodies."

"You're right, no point in returning to him empty-handed. There's still time to make it to the jeweller's district before dusk." Pine searched for the sun through the gaps in the overhanging roofs. "If we can find our way back to the stairs."

"We took two lefts, a right, then another two lefts," Selene said, playing with the chain of her necklace. "A five-year-old could work it out."

Pine shook his head. "Fine. Then, by all means, lead the way."

⌘

The artisan district was wedged between the overpacked residential levels and the smoke-filled grime of the furnaces and charcoal pits. Labourers toiled up and down the wide central staircase that separated the two, many of them bent double by the weight of the baskets strapped to their backs. Over the years, the citizens of Keselgraad had attempted to transport goods via pulleys, cranes, or even cattle, but in the end, the cheapest way to send something from one level to another was to hire the steady feet and broad shoulders of a carrier.

Pine allowed himself to be pulled along by the current. His dented breastplate and injured cheek drew a few inquisitive stares, but most of the travellers were concentrating on keeping their baskets level and upright. He soon arrived at the wide arch that led into the artisan district. Selene was waiting for him, munching on a fouace.

"Sorry, Captain," she mumbled through a mouthful of bread. "Some lad was selling them on the stairs and …"

"He sets up shop there because he doesn't have a guild

licence," Pine said. "Mists, that could be filled with rat meat for all you know. Or worse."

Selene swallowed. "Still tastes better than some of the stuff the house chef used to make me."

"House chef? You had a … never mind, I'll take your word for it. Where shall we start?"

"Well, as you took a *very* long time to meander down those stairs, I've already scouted the main street. There are only three jeweller's workshops. It stands to reason that Spritt must have either owned or been employed by one of them."

The first two places had never heard of the deceased craftsman. Pine plodded on towards the final building, willing for his luck to change, his officer's cloak trailing through the muck behind him. He rapped on the entrance with his knuckles. There was a pattering of feet from somewhere inside, and the door was jerked open to reveal a small, bandy-legged man with half-moon glasses and a shock of white hair.

"Yes?" he enquired shrilly, peering down the length of his nose. "Are you here to deliver the silver?"

"City Watch, Sir. May we come in?"

"What? Oh, yes, of course, Officer. Um, please excuse the mess."

He wiped his hands on his leather apron and ushered them inside. The room was dominated by an enormous workbench, its entire surface covered with cogs, gears, springs, and various other bizarre pieces of machinery. They seemed to be piled on top of each other haphazardly, creating a miniature diorama of vertiginous peaks and deep valleys. Behind the table, a set of creaky shelves bore even more strange paraphernalia.

"You're a jeweller?" Pine asked, searching the interior for something resembling a ring or necklace.

"Hmmm? Yes, well, um, not really, not anymore. The revolution is upon us, my boy! A multitude of new ways to facilitate the most mundane tasks."

"I see. So, these are all … parts?"

"Indeed," the old man beamed. "Most of them my own inventions. The name Bendel Spritt will soon be known to all of Keselgraad."

Pine felt his heart drop. "Spritt? Are you by any chance related to a Jethro Spritt?"

Bendel rolled his eyes. "My cousin's son. Quite talented, I must admit, but severely lacking in imagination. No soul! No vision! And not very punctual. His shift started hours ago."

"I'm afraid he won't be coming in at all. We found him dead in his quarters this morning."

"Dead? Jethro? That's most unfortunate."

"Yes, it is upsetting news. The loss of a loved one can be—"

"No, no. I mean for the piece he was working on. The client was quite adamant that it must be delivered by tomorrow. With Jethro gone, I'll have to finish it myself."

Pine shared a brief look of disbelief with Selene. "May we see what he was making?"

"I suppose so. But then I will have to ask you to leave. I'm already behind schedule as it is."

Bendel led them through an opening in the rows of shelves to a second, much smaller room containing a desk and stool.

"This is … *was* Jethro's atelier," he said. "Just as he left it."

The table was significantly less cluttered than the workbench. At its very centre sat a strange-looking apparatus: two long curved prongs joined together at one end to resemble a pincer.

"What does it do?" Selene asked. "It looks like a compass."

"A what?"

"A compass, a device my tutor used to draw circles."

Pine pointed to the hooked tips. "I don't think so. A weapon of some sort, maybe? Bendel! What in the Mists is this thing for?"

The jeweller made a popping sound as he shook his head. "No idea. Isn't it fascinating? We were only told to follow the instructions as precisely as possible."

There was a torn scrap of paper next to the pincer, covered in hastily drawn sketches and measurements. A long string of symbols was inked into the top-left corner.

"Paper," Selene said. "An expensive commodity. Probably means that the order came from one of the upper levels. What do you think, Captain?"

Pine was too busy staring at the numbers to reply. "I've seen this before," he murmured, tracing the code with his index finger. It had been stencilled deeply. "A decade ago. I never thought I'd see it again. Who commissioned you?"

Bendel shifted his gaze. "I'd rather … I'd rather not say."

"Jethro is dead," Pine growled back at him, losing patience. "And I'm becoming more and more convinced that it wasn't accidental. Someone must have given you these instructions. Who was it? Who's paying you?"

The jeweller's reply was almost inaudible.

"The … the Keeper of the Peace. Lord Matellas Thane."

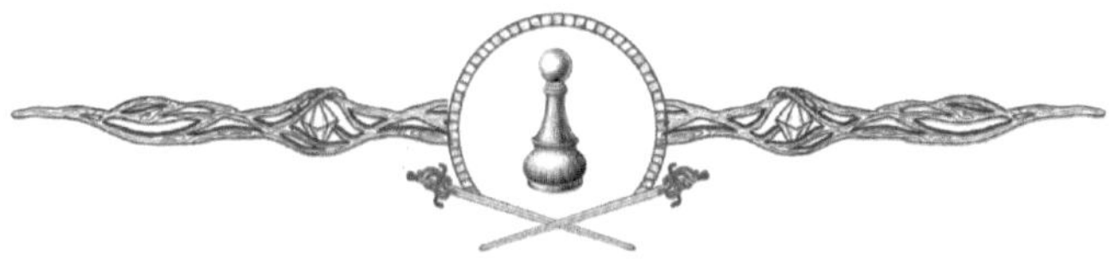

FIVE
THE INSECT KING

"Trust me when I tell you that I feel your pain. The Collapse has not only claimed the lives of many hard-working citizens, it has also buried countless subterranean galleries and the exploitable veins of ore they contained. It will take years for Keselgraad to recover from this tragedy. Yet, we will not falter. We will not despair. We will endure, and, by the Mother, I pledge to you to do everything in my power to make this fair city shine again, greater and brighter than ever before."

Lord Matellas Thane, 823rd Year of the Mother

ROE CRIED OUT in pain as the birchwood stick thwacked against his naked buttocks. Krabbon exacted his punishment expertly, each blow landing close enough to the previous one to create a single bruised line of flesh. On the fifth strike, the skin split open. Roe could feel the blood trickle down between his legs. He gritted his teeth and steadied himself against the whipping post.

I deserve this, he thought. The bitter grief in his heart hurt far more than the lash of the stick. Ant was dead. And it was all his fault.

Krabbon had pounced on him as soon as he had returned

to the orphanage, rousing the other boys and girls from their beds and dragging them out to the yard to witness the consequences of insubordination. They now formed a rough semi-circle around Roe, shivering in the cold night air. Some of the younger ones flinched at every resonant crack.

After bringing his cane down for a tenth and final time, Krabbon stopped. He was breathing hard from the effort, his wheezes chilling to a fine mist as he exhaled.

"Pull your trousers up, Roach," he growled. "Castigation's over for today." He sniffed and scratched at his beard; an enormous, greasy thing that exploded from his pudgy face and spilt down his chest in a mass of unruly curls. "But mark my words, whenever Ant turns up, he'd better have a damned fine excuse for his tardiness."

"I told you, M'Lord, he was taken by the Mi—"

"ENOUGH!" Krabbon roared, throwing his cane aside and stabbing a meaty finger towards Roe. "If you're going to try and lie your way out of a beating, at least put some effort into it. I taught you better than that."

"M'Lord, I—"

"I've been around a long time, Roach. Longer than all of you. I've seen a good many criminals tied to the cross and gifted to the Mists. Screaming and pulling against their bonds as they were lowered into the Sea of Retribution. No one would go near the edge of the city wall voluntarily. Not even a pair of moronic bugs like you."

Roe laced up the front of his trousers and stared at Krabbon defiantly. "They killed Pearlton."

"Really?" The self-styled Insect King spread his arms wide. Moonlight glinted off his bald pate, giving him a silver halo. "The first thing I did after hearing your ludicrous tale was to send Spider to the market place. Let him tell you what he found."

A willow-thin boy with jet-black hair stepped out of the circle of onlookers; his pasty-white skin was covered in goose bumps. "Nothing," he murmured in an unhurried monotone.

"That can't be right," Roe retorted. "I saw him. He had been packed into a burlap sack like a haunch of dried meat. The warden must have disposed of him."

"The warden," Krabbon stated flatly.

"Yes."

"A custodian of Keselgraad. A guardian of the city. Reporting directly to Lord Thane himself. The same warden who presumably attempted to kill you and Ant."

"Yes."

Krabbon's smile revealed a row of crooked, yellow-stained teeth. "Spider, you are one of our oldest. Remind me, if you would. Since when has this fine establishment existed?"

"Ten years, M'Lord."

"Aye. That sounds about right. Just after the Collapse. Mist-spawned thing made a lot of orphans."

Roe shifted uncomfortably. His buttocks felt like they were on fire. "I know what you're going to say—"

"Quiet, Roach. A *decade*. Most of you were still in swaddling, pissing yourselves day in day out with reckless abandon." He closed his eyes theatrically. "So long ago I can barely remember it myself. And for all that time, our generous patron has kept us afloat. Put food in our bellies. Provided wood and animal dung to keep us warm. Without him, we would have all starved to death. Now, tell me, Roach. Who is our patron?"

"Lord Matellas Thane." Roe spat the words out, hating himself as he did so. He could still hear the crossbow bolt whistling by his ear. Ant's scream as the Mists tore him apart.

"Lord Thane," Krabbon repeated, still smiling. "The wardens never act without his knowledge. Why then, little cockroach, would the person who has been keeping you alive ever since you were born now want to kill you? Doesn't sound like a very good investment to me."

He crossed his stubby arms over his untamed beard and waited expectantly.

Roe's fiery pain was eclipsed by an even greater conflagration; a roaring, twisting maelstrom that sputtered to life in his belly and crackled up his chest to lodge itself firmly in his brain. Everything else faded except Krabbon's sneer of disbelief. His fingers clenched into a fist.

I'll make him see, he thought. *I'll pummel that smug bastard until he begs me to stop.*

One of the orphans rubbed her red nose and sniffled. It was June, the youngest, a little girl no older than eleven, her patched tunic scarcely reaching her knees. Her bare feet were white as alabaster against the muddy grit of the yard. She was freezing to death. They all were.

"Well?" Krabbon asked. He was wearing a thick leather doublet and boots, untroubled by the cold.

Roe hesitated. He knew what would happen if June grew ill. He had seen it before. There was no coin for a physician. Nor for herbs or poultices. Or, at least, nothing that the Insect King would want to share. He would stand by and allow the disease to do its work, until her frail body drew its last breath, and then sell her corpse to the Keeper of the Fields. Food for the crops and forests of the upper levels.

For that is all we are to him, Roe reminded himself. *Merchandise. Resources to be exploited. Thrown aside when we are no longer needed ... or no longer profitable. That is why Ant's disappearance means nothing. A mere annoyance, like mislaying a tool or a belt.*

He scanned the row of pale faces.

Instead of fighting for those who have died, I should be fighting for those who live.

Roe unclenched his hand and bowed his head. "You are right, M'Lord, of course. It was getting dark. Perhaps my eyes betrayed me."

Krabbon clapped his hands together with a crack almost as loud as his cane. "Aye, that must be it. Never forget where Thane found you, Roach. Down in the Depths covered in your own piss and vomit. Bawling for your mother. A little runt, born in the shadows." His voice grew low. "That's where you belong. Far from the light. Right! Back to your beds! All of you! The sun will soon rise on a new day, full of opportunities!"

He clumped away, back to the warmth of his small fire and the bottle of whatever foul-smelling barley mash liquor he had managed to procure for himself.

Roe stared daggers into the man's retreating back. His anger was still there, hot and heavy in the pit of his stomach, like a piece of smouldering coal.

"Aye, I was born in the shadows," he whispered. "But I no longer fear the dark ... and I no longer fear you."

⌘

"Hurry, Roach, hurry!"

He awoke with a groan, his eyelids stuck together like glue. He pried them open to see June's blurry face peering down at him, her straw-coloured hair sticking out in all directions.

"Umph."

"Time to get up!"

"Don't call me Roach." Krabbon renamed all the orphans he brought into his kingdom, like an owner with a new pet. Old identities were stripped away and forgotten, replaced by the name of whatever insect tickled his fancy on that particular day. Spiders, wasps, ants, bees, and beetles. Some of the new arrivals were fortunate enough to inherit passable monikers, like June Bug. Others, who had the bad luck to catch Krabbon in a foul mood, were dubbed Worm, Louse … or Roach, which, even shortened to Roe, sounded like something you would scrape off the sole of your boot.

"Sorry," June said in a small voice. She was clutching a doll that she had made herself. Balls of dirt stuck together and then left to dry in the sun.

"That's all right. What is it?"

"The King is already awake. He's asking for you."

"He's not our King any more than we're his bugs," Roe mumbled, rolling onto his back and immediately regretting it. "Mother's Grace! My arse feels like it's been run over by a rickshaw."

"Hmm. Have you tried mud?"

"What, on the wound? Are you mad? We empty the chamber pots into the yard, June. I'd be slathering myself with …"

"Not just any old mud, silly. I'll try and bring you back some clay next time I'm down in the Mines."

"Steal some clay, you mean. That's not a good idea. If you—"

"Don't worry. No one ever notices me. I'll be fine. Which is more than you'll be if you don't get a move on."

Roe stood with a moan and patted down his springy hair as best he could. "I wonder what he wants with me now. It's already hard enough to keep myself upright." He hobbled out of the tiny room he used to share with Ant and dragged his aching frame down the corridor to the large living space that the Insect King had dubbed 'The Grand Hall'. It was from here that he lorded over his subjects, comfortably installed in a high-backed chair that he seemed to think was some sort of throne.

"You're late," he growled as Roe arrived. His frown sent ripples up his shaved scalp. "Again. I thought you would have learnt your lesson after last night."

"Apologies, M'Lord. I seem to have some difficulty walking this morning. It's making me slower."

Krabbon chuckled, his beard bouncing up and down on his belly. "Always a riposte, hey, Roach? If we were duelling with swords, you'd have cut me nice and good." He drew a dagger from his belt. It looked tiny in his meaty fist. "Now, come closer."

Roe took a few nervous steps. A stocky arm reached out and caught his wrist. "Ant's still missing. A pox on the lucky bastard who finds his body. I'm never going to see the shine of that corpse-coin, am I?"

"M'Lord, perhaps—"

"I wasn't asking you, Roach. We're still not square, you

and I. Rules are rules, after all. You came back with a mouth full of lies and a pouch emptier than an ugly whore's bedchamber. No one sleeps here for free."

Roe glanced at the knife. "So, you're going to take what you're owed from my flesh?"

A flash of crooked teeth. "In a manner of sorts."

The blade sang, carving three horizontal lines into the skin of Roe's forearms. They began to weep blood.

"Play to your strengths," Krabbon said, examining the wounds. "People think the best way to get coin from someone is to steal it, but they're wrong. The best way is for them to *give it to you*. I've been a bristler. A trickster. A whipjack and a drummer. I've worn the clothes of a ruffler and lit lamps as a bat-fowler. Today, you'll be my clapper."

He squeezed hard to make more red liquid leak from the gashes. "All beggars need a gimmick. One that both attracts attention and inspires pity. Go find a disused tunic and tear it into strips to make bandages. Don't wrap them too tightly, mind you, the blood needs to seep through and stain the fabric."

Roe tried to concentrate. "You think this will actually work?"

"Think? I know it will, Roach. Tried it myself once or twice when I was your age. The younger the better. There's something about seeing a sickly little child that tugs at the heartstrings."

"What if they ask me what happened?"

Krabbon cackled. His breath stank of alcohol and rotten meat. "You showed me last night that you can spin a convincing tale. Tell them whatever you want. Perhaps your arms got caught in a mining accident. Or you were struck down with some terrible disease. As long as they cough up the coin."

His eyes narrowed. "And you'd better hope they're feeling generous, little cockroach, or you'll be sleeping in the yard."

"Yes, M'Lord."

Krabbon tightened his grip, his fingers like a vice crushing Roe's wrist. "Perhaps I should send someone with you, just to be sure. Spider!"

The slim, ashen-skinned boy was sitting on one of the benches that dotted the Great Hall, scrubbing the bottom of a cooking pot with a dirty cloth. He looked up, a bored expression on his face.

"Hmmm?"

"Roach here needs a new partner. You're volunteering."

Spider shrugged. "As long as he doesn't get me killed."

Krabbon considered this, then threw the dagger he was holding. It thunked into the table next to the pile of unwashed pots, Roe's blood still smeared on the blade.

"Take that with you. Open a few holes in him if he tries anything."

Spider pulled the weapon free and stuck it in his belt.

"When do we leave?"

⌘

After a few hours combing the market place, Roe was forced to admit that Krabbon was right. His wobbling gait and bandaged arms drew a host of curious stares. It was easy enough to identify those who were sympathetic to his plight and reel them in. He found himself changing his story depending on his mark: to a miner's widow he had been the victim of a cave-in, to a tanner's sister he was burnt from the liming … as long as he kept a slight tremble in his voice and a tear in his eye, a handful of coins eventually found their way into his pocket.

Spider was never far away, watching him from behind one of the many run-down stalls or from the shadow of the city wall that dominated the Slums with its austere presence. His demeanour ranged from apathy to disinterest, his impassive face impossible to read.

Roe surmised that they were roughly the same age, yet his fellow orphan appeared older somehow, the flatness of his features and the dullness of his eyes creating an overwhelming sense of world-weariness. It was as if he had already lived a long, tedious life. And maybe he had. Spider never joined the others in the yard and rarely ate with them. Even when he did, he never engaged in conversation, content to sit and listen in silence. Roe realised that despite having shared the same roof for over a decade, he knew little to nothing about his new partner.

After several hours of grifting, Roe's pouch was jingling with more than enough coin to satisfy the avaricious Insect King. He stopped at one of the stalls and picked out a large loaf of rye bread, carefully checking it for mould and maggots. Spider was waiting for him at the entrance to an alleyway. Roe's footsteps slowed as he recognised it as the same place where he had sat and waited to steal the apple, what seemed like a lifetime ago.

The bread suddenly felt dry and flaky in his mouth. He swallowed with difficulty and tore off a large chunk to offer to Spider.

"Your cuts have scabbed," the other boy remarked blandly. He was attempting to balance Krabbon's knife on his middle finger. "We'll have to open them up again if you want to appear convincing."

Roe grunted, his eyes drawn to a dark patch near the empty remains of Pearlton's stall.

"There was no body," Spider said, following his gaze. "That much was true. But there were signs of a struggle. And I found a shattered shaft that could well have come from a crossbow bolt."

"You … lied to Krabbon."

"I twisted the truth. It must be obvious why, even for a dullard like you."

The anger returned, a dull drumming sound that filled Roe's ears. "You really don't care, do you? I thought the blank expression was all an act, but it's not that. You just have a block of ice in place of your heart." He gestured towards the wall. "Ant died less than a hundred feet from where we're standing, yet your fear of the Insect King means his killer will never be brought to justice."

Spider calmly finished his piece of bread and returned the dagger to his belt. "Follow me."

They walked back through the Slums, past the piles of decomposing refuse, the gaping tunnel to the Mines, the nauseous streams of sludge and muck that dribbled down from the upper levels; this awful, stinking dirt-encrusted scab of sick and mud that clung to the base of Keselgraad like manure to the sole of a shoe.

Spider forged onwards, past the street that led to the orphanage, before stopping in front of a gaudily painted building draped in dyed red and purple sheets.

"A brothel," Roe stated. "You've brought me to a brothel."

"It is not what lies inside that interests us. Come."

A tall wooden fence surrounded the rear of the building. A way for its occupants to enjoy some privacy perhaps, or an attempt at a garden, not that anything would flourish down here so far from the light.

Spider put a finger to his lips and pushed gently on one of the planks. It slid sideways, allowing Roe to peer through the gap.

Krabbon, the Insect King, stood in the middle of a tiny courtyard, his shaved head bowed as he conversed with a figure whom Roe instantly recognised.

A flat-topped hat, long black robes, and a viciously curved beak-like mask.

A warden.

SIX
THE GNAWING OF RATS

"My daughter's favourite toy was a simple thing. A piece of wood with three differently shaped holes: round, triangular, and square. And there were pegs, of course, carved to fit perfectly into each opening. She solved this trivial puzzle in minutes, and I thought that would be the end of it, but she continued to play, day after day, attempting to force the wrong pegs into the wrong holes. She refused to believe that there was only one way to win, do you see? She believed there was something ... more."

First Technologist Arniel Sin, The Time Before

T HANE STARED AT the two pieces of crystal. A dozen distorted versions of his own image glared back at him, diffracted by the multitude of colourless facets. *It's too soon. Far too soon.*

"It's getting worse," Nayelle whined, echoing his thoughts. "Why is the Mother abandoning us?"

Thane wrapped his fingers around the brass sphere that formed the pommel of his cane and tightened his grip. The walking stick was an incongruous heirloom of House Quellion, passed down from generation to generation, the metal worn smooth by a score of Noble hands. He could feel the polished surface through his leather gloves. It reminded him of all those who had come before. Lord after Lord, all heroes of Keselgraad. All working tirelessly to keep the city safe. He would not be the first of his line to fail. He would live up to his name. And his legacy.

The glass shards glittered. Mocking his promise. He snatched them up and concealed them in the outer pocked of his overcoat.

"They can be repaired," he said soothingly. "Just like before. In time, their light will shine out from the spire once more."

The Keeper of the Faith wiped her dribbling nose with the sleeve of her robe. "Six years ago, the first amethyst failed," she said. "Three years ago, the second. Two years ago, the third. Six months ago, the fourth. And now … two at once. The intervals are decreasing, my Lord. I fear there will come a time when the jewels will fade faster than you can fix them. What have we done to offend the Mother?"

"This has nothing to do with the Mother," Thane snapped, losing patience. "This is the work of the Mists. They scratch and claw at our door like rats, desperate to be let in. If not for her protection, we would already be dead."

"We should have left it," Nayelle whispered. "We should have left the relic where we found it."

Thane grasped the brass pommel even tighter.

How could someone so weak hold the title of Keeper? he fumed. *So emotional. So frail. So plagued by self-doubt.*

"May I remind you that it was the Mater Sorores who petitioned for the gem to be moved from the Depths up to the Church? An idea I strongly opposed. Quite why the other members of the Council chose to vote in your favour, I'll never fully understand."

Nayelle looked out over the herb garden and its myriad rows of plants, swaying softly in the breeze.

"To give people hope," she replied in a quiet voice. "This city is full of sadness and despair. You have been to the lower levels, my Lord. You have seen the poverty. The squalor. Over two-thirds of Keselgraad's inhabitants cannot afford to eat on a daily basis. Or heat their homes. Their lives teeter on a knife's edge. One wrong step will send them plummeting into the abyss."

"I am not a supplicant to be sermoned, Sister. I am well aware of the current situation."

"You are aware of the statistics. The number of deaths. Crop yields. Rations. Winter supplies. You have not visited the Slums. Seen the orphaned children. These are the people that need something to believe in, my Lord. That is why we wanted to add the amethyst to the Church spire. So that it might be visible to all of Keselgraad. A shining symbol. A beacon bringing light to those tempted by darkness. A sign of *hope*."

Her gaze shone with fervent zeal.

She believes it. All this nonsense about divine providence. Pathetic.

A trio of nuns hurried past, their heads masked by their white wimples, their robes swishing on the stone. Thane waited for them to pass before clearing his throat. "I believe that the same rejuvenating procedure I employed previously will still give the desired results", he said. "Although I am already trying to keep so many balls up in the air, I fear that if I add another, I may end up dropping them all."

"Of course, my Lord. Of course. Perhaps some sort of

monetary donation for your office may help you bear the load?"

Thane made a show of considering the proposal. "A fine idea. However, funding has never been an issue. My family's coffers run deep, and the Keepers Council has always been most generous in its support. No, the problem, I'm afraid, is a simple matter of manpower. I need more loyal citizens to help protect Keselgraad."

Nayelle was nodding vigorously. "Forgive me for my foolishness. I'm sure the Council would have no objection to an expansion of the City Watch. It's well overdue."

"I was … I was not talking about the Watch. The tasks I have in mind can only be entrusted to the most skilled and resilient soldiers. Strong, fearless guardians able to resist the corruption of the Mists."

Her face fell. "The wardens. You wish to recruit more wardens?"

Thane took her hands in his. Her fingernails were incrusted with a black tarry substance that stuck to the leather of his gloves. He fought the urge to pull away.

"Nayelle," he said in a firm tone. "Sister. If we are to defeat the Mists, we must first *understand* them. And who better to carry out such a perilous undertaking than the only ones who have the courage to leave the city walls and venture forth into that nightmarish fog?"

"Yes, but you increased their number the last time this happened. I've seen with my own eyes what becomes of them after the trial. I don't—"

"Because it was necessary. And it has become necessary again. Lady Hellington knows this. I know this. Lords Jeckle and Potsworn will vote against me, as they seem to do almost systematically these days. Which means that …"

"… I will cast the deciding vote," Nayelle finished glumly.

Thane attempted what he hoped was a conciliatory smile. "You hold Keselgraad in the palm of your hand, Sister. You can either help me to protect it or let the rats gnaw their way inside. Which will it be?"

She returned his smile, and he knew, in that instant, that he had her.

"The Mother stands by you, my Lord. She guides your hand, just as she guides mine. May she keep us from harm."

He squeezed her blackened fingertips. "With your help, I know she will."

⌘

Thane walked down the central aisle of the Church of the Mother, the tapping of his cane resonating off the ostentatious marble columns. A thousand different thoughts whirled around in his head, jostling for dominance. He had been prepared for more of the shards to fade; it was the logical continuation of the terrible cycle of self-destruction that the Mater Sorores had set in motion ten years ago by requesting the relic's removal from the Depths. But two losses in *six months*? The increase in crystal degradation was beyond his most pessimistic calculations.

He would have to increase the siphoning process. Exponentially. Which meant more raw materials. Materials that the Keepers Council would never authorise. That was the real issue. Thane was forced to wage two wars at the same time: one against the insatiable hunger of the Mists, the other against a bunch of preening, parasitic peacocks who refused to see anything past the end of their considerable noses.

Those were the shackles he bore, forged from fear and hubris. There was a way for him to be free, but it required more wardens. Many more.

Thane pushed through the arched double-doors and hurried down the steps, the broken amethysts clinking in his pocket. He could feel the chiselled gaze of Keselgraad's nobility boring into his back, his own ancestors among them.

I will be worthy, he thought. *I will be worthy of my lineage.*

"Keeper of the Peace!"

Lord Jeckle stood with his feet firmly planted on the strip of grass, surrounded by three saffron-clad members of his honour guard. The Keeper of the Anvil was small and stubby as if a grown man had been squeezed into the body of a child. He was wearing a green puff-sleeved doublet and yellow hose. A frilly ruff ringed his undersized neck, tickling the tips of a drooping moustache that had quite visibly been bleached with lye soap.

Jeckle's questionable choice of garments was completed by a thimble-shaped plumed hat, its feather dangling as limply as his facial hair. The Keeper told anyone who would listen that it was from the wing of a now-extinct bird of prey. To Thane, it looked like it had been plucked from the arse of a goose.

"Keeper of the Anvil."

"What were you *doing* in there, Thane? I've been waiting out here for Mother-knows-how-long."

"An urgent matter that needed my attention."

Jeckle's nose twitched, making his moustache dance. "*Urgent matters* are to be brought before the Council, not discussed in secrecy. This whole thing reeks of conspiracy."

Thane fixed him with a flinty stare. "Are you suggesting that the Sister Superior is untrustworthy?"

"No, no, of course not. But these things must go through the proper channels. Otherwise, we are no better than the bloodthirsty despots our ancestors fought so hard to overthrow!"

Ah, the so-called despots, Thane thought. His fellow Keeper was referring to the Kings who ruled Keselgraad before the infamous Uprising. Single sovereigns, heads of both state and Church, supposedly blessed with a direct link to the prophecies of the Mother herself. No Council. No bureaucracy.

It sounded exquisite.

"My own forebear led the charge over the barricade, as I am sure you're aware," Jeckle continued, his chest thrust out like a pigeon in mating season. "Wearing this exact same hat. It was pierced by a flurry of crossbow bolts, yet his resolve never wavered! We have him to thank for making Keselgraad the proud democracy it is today."

The oligarchy, you mean, Thane corrected silently. *The only thing the Uprising did for the lower classes was to multiply the number of people controlling their lives.*

"I have a long day ahead of me," he said aloud. "Perhaps the history lesson can be saved for another time."

Jeckle bristled. "There you go again, trying to shirk your responsibilities. Whenever I try to arrange a meeting with you, there's always some excuse. Well, not today! I have you cornered, Keeper of the Peace, and you *will* answer my questions!"

The honour guard closest to him placed a hand on the pommel of his sword. The air hummed with unresolved tension.

"Fine," Thane said. "Ask away."

"You have been stealing from me."

"That's not a question."

A red flush appeared on the fringes of Jeckle's frilly ruff. "Don't you dare mock me, Thane. I've tolerated your snide remarks and crude attempts at undermining the will of the Council for long enough. Where are my supplies?"

"I have no idea what you are talking about."

Jeckle snapped his fingers. One of the guards produced a wafer-thin scrap of vellum covered in minuscule text. Parchment of any sort was an expensive commodity and was often washed and reused two or three times until the surface became too scarred to be legible.

"Two crates of iron ore. One crate of silver. Five pots of clay slurry. Four barrels of charcoal, a drawplate, a pair of fullers, three boxes of nails, and … an anvil! An entire anvil! And that's just the raw materials and equipment. At least two of the smelters have spoken to me about work orders that I certainly didn't sign off on."

Thane sighed. Perhaps he had slightly underestimated Lord Jeckle. The man was a bumbling half-wit but also tremendously tight-fisted. A fool, yet a miserly fool, which made for a dangerous combination.

"Every single item was required for city business. I would be happy to explain—"

"It's too late for that," Jeckle interrupted, fuming. "You

have no right to commandeer my merchandise or instruct my workers." He tapped the gleaming badge pinned to his chest; a hammer crossed with tongs. "*I* am the Keeper of the Anvil. *I* have complete authority over anything that is brought up from the Mines and—"

Thane gripped his cane as hard as he could to calm his own annoyance. "It is not *your* merchandise; it belongs to the city of Keselgraad."

"And therefore, it must be distributed according to the contracts signed by the guilds and validated by the Council. Clearly, something you have forgotten. What's even worse is that I spoke with Lord Potsworn this morning and it appears that you have been stealing from him, too! Men sent off to Mother-knows-where without justification. A whole stack of tanned leather hides diverted from their original destination. It cannot stand! I will not allow it! You will return everything that you have taken. Immediately! Or suffer the consequences!"

It took every ounce of self-restraint for Thane not to slam his fist into the greedy little man's face.

"That is impossible, I'm afraid."

The crimson tint continued its inexorable climb up Lord Jeckle's face, setting his cheeks aglow. "Do not *presume* to tell me what is possible and what is not. You have gone too far this time, Thane. Both Potsworn and I agree that you have overstepped your boundaries. And once I show the receipts to Lady Hellington, she will support our claim. The next meeting is in two days, and if—"

"You threaten me with ostracism?" Thane cut in, his voice dagger-sharp. "You would seek to … remove my title?

House Quellion has held a seat on the Council for over a hundred years. How dare you even consider such a thing?"

"I have the votes."

"You do not. Removing a Keeper from office necessitates a unanimous agreement from the other Council members. Who include Sister Nayelle."

Lord Jeckle paused mid-retort, his moustache squirming on his lip as he digested this new piece of information. "A mild inconvenience. I'm sure the Sister Superior will see reason once I expose the damage you are doing to this city. And I have two days to convince her."

Thane gave a sniff of disbelief. "You and I both know that's not true. Do what you will. I believe this conversation has run its course, Keeper of the Anvil. Good day to you."

"We're not done yet, Keeper of the Peace. I require compensation for everything you have taken from me."

"Send your claim to the Stables and I'll look it over." Thane stepped around the quivering Lord Jeckle and made for the flight of stairs leading down to the next level. A guard moved to block his path.

"*Compensation*," Jeckle squeaked like a petulant child. "You're not leaving here until I get my money, Keeper."

Mists take him, Thane cursed. *He preaches honour and loyalty, yet he is no better than one of the Slums' petty criminals. Since when had the Keepers Council become so hypocritical? So corrupt?*

He ignored the badly dressed, over-privileged moneygrubber and focused instead on the soldier obstructing his path. The man's conical helmet had been buffed to a fine sheen; the cassock draped over his breastplate was embroidered with a diving hawk motif. His boots were so spotless that they appeared new. Thane dropped his gaze to his opponent's hands. They were smooth and unblemished, the nails clipped and regular.

Much could be learnt about someone from the state of his palms. It was one of the reasons that Thane often wore gloves. They hid the scars from a part of his life he would rather not remember. The blisters from his cane. And the calluses earned from his daily sparring lessons. Thane knew how to fight. He knew how to kill. The man in front of him did not.

"Move aside."

The guard stood his ground. A bead of sweat escaped the confines of his helmet and rolled down his cheek to drop onto his boots.

Thane twisted the brass sphere at the top of his cane. There was an almost imperceptible click. He pulled a long, rapier-like blade from the wooden scabbard. It made a soft whining sound.

"Move aside or draw your sword. Decide now."

The soldier's fingers twitched. He began to reach for the hilt of his blade. A part of Thane wanted him to do it. Wanted him to touch the leather grip so that he could have an excuse to cut through the thin flap of skin just below the chin and watch the man's lifeblood sluice down his styled cassock to colour the grass crimson.

The hand slowed. Then stopped. The guardsman took a step back and let his arm fall to his side.

Thane sheathed his weapon and began to descend the stairs, impervious to the sputtering insults hurled after him by the red-faced Keeper of the Anvil.

"Don't turn your back on me, Thane!" Jeckle was

yelling. "Never turn your back on me. I've killed men for less. Thane. THANE!"

There it was. No more euphemisms. No more thinly veiled threats. The man was no longer simply an annoyance.

He was an enemy.

And like all enemies of House Quellion, he would be battered, beaten, and *broken*.

Until there was nothing left.

SEVEN
GHOSTS OF THE PAST

"Do not be swayed by lust or greed,

Do not attempt to dig too deep,

For there are things that lie in wait,

Trapped in the earth beneath your feet."

Keselgraadian mining song, 810th Year of the Mother

THE DRIPPING BUCKET was a tavern only in the very loosest sense of the word. The bar was a plank of wood balanced on two old barrels that smelt of fermented wine; the tables were a motley collection of rotting crates, disused rickshaws, and what appeared to be an overturned wheelbarrow. An unsettling odour of sweat and dried vomit pervaded every corner of its dingy interior, from the termite-riddled rafters to the straw-covered floor.

The balding barkeep was lighting sets of tallow candles as Pine and Selene arrived, the stink of burning animal fat only adding to the ambient stench. His happy expression at the prospect of new customers quickly changed to one of dour apprehension when he saw the crimson tunics and bronze breastplates.

"City Watch," he spat, somehow managing to make

the words sound like an insult. "What in the Mists are you doing here?"

"Unofficial business," Pine replied easily, his scarred palms raised. "Just looking for a nice spot for a drink."

"In the middle of the day?"

"A dry throat is a dry throat. Besides, my partner and I have just had a rather nasty encounter with some of the less polite members of the residential levels."

The barkeep blew out his wick. "I don't give a rat's arse. I'm not serving no coppers."

Pine laughed. "By the Mother, you really don't recognise me, do you, Fletch?"

The other man grunted and brought one of the candles closer. His eyes took in the greying hair and marked face, then widened in amazement. "M … Mists take me. Aldin? Aldin M. Pine? Is that really you?"

"The very same."

Fletch grinned. "By my hairy bollocks, I thought ya were dead! After the Collapse, we lost so many of your lot. And when ya didn't show up here no more, I reckoned you'd been buried down there with the rest of them."

"I know. Sorry, Fletch. I just … I just needed some time to—"

"*Time*? It's been ten bloody years, Aldin! Enough for all my hair to fall out and my belly to swell to the size of a pig's arse! It wouldn't have cost ya much just to stop by."

Pine remembered. The deafening crack exploding in his ears. The panicked cries for help. The clogging smoke and dust filling his lungs, choking the life from him. The swirling of amethyst stars. The blood covering his hands, his arms, his face. Every inch of exposed skin weeping crimson tears as the world collapsed around him.

Bera. Hale. Lyle.

Fate and fortune.

"It was … harder than you might think," he managed.

Fletch held his gaze for a moment, then nodded. "Aye, lad. I understand. Much was lost that day." His eyes flickered to Selene, and his demeanour brightened considerably.

"And who might you be, lass? Some poor woman forced to suffer under this curmudgeonly bastard? I pity you, I really do."

"Selene Eckelston. You're right, he's a bit of a grump, but he does have his moments."

"I'm sure he does. Lad used to come in here most nights. Laughed the loudest, if I recall. Could down a pint of ale faster than patrons twice his age."

"Interesting. I've never seen him drink anything but water."

"Well, you're missing out. Eckelston … I've seen that name stencilled on crates around the tanneries. You're from one of the Noble Houses." Fletch tapped the top of the bar. "Probably the first time you've been in a place like this, eh?"

The corners of Selene's lips jerked. "You'd be surprised."

"Aye, lass. I don't doubt that I would. Now, what brings you two fine figures of the City Watch to my humble establishment? I have an inkling it's not just for a pint of my infamous ale."

"No." Pine scanned the tavern. Apart from a couple of morose patrons nursing cracked tankards in a shadowy corner, the place was empty. "I'm looking for Gamin. I imagine he still frequents this place?"

"He does," Fletch replied with a hint of sadness. "Poor bastard. He's usually already here, but he had a particularly rough one last night. I expect he's sleeping it off." He gestured to a rusting old mine cart that had been repurposed into a table, complete with a set of benches. "That there's his spot if ya want to wait for him."

"We do. Thank you, Fletch. How about two pints of your best brew to keep us company?"

"With pleasure, Aldin, with pleasure. In my cleanest tankards."

Selene selected one of the benches and sat down with a relieved sigh. There was a glob of something wet and sticky on the surface of the table. She wrinkled her nose and flicked it away with her thumb and forefinger.

"Well, Captain," she said. "You sure know how to show a woman a good time. It smells worse here than in Spritt's house."

Pine took a seat opposite her, banging the scabbard of his sword against the wood in the process. "Pinch your nostrils shut," he shot back testily. "We're here on business."

"Ah, the mysterious Gamin."

"Yes."

"So, you were a miner before becoming a watchman?"

"As I'm sure you already know. Stop interrogating me like one of your suspects."

Fletch arrived with two tankards filled with something dark and frothy. He set them down with a clank and waved away Pine's offer of three copper coins.

"Your money's no good here, Aldin. Just don't take another decade to come back again, eh?"

He gave Pine a hearty slap on the shoulder and wandered

away, whistling. Selene pushed a lock of auburn hair back behind her ear and took a cautious sip of ale.

"It's … it's surprisingly good," she admitted, a foamy moustache gracing her top lip.

"It certainly has character," Pine agreed, the bitter taste in his mouth bringing back a host of old memories. Coming up from the tunnels so bone-weary he could barely walk, his eyes burning from the dust, fresh blisters on his hands, enough grit in his hair to turn it grey. Staggering into the Dripping Bucket to reunite with the others. Friends closer than brothers.

All of them gone.

"So," Selene began tentatively. "You were in the Mines ten years ago? During the Collapse? I wonder if—"

"Why are you here?" Pine countered.

"What do you mean?"

"What's a rich, pampered young woman doing down here in the sludge and piss? Pretty much everyone in the Slums would dream of seeing the sun for more than a few hours and breathing air that didn't taste of charcoal. No one *asks* to come to this Mist-spawned place. No one except you. Why is that?"

Selene shifted uncomfortably. "I have my reasons."

"I'm sure you do."

"I … I was just trying to make friendly conversation."

Pine took a long draught of ale. "Except we're not *friends*, Watchman. I don't have any friends. Not anymore. And I don't want any new ones."

"How very stupid of you."

"Careful how you talk to your Captain. It's not stupidity,

it's practicality. We both know that in a couple of months, you'll be missing your feather mattress and pretty gas lamps."

Selene's eyes flickered, and Pine realised guiltily that he had gone too far.

Mists take me.

"I'm sorry," he began. "You didn't deserve—"

"Aldin?"

An old man stood silhouetted in the doorway of the Dripping Bucket, his bloodshot gaze wavering between anger and confusion. Worry lines and wrinkles cut deep into his aged face, forming a web of cracks and fissures. His left arm and bandy legs were more sinew than muscle, the skin stretched tight and thin over ropey tendons. The right arm ended in a mass of badly healed scar tissue just below the elbow.

He shuffled closer, his bony jaw moving as he considered his next words.

"You're in my spot," he said finally.

Pine patted a space on the wooden bench next to him. "I saved you a seat."

Gamin grunted and joined them with a crack of arthritic knees. "Been a while."

"It has."

"You owe me a pint."

"I owe you more than that," Pine said softly. "I owe you an explanation. I owe you an apology. I shouldn't have—"

"Bollocks," Gamin interrupted with a wave of his remaining hand. "A man grieves in his own way and in his own time. You needed to get away and forget."

"I did."

Fletch appeared silently and set down a third tankard.

Gamin gave him an appreciative mutter of thanks and lifted the ale high in a toast.

"Fate and fortune."

"Fate and fortune," Pine mumbled back, hating how hollow those words sounded now.

Gamin drank deeply. "Did it work? Stop the nightmares?"

Screams of fear. Weeping blood from every pore.

"No."

Another grunt. "My own plan was to drink enough of this piss-poor pigswill to drown my guilt."

"Any success?"

"None yet. But I'm still trying."

They sat in silence for some time, nursing their tankards of ale while Selene watched them, fingering her necklace. The other two patrons finished up their drinks and left, one of them flicking a couple of coins at Fletch as they passed. The barkeep loitered close by, surreptitiously cocking an ear as he half-heartedly cleaned a pewter cup with a dirty washcloth.

"I need your help," Pine admitted finally. "A man was found dead this morning. Possible murder. We're wondering if this might have something to do with it." He reached into the pocket of his tunic and produced the piece of paper confiscated from the jeweller earlier that day.

Gamin reached over and took it with a frown. "I gathered as much. You certainly didn't come here just for the pleasure of my company. I don't recognise any of the sketches." He rubbed at one corner with his thumb. "Mother's Grace, Aldin, this isn't vellum!"

"I know."

The older man dropped the scrap in disgust. "Then, you know where this is from. The Depths."

Selene's breastplate creaked as she leant forwards across the table, an expression of interest on her freckled face. "The Depths? Really? But they've been closed …"

"… since the Collapse," Pine finished. He studied her pensively, wondering just how much he trusted her. In the six months they had spent together, she had never given him any reason to doubt her sincerity. She was inquisitive, resourceful and, as she had once again proven today, a competent fighter. Her constant poking and prodding at his past was annoying yet seemed to come from a real desire to know him better. He glanced over at Gamin, who gave him an almost imperceptible nod of consent.

"I wasn't a miner," he said, feeling a weight lift from his shoulders. "Or rather, I was at first … then Gamin found me. He was looking for volunteers. To go beyond the Mines. Into unexplored territory."

"The Depths," Selene whispered.

"Far from the Mother's light," Gamin replied faintly. "To a place full of shadows and misery. The things we saw down there in the dark. Ghosts of the past …"

"These symbols," Pine pressed, holding up the paper. "I've seen them before, stencilled into the relics we found. What do they mean?"

Gamin took a mouthful of bitter ale and peered reluctantly at the markings. "I'm not sure."

"You must know something. Please."

"I … Mists take you, lad, you won't leave it alone, will you? It's some form of identification. Numbers. The first's a floor."

"A floor?"

"A level. The higher the number, the deeper the level. Second set's a room. No idea what the rest means." He wiped the froth from his lip and squinted. "Nine, one, zero, one."

"Mother keep me!" Selene exclaimed. "Nine levels down?"

"Aye. That's where it came from. I'd burn it though, if I were you."

"Why?"

Gamin scratched at the puckered stump of his right arm. His hand was trembling. "It wasn't much at first. A flicker in the corner of your eye. Tools missing from the spot where you left them. Gas lamps emptied of their fuel. Shadows … shadows among shadows."

"I don't think she needs to know—" Pine began.

"Pfff. Quiet, lad. You felt the same thing. We all did. We were just too scared or too stupid to talk about it." He tapped Pine's breastplate with a long-nailed finger. "Look at you, burying yourself away in another life, pretending nothing ever happened. That you weren't a part of it. As if that will stop the nightmares. Do you know why most people run? It's because they are being chased. So, why are you still running, Aldin? Who's chasing you?"

Bera. Hale. Lyle.

Ghosts of the past.

Pine snatched up the piece of paper and rose to his feet. "It was a mistake coming back here," he said, surprised at how bitter he sounded. The room swam, and he placed a hand on the table to steady himself. His tunic pressed tightly against his chest, making it hard to breathe. He had to get out. He had to get some air.

"Come on, Selene, we're leaving."

Gamin chuckled. "Hah. You're only proving me right, lad."

"Stop calling me lad. I'm not that Mist-spawned little boy anymore." Pine's voice was growing louder as he became angrier. Fletch had given up any pretence of cleaning his cup and was watching the exchange with interest.

Gamin drained the last of his ale and stood. His head barely reached Pine's shoulder.

I remember him being so tall, Pine thought. *So strong. A force of nature. But he's nothing. A crazed, doddering old man.*

"Selene," he repeated.

He was nearly suffocating now, his breath escaping in short, sharp gasps.

"No longer a boy, yet still running," Gamin said calmly. "And I wager what's chasing you is the same thing that's chasing me. It's your *guilt*. The shame of having survived when so many others did not."

"Mists … Mists take you."

"Aye. There are days when I wish they would. I even bribed my way up onto the city wall once. Looked out over those rolling white swirls. It would have been so easy to succumb to their embrace."

"Then, why didn't you?"

Gamin smiled. "I kept thinking of all those who died. How they must have prayed to the Mother for one more moment of life. One more chance to see their loved ones. We were lucky enough to be granted that second chance, Aldin. It would be a terrible dishonour to their memories to squander that."

Pine gazed at his scarred palms. "You're right," he said,

the anger draining from him. "It … it doesn't stop the dreams."

"I know, lad. I know." Gamin sighed. His next words were slow and measured as if causing him physical pain. "I went down as far as the ninth level once or twice. I still remember the way. If the Collapse hasn't rendered the tunnels inaccessible, I'll take you there."

"W … why?"

"Maybe it's time we stopped running and turned to face our fears. Maybe the Mother saved us for this very purpose. So that we could help others. I can't force you, lad, but if ever you need a guide, this is where you'll find me." He picked his empty tankard up off the table and shook it hopefully in Fletch's direction "Barkeep! More ale! My throat is drier than a constipated rat's arse." He paused, then turned back to Pine. "You never told me where you got that Mist-spawned thing, did you?"

"The victim was working on reproducing one of the designs. On orders from Lord Thane."

"Thane. As in the Keeper of the Peace? As in your *superior*? Why is the Protector of the City and the Commander of the City Watch dabbling with relics from the Depths?"

"I don't know," Pine replied grimly. "But I intend to find out."

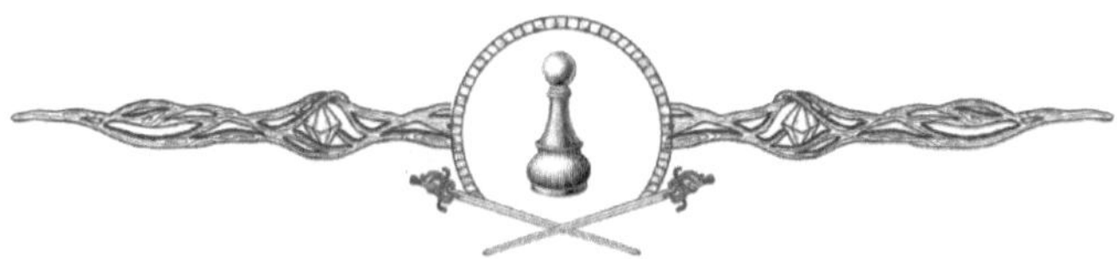

EIGHT
THE LIST OF THE DEAD

"She was back in my study again today, still playing that ridiculous game of hers. I was about to lecture her once more on the concept of inalterability when I realised that something was different. She had changed the shapes of the holes. It must have taken her hours. Days, even. Scraping diligently away at the wood with whatever tools she could find. Yet, she had persevered. Despite my constant remonstrations. She had not given up. And in doing so, she had opened up new possibilities. New ways to win. I think it was at that precise moment that my mindset began to change. For if my daughter has the strength and courage to deny the inevitable, then why shouldn't I?"

First Technologist Arniel Sin, The Time Before

R OE LET HIS breath out in a long hiss. What in the Mists was Krabbon doing with a warden? He felt Spider's hand on his shoulder. The older boy was motioning him to move away.

"Do you see now?" he said, once they had made their way back to the main street. "If I had confirmed your story, I would have been strung up next to you on the whipping post. Or possibly worse. We might have simply disappeared."

The cuts on Roe's arms stung. His head throbbed. He

closed his eyes, only to see Ant's scared face scream out at him from the depths of his troubled mind.

"Why punish us for telling the truth? A warden tried to kill Ant and me. Krabbon is constantly reminding us that we are an … investment to him. The coin we earn allows him to thrive. Even if he doesn't like us, he needs us."

A rickshaw rattled past on shaky wheels, pulled by a woman with a crooked back and balding head. The two orphans pressed themselves against the wall of the brothel to avoid being run over.

"Another question with an obvious answer," Spider said. He had his dagger out again. "If Krabbon doesn't want to pursue the matter any further, it can only be because he values his relationship with the wardens more than he values us." He held up his finger, his blade balanced across the tip. "Imagine a set of scales. On one side, exploitation. On the other, coalition. Krabbon must be careful to keep them both level." Spider flicked the knife into the air and caught it deftly. "Come on. He'll be leaving soon, and we don't want to be here when he does."

Roe plodded morosely back towards the marketplace considering what Spider had said. For how long had Krabbon been dealing with the wardens? And what exactly did he gain by doing so? He hefted his money pouch thoughtfully, hearing the clink of bronze pieces. It couldn't be for the money; his little gang of insects collected more coin in a day than a miner would make in a week. Prestige, then? Or something else?

"Feel her light," a voice called shrilly. It belonged to a member of the Mater Sorores, standing on the steps outside a crumbling chapel of the Mother, her once-white wimple now as soot-stained as her robe. She saw Roe looking at her and beckoned him with a wan smile. "Come, child. Come inside and let the Mother ease your pain."

"Another time," he replied a tad too hastily, running to catch up with Spider, who was scanning the entrance to the marketplace.

"It's half-empty," the chalk-skinned boy murmured. "Perhaps we should try the tunnels instead. The miners will be coming back up soon. We could put together some sob story about you getting your hands crushed by a collapsing shaft. Or abused by an alcoholic father. Whatever gets those pouches to open."

Roe nodded absently. "How did you find out?" he asked.

"About what?"

"Krabbon. The brothel. How did you find out?"

Spider gave a disinterested shrug. "He trusts me more than the rest of you put together."

"Because you don't ask any questions."

"That's probably one of the reasons. He sends me there every month or so with a sealed missive for the owner. My curiosity eventually led me to take a peek inside."

"It's a good place for a gathering," Roe added. "Anyone who sees Krabbon going inside will assume he's just … whetting his appetite. Hmmm. How long do these meetings normally last?"

"An hour or so. Sometimes more."

"Interesting."

"No."

"What?"

"I know what that tiny mind of yours is plotting. You want to rifle through his room while he's out. Bad idea."

"Oh, come on. Don't tell me you've never thought about it."

"I have. Then I remember the names of all the little insects who have gone missing over the years. Scarab, Moth, Mantis, Wasp, and now Ant. I have no desire to be the next name on that Mist-spawned list."

Roe was starting back towards the orphanage. "Fine. I'll do it by myself. You can stay outside and be my lookout. Whistle or something if you spot the bastard's shiny bald head."

Spider gave a long, exasperated sigh. "I'm already regretting taking you into my confidence."

"No, you're not. You're enjoying this. I've never heard you talk so much in all the years we've known each other."

"I had no reason to. No one spoke to me."

Roe felt a pang of guilt. "I … I suppose we didn't, did we? I'm sorry for that. We should have been better— Ah, we're here."

The austere facade of the orphanage loomed. It was the only stone building in the neighbourhood, a vestige of a long-forgotten age before the Mists had spread across the land and the upper classes still populated the lower levels. Two cracked statues guarded the ancient double doors, the left split almost in two by a gaping fissure, the right missing its head. Figures of Keselgraad's past, condemned to obscurity.

Roe hurried up the chipped steps and pushed his way inside, his hand leaving a bloody smear on the handle.

"Hello?"

The interior of the orphanage was just as bleak as its exterior. A single high-ceilinged arcade surrounded a square courtyard, currently empty save for its central whipping post and a collection of chamber pots stacked in one corner. Doors lined the opposite side leading to the sleeping quarters, pantry, and inaptly named Great Hall.

Roe traipsed across the yard, the mere sight of the post awakening a flare of pain in his buttocks. He recalled the silent stares of the other orphans, subdued and afraid. Krabbon's yellow-toothed leer as the birchwood stick rose and fell. He realised that there were no happy memories here. This was not his home. It never had been. It was a prison where he had been locked in for the last decade; every year stripping more of his humanity away until, eventually, he would become like Spider. Without emotion. Without hope.

Another docile subject of the Insect King.

He entered the Great Hall. It was darker inside, the only source of light the soft glow of the embers smouldering in the huge fireplace. Much to his relief, the place was deserted. Krabbon's ridiculous throne of carved wood lorded over rows of vacant benches.

Roe made for the end of the room, pausing to spit on the cushioned seat as he passed. A small opening led to the Insect King's chambers and a luxurious four-poster bed, its opulence slightly marred by the streaks of grease and other unidentifiable stains that covered its straw mattress. A cupboard stood in the opposite corner, its doors hanging open to reveal various disguises that Krabbon used to ply his trade, most of them crumpled and unwashed. Empty pewter bottles littered the floor, the fermented dregs adding to the rancid smell of sweat and dirt that permeated the air.

Roe began his search, not completely sure what he was

looking for. The space beneath the bed was empty. The over-turned mattress held no hidden secrets. He briefly considered splitting the fabric open to rummage among the straw, but that would be a surefire way to find himself back on the whipping post. The back of the cupboard had no discernible panels. There were no loose flagstones. No concealed pockets in Krabbon's moth-eaten clothes. He tapped all four posts of the bed, but none sounded hollow.

He grunted in frustration. There had to be something. Perhaps all he needed was some divine intervention. He closed his eyes.

"Mother keep me. Mother show me the way."

"Stop talking to yourself."

Roe gave a yelp and spun on his heel to see Spider staring at him from the doorway with his arms crossed and a bemused expression on his face.

"Mists take you," Roe spluttered. "You almost made me piss myself."

"From the terrible smell in here, I thought you already had. Time's up. We have to leave."

"A few more minutes."

"We don't have a few more minutes. There will be other meetings. Other opportunities."

Roe hesitated. "I'm not sure there will. Not for me. I … I think … I think I'm done."

"Done with what?"

"Krabbon. The orphanage. All of it. This place has brought me nothing but misery."

Spider looked unsure. "He is not the kindest of Masters, I admit, but I fear you are once again allowing your naivety to cloud your judgment."

"You're wrong." Roe pushed past the other boy, back into the Great Hall.

"I am not. I have considered leaving this place behind many times, only to conclude that the risk is too great. You … you fail to comprehend the extent of his influence. We are never hassled by the other gangs. Never bothered by the City Watch. Krabbon is a staple of the Slums. He has made deals with all the right people."

"I don't care," Roe replied, the orange glow of the fire deepening the lines in his face.

"You should. The Slums are not so different from the Mists, full of unseen terrors, watching and waiting, preying on the weak. As soon as you step out from behind the shield that Krabbon has built for us, they will devour you." Spider pointed at the carved throne. "All eccentricities hide a kernel of truth. No matter what you believe, he is our *King*."

"NO!" Roe shouted, his anger bursting free, raw and untamed. He grasped the arm of the chair and pushed, toppling it from its pedestal onto the floor. Both front legs broke off. The upholstered cushion tumbled free. The wooden seat cracked.

"That was … unwise," Spider remarked, brushing splinters from his tunic.

"This city is full of people like you," Roe seethed. "Those who believe things cannot be changed. It is why Keselgraad is dying from the inside out. But we can escape our fate, don't you see? We just need to fight hard enough. The Mother will show me the way."

"I think," Spider said, looking at the broken chair. "I think she already has."

A rectangular box protruded from the wreckage of the

seat, small and unadorned, with no discernible lock. Roe moved a couple of slats aside and bent to pick it up. He removed the top with little effort and peered inside.

"Coin," he said in disappointment.

"A lot of coin," Spider corrected. "And there's some silver mixed in there with the bronze. No one in the Slums pays in silver. It must come from the upper levels."

"Lord Thane's stipend, perhaps." Roe sifted through the metal pieces, most of them so chipped and worn that the stamped effigy of Lord Keselgraad was no longer visible. His fingers brushed against something at the very bottom of the box. A piece of frayed vellum. Words had been scratched into the surface, too faint to read. He frowned and moved closer to the dying embers.

"What's that?" Spider asked, craning his neck to see.

The rarity and cost of parchment, especially in the Slums, meant that the same scraps were used over and over again, either by washing the ink from the material with milk and oat bran or by scraping the surface with pumice. If the vellum was only washed, a slight imprint of the former writing could remain. A shadow.

The scrap that Roe was holding had obviously gone through the process numerous times, becoming so thin that it was nearly transparent. The first few lines were too faded to read. He brought the parchment even closer to the fire, squinting.

"I can't quite make it out ... Scab? Skarn?"

"Scarab," Spider said, his voice cold. "Remember him? Long hair and an infectious grin. Went missing two years ago. And underneath?"

"Dragonfly. Mists take me, it's a list of names."

"Worse. It's a list of the dead."

Roe's eyes dropped to the bottom of the parchment. The last line of text was bolder than the rest, written recently. His heart sank. Two words.

June Bug.

"No," he whispered. "Not her."

"I'm ... I'm sorry," Spider said, the word sounding strange in his mouth.

"We can still stop this!" Roe said. "We can find her and warn her. We can—"

Whatever he was going to say next was silenced by a deep, booming voice. "It's too late for that."

Krabbon stood framed in the doorway of the Great Hall, his wide shoulders brushing against the uprights. His beady little eyes glittered like buttons in the depths of his round face.

Roe dropped the box, scattering bronze and silver coins over the floor. He licked his dry lips and fixed the Insect King defiantly. "What are you going to do to June?"

"You are meddling in things you do not understand, Roach," Krabbon replied, slowly removing his gloves and overcoat. "It is for the good of the city. Everything I do is for the good of the city."

"She's only a child. Whatever you have planned for her, she doesn't deserve it."

"*Deserve?*" Krabbon spat. "Who are you to question the Mother's will? You are the mud on her boots. You are the insect at her feet. The ... roach." He rolled his neck, making his cervical bones crack. "We are at *war*. At war against the Mists. And like in all wars, there will be casualties on the long road to victory. There will be *sacrifices*."

He took a menacing step forwards. Roe's gaze flickered desperately around the Great Hall, searching for an escape route. A weapon. Anything.

"I am no sadist," the Insect King continued. "I take no joy in what I do. I only wish to serve the Mother. You are her enemy. I see that now. Sowing dissension among the other orphans. Trying to turn them against me with your lies. You seek to undermine our efforts to save this place. To undermine *her*." Spittle leaked from his lips, dribbling down into his beard that was writhing and crawling as he grew more agitated.

"I ..." Spider began, his normally monotone voice tinged with fear.

"Stand aside," Krabbon said. "I am most vexed by the part that you have played in this."

"But—"

"STAND ASIDE!"

Spider's jaw slammed shut, and he stepped away, hanging his head.

"No," Roe murmured, his own fear a ball of iron, round and heavy in his gut. "Help me. Please, help me."

Then Krabbon was there, his eyes filled with thunderous zeal, his fists raised to exact his retribution. Roe managed to dodge the first blow but could do nothing about the second, which hammered into his diaphragm hard enough to drive the air from his lungs.

"Please," he wheezed, blocking the return sweep with his bandaged forearm. A whistling right hook caught him on the side of the head. His vision blurred.

"Spider ..." He attempted to fight back, sending a frantic flurry of blows into Krabbon's flabby stomach. The Insect

King shrugged them off with a laugh and stamped on Roe's foot with his boot, sending a fresh jolt of pain up the boy's leg.

"The Mother will forgive you."

Roe screamed back at him, throwing a wild punch that was batted away with little effort. A knee slammed into his groin, and he doubled over, vomit mixing with the saliva in his mouth.

"It is finished, Roach," Krabbon said softly. Roe felt two strong hands encircle his neck and begin to squeeze. Terror filled him. He pulled at the fingers crushing his windpipe. Scratched at the wrists holding him prisoner. It was like trying to move marble. He gasped for air. His lungs burned. His lips formed a word he could no longer say.

Please.

"I envy you," Krabbon murmured. "You will soon stand in her light whereas I must remain here to do her bidding. Until every single insect has been sent to her loving embrace."

He applied more pressure. A black curtain was falling across Roe's eyes. He could no longer see the fire's embers. His arms dropped limply to his sides. Ant's scowling face shimmered in the darkness, berating him.

I'm sorry, Roe thought. *I tried.*

"You will make a fine gift for the Keeper of the Fields," Krabbon murmured. "You have failed this city in life, but you will serve her in death. Your corpse-coin will allow me to—"

Something hot and sticky spattered over Roe's head. The iron grip around his neck relaxed. He could breathe again. Ant's face disappeared, to be replaced by that of a wide-eyed man with a beard of crimson. Meaty hands were thrust into that mass of black hair, searching. Feeling.

Krabbon coughed, showering Roe with more steaming droplets. Blood. It was blood. Running from the King's open mouth, clogging his beard, drenching his thick fingers, and pouring from his throat in a stream of red. It reminded Roe of one of the many sewer pipes that spat their filth into the Slums, polluting the earth with their corruption.

The Insect King collapsed with a gurgle. Spider stood behind him, breathing hard, his expression a mix of fear and elation, his gore-caked dagger wavering in his grasp.

"*Every single insect,*" he said faintly. "You heard him. He was going to kill us *all*. I had no choice ..."

Roe stepped carefully over Krabbon's juddering form and took the blade from Spider's unresisting hand. "I heard. You saved them. You saved us."

"No choice," Spider repeated, making the words a mantra. "No choice." He looked down. Krabbon was still breathing. Short, gurgling gasps. "May the Mother keep him."

"June," Roe said suddenly, remembering. "It might not be too late! We have to warn her!" He bolted for the door, pulling Spider after him and leaving the Insect King to bleed out on the dirty floor of the Great Hall, surrounded by a twinkling tapestry of blood-stained coins and the shattered remains of his fallen throne.

NINE
THE STABLES

"Every Keeper on the Council will argue that their role is the most important. Potsworn will tell you that without food, the city will starve. Jeckle will point out that without wood and ore, our people will be neither housed nor clothed. Hellington will vaunt the merits of the taxes and tithes that allow our economy to flourish. They are all wrong, of course. I am the protector of Keselgraad. I am the Keeper of the Peace. And if there is no peace, then there is nothing. Only chaos."

Lord Matellas Thane, 832nd Year of the Mother

THANE STEEPLED HIS fingers and studied the relic that was reverently placed in the centre of his desk. It had been one of the very first objects that his excavation teams had found in the unexplored wonders of the Depths and was, as far as he knew, unique. Yet, despite many subsequent expeditions, its purpose remained frustratingly inscrutable.

A board covered in alternating black and white squares to form a chequered pattern. Eight rows. Eight columns. Then there were the black and white pieces. Exquisitely carved. Towers. Horses. Taller figures wearing crowns. Others, more numerous, with domed heads like the pommel of Thane's cane.

The relic had been found with the pieces already placed on the squares, grouped on either side like two opposing armies with the smaller figures making up the first line of defence. He picked one up and studied it carefully. Was it a tool to help devise battle tactics? Was it a game? A toy?

Thane set the piece back down with a scowl. The relic always awakened two conflicting emotions; an insatiable curiosity to learn more, and a deep annoyance at not being able to solve this particular mystery. He had always had an irrepressible urge to understand how things worked. Not just so that he could use them. So that he could *control* them. The city was no different.

He tapped his finger on the black king's crowned head and smiled.

One day. One day, he would reign over it all.

A tentative knock at the door heralded the arrival of his manservant with Thane's single and prohibitively expensive vice. He accepted the pear-shaped glass and downed its contents in one sip. The alcohol slid down his throat like liquid fire to settle in the pit of his belly. He motioned for the man to pour him another, fully aware that the bottle was probably worth more than a thousand casks of ale.

Control. He who controlled the Council controlled Keselgraad. Another problematic conundrum that he had not quite solved.

Mist-spawned Jeckle and his Mist-spawned empty threats.

Thane had done his research on the puff-sleeved prancer just as he had for all of his fellow Keepers. Jeckle's reputation was squeaky-clean, which meant that either he was an honest, upstanding citizen of Keselgraad or, more likely, he was exceptionally good at hiding his past. One thing the wardens *had* managed to dig up was a certain rumour pertaining to Jeckle's legitimacy as a member of House Grintov.

Council membership was hereditary; a rather ironic fact considering it had risen from the ashes of a revolution that had been driven by discontent with the previous totalitarian regime. The title of Keeper was passed from father to son. If there were no male heirs, the eldest daughter was chosen. And if the current incumbent had no children … things became complicated. Theoretically, whoever was next in line could claim the Council seat, although in practice, when the Grintov patriarch had died and been gifted to the fields, a host of pretendants had crawled out of the woodwork, all seemingly holding irrefutable proof of their legitimacy.

Jeckle had been the only candidate from the lower levels, a self-proclaimed mediator who brokered deals between the smelters and metal workers. His claim was also among the weakest, a vague assurance that his bloodline could be traced back to one of the deceased's distant cousins. He was quickly dismissed. Then, strangely, the other pretendants' applications began to fall apart. Claims were proved to be false or withdrawn without explanation. Two of them simply disappeared without trace. One by one, they faded away like shadows in the mist until, finally, only Jeckle remained.

The gaudy clothes were a disguise. Just as Thane's sword was concealed within his cane, so was Jeckle's true nature masked by buckled shoes, golden embroidery, and a frilly ruff. Until now, Thane had tolerated the man, but if the amethysts continued to fail more and more rapidly, he would have to be dealt with. Carefully.

Thane downed his second glass and rolled his tongue around the inside of his mouth. An excellent year. Bottled shortly before the arrival of the Mists. As if that impending tragedy had somehow made the distillers work harder. He smiled to himself.

"I will be spending the remainder of the day at the Stables," he informed the servant, reaching for his gloves. "Send a runner to the Den and request that Warden Devrard join me there. He will be pleased to know that his constant demands for more acolytes are finally going to be answered."

⌘

The City Watch House bordered a wide, open square on the twenty-second level, far below the Noble Quarters, fields and woodlands, yet sufficiently distant from the workshops and furnaces not to be troubled by their acrid smog. There was no need for mirrors here, and sunlight streamed down from the cloudless sky as Thane crossed the paving, sparing a quick glance at the statue that dominated the centre: a cavalry officer sitting proudly on his steed, his sabre raised in triumph. The oxidised metal had turned his face a sickly green, the eyes and nose worn smooth with the passage of time. Another vestige. Another long-forgotten hero.

The silent effigy hinted at the Watch House's previous role; the building had originally been a stable block to house the cavalry wing of Keselgraad's army back when the city had been surrounded by grassy plains instead of stifling Mists. As soon as the deadly white tendrils had reached the defensive walls, however, horses had lost all value. Too large to navigate the central stairway or winding alleyways. Too heavy to be allowed on the lifts. They had quickly become a luxury, a frivolous commodity displayed by the wealthy until, mal-treated and undernourished, they had died out completely.

The boxes were now barracks, the stalls were holding cells, and the outdoor arena a training yard, while the multi-storey administrative building had been converted into offices for the Watch captains and the Keeper of the Peace.

Thane stalked up the stairs to the second floor, returning the salutes of the guardsmen he passed with a crisp gesture of his own. The door to his study opened and closed with a well-oiled click. He removed his greatcoat, smoothed down his purple doublet, and settled into the stiff-backed chair behind his desk. A dozen sheets of rough vellum awaited his appraisal. Requisition forms, criminal sentencing, and daily reports laboriously transcribed by the Watch captains and physicians. He shuffled through them listlessly, then stopped as he saw a name he thought he recognised.

Jethro Spritt.

His eyes narrowed. He brought the vellum closer to his face to peer at the tiny script. An autopsy report, requested by Captain Aldin M. Pine. It appeared that Spritt had been dead for some time when they found him, making the pro-cedure more interesting. The stomach cavity was empty but blistering had been found along the inner lining as far as the lower intestines. Redness around the mouth and lips too. Thane skipped to the physician's conclusion. Possible poisoning.

Mists take me. Spritt. Dead ... poisoned.

It could not have come at a worse time. There was only a handful of artisans who could follow the instructions on the archaic sketches correctly and if—

Wait. Only a handful.

He rifled through the documents. There! Another name he recognised. The corpse of a welder found in the gutter outside a tavern in the Slums. And the previous week, a swineherd, his decomposing body discovered face-down in his sty, half-eaten by the pigs that he used to raise. All in Thane's employ. This was no longer a coincidence. This was deliberate sabotage. Someone knew what he was doing and was attempting to stop it.

Whoever it was, they were committing suicide. For if Thane could no longer repair the damaged amethysts that powered Keselgraad's protective barrier, there would be nothing to stop the Mists from entering the city and devouring its inhabitants.

A sharp rap on the study door.

Devrard. Finally. They had no more time to waste.

"Come in, Warden" Thane ordered. "Things are coming to a head. We must—"

"Apologies, my Lord. It's Captain Pine."

Mists.

"I'm very busy, Watchman."

"It's important."

Thane set down the sheets of vellum and massaged his temples. He could feel the all-too-familiar throb that heralded the beginning of a raging headache. "Five minutes."

Pine entered, his scarred face haggard, a fresh cut scabbing over on his cheek, and a new dent in his breastplate. His partner, Selene Eckelston, followed, the entire right side of her tunic a bloody mess.

"You seem to have run into some difficulty, Captain."

"We were chasing down a lead, my Lord. Quite literally, in fact." Pine saluted in an off-hand fashion.

"Ah, yes. The Spritt case."

"Murder. The Spritt *murder*."

Thane tapped the sheet of vellum. "I read the report. Marks on the deceased's lips and intestines are not irrefutable evidence of poison, Captain. You've been doing this job long enough to know that. Where did the trail take you?"

"A workshop on one of the lower levels, my Lord. We found a couple of interesting items." He reached into the pocket of his tunic and laid the prong-like contraption and piece of paper down on the desk.

He finished it, Thane jubilated. *Spritt actually managed to finish it!* He looked up to see Pine studying him carefully, searching for a reaction. Thane gripped the armrests of his chair tightly. The last thing he needed was more people trying to undermine his project. He held the other man's gaze calmly. "What is it?"

"We're not sure, my Lord," Selene said. "Neither of us has seen anything like it before. The paper, however, is a different story. The symbols are numbers, and they appear to allude—"

"I'm sure the Keeper of the Peace is only interested in information pertaining directly to the case," Pine interrupted, his eyes never leaving Thane's face. "Isn't that right, my Lord?"

I remember you, Thane thought. *When I found you, you were lying on your back in the dirt. Then you crawled up out of the Depths like a rat to beg me for a new life. A new beginning. Anything to keep you away from those dark tunnels. You owe me. You owe me everything.*

"I'm curious," he said to Selene. "What did the numbers tell you?"

"That the sketches most likely originate from deep underground. A place called the Depths."

"Lord Thane knows all about the Depths, Watchman," Pine said. His voice quavered. "Any expeditions had to be validated by the Keepers Council. Before they were closed, of course."

"True. You remember it well, Captain. Which is surprising, as I seem to recall you wished to join the City Watch to help you forget."

Pine glanced down at his scars. The same scars that Thane kept hidden under his leather gloves. "Some memories will never fade," he said. "I still hear the voices. Do you … my Lord?"

"Of course not," Thane scoffed. "Your five minutes are nearly up. Where are you going with all of this?"

"The expeditions to the Depths were validated by the Council, and it was also mandatory to submit any of the relics recovered for inspection. A Council that you are part of. Do you … recognise either of these two items, my Lord?"

"No."

Pine leant forwards, planting both his hands on the varnished desk, their palms flat. "We met with the workshop owner, a certain Bendel Spritt, who told us the piece had been commissioned by Lord Matellas Thane. Take another look."

"Am I under investigation, Captain?"

Selene coughed loudly. Pine ignored her.

"You forget how well I know you, my Lord. We have

travelled in the same circles, you and I. Seen the same things. Take another look."

Thane could smell the faintest hint of alcohol on the other man's breath. The scab on Pine's cheek had broken open and was leaking blood. He could have been mistaken for a tavern drunkard if it were not for those piercing dark blue eyes, flecked with indigo sparks. Sadness had made its home there, buoyed by melancholy and guilt. They were the eyes of a war veteran. Of someone who had survived a great tragedy and was still struggling with the horrific aftermath, day after day.

Such a man could not be threatened. Or bribed. Or cowed into submission. His fear had been numbed by the events of the past. It made him dangerous.

"I cannot help you, Captain," Thane said.

Pine's thin-lipped smile was devoid of mirth. "The Watch has a duty to uphold the laws of this City, my Lord. I believe you swore the same oath as I did. Jethro Spritt deserves justice."

"I could not agree more."

The desk creaked under Pine's weight. "Then, tell me—"

He was interrupted by three precise, orderly taps on the doorframe. Warden Devrard stood in the study entrance, his long-beaked mask obscuring his features. "Is everything all right, my Lord?" he enquired. His voice was soft and slightly muffled, yet somehow managed to convey a hint of menace.

"Ah, Devrard," Thane said, releasing his grip on the armrests of his chair and standing up swiftly. "Everything's fine, isn't it, Captain?"

"I have not finished," Pine countered hotly.

"Then, we will have to continue this conversation

another time. The warden and I have pressing matters to attend to. You are dismissed."

Pine made to pick up the metal tongs and paper. Thane motioned for him to stop. "You can leave those with me, Captain."

"I don't—"

"That's an order. Unless, perhaps, you are no longer capable of following them? In which case, I'm sure Watchman Eckelston will be happy to take over your duties."

"But—"

"Go home. Both of you. You are overworked and not thinking straight. A good night's sleep will help shed new light on this unfortunate misunderstanding."

Pine's gaze flickered to his officer's sword, and for an instant, Thane wondered if he was going to tear it from its scabbard and launch himself over the desk. Then, his expression changed, and his shoulders sagged. "As you wish, my Lord."

Another half-hearted salute and he turned away. Thane waited until both watchmen had left the study then pocketed the metal apparatus and went to put on his coat.

"Things are accelerating," he said to Devrard. "We lost two amethysts this morning."

The warden cocked his head in a strangely bird-like gesture. "Two?"

"Yes. We will need more raw materials. I trust that will not be an issue?"

"Supplies are running low."

"I know. Sister Nayelle has promised to support my request for more wardens. That should facilitate your harvest."

"Indeed."

"We can take the same elevator to the lower levels. I must visit Bendel Spritt before nightfall. It appears that his tongue has worked its way loose from its knot."

"Hmm. If the carrot has failed, perhaps the stick will be more effective."

Thane thought back to the chequered board and the black king, lording over his row of soldiers. All great deeds demand sacrifice.

"You're right," he said. "The stick it is."

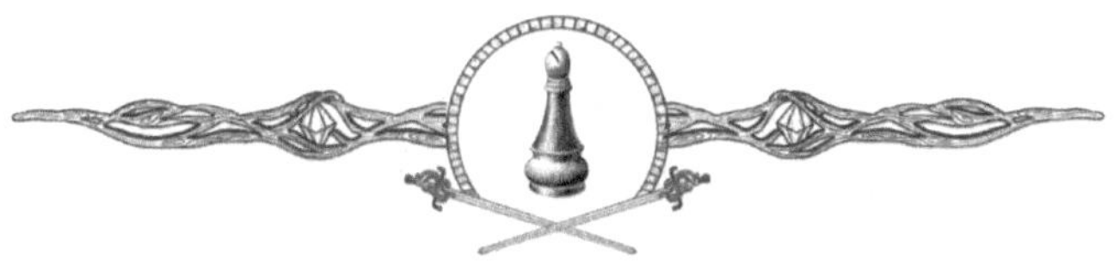

TEN
UNDER THE ALTAR

"I am often asked why the Mother, in her infinite power and wisdom, does not simply destroy the Mists that encircle our beleaguered city. The truth is that I do not have a definitive answer. Her plans for us extend far beyond anything we mere mortals can comprehend. What I believe, however, is that she cannot banish the Mists because it is we who created them. That they are the manifestation of all our corruption and sin. The more we sin, the stronger the Mists become, and it is only by seeking absolution that we may hope one day to be free of them."

Sister Nayelle, Keeper of the Faith, 833rd Year of the Mother

S ISTER SUPERIOR NAYELLE ripped the offending weed out of the soft soil, checking that she had removed all of its roots. No matter how long she spent scouring her herb garden clean, the unwanted plants always seemed to return. An ever-present menace to her beautiful flowers, much like the Mists constantly threatened Keselgraad.

She loved working in the garden. It was one of the few peaceful spots in the entire convent, silent save for the soft humming of the bees as they buzzed among the lavender, foxgloves, and buttercups. A place to forget the weakening of the amethysts set into the Church spire, the increasingly worrying demands of Lord Thane, and everything that the Mother required of her.

She brushed the dirt from her fingers and studied her hands. There was still some of that awful black substance stuck under the nails. She had scrubbed her skin almost raw trying to remove it last time. It was as if it had been inked into her flesh.

Perhaps it is a mark, she thought, reaching for her trowel. *A sign that I am one of the Mother's Chosen.*

The Keeper of the Faith was the only position on the Keepers Council that wasn't hereditary. Instead, upon the death of the previous incumbent, a half-dozen nuns selected by their peers were sent into the chambers under the Church. Of the six who entered, only one returned with her mind clear and her fingers stained.

Nayelle removed another tenacious weed from the base of a bright yellow calendula. Something wet splashed onto the freshly unearthed soil. A tear. She was crying. Why?

Because I hate that place. That subterranean chamber. And I've been trying to ignore the fact that I have to go back.

The wardens. She had promised Lord Thane that she would support his request. Which meant more of the philtre for the initiation process.

Nayelle set down the trowel and stood, readjusting her long robes. It was time. She left the garden and passed through the cloister into the Church of the Mother. The pews were almost empty at this time of day, with only a handful of supplicants conversing with the nuns or kneeling in prayer. The magnificent stained-glassed effigy of the Mother watched over them all, her shining golden locks forming a halo around her serene face.

Nayelle paused in front of the central aisle and stared up at the representation of her goddess, gathering her strength. She was Chosen. She was the Mother's emissary. Her voice. Her right arm. The other nuns would give anything to be in her place. To wield the power that she had. She should be exultant. So why did it take every ounce of her fortitude to return to that chamber?

Mother keep me.

The entrance was a simple trapdoor located behind the altar. There was no lock, only a triangular indentation that fitted perfectly the medallion she wore around her neck. A rusty ladder with two missing rungs led down into a short corridor that ended in another closed door.

Nayelle's hand was trembling as she pressed her necklace into a depression near the handle. Something clicked, and the hinges moved of their own accord, revealing the room beyond. It was small and simple; four featureless stone walls lit by a lightwell set into the ceiling. In the centre, on a raised dais, sat an octagonal font. Seven of its sides were carved with religious imagery representing the Mother blessing Lord Keselgraad as he claims the land that will be the site of his city. Watching from the heavens as the levels rise. Protecting those working tirelessly to erect the spire. The eighth side was void of sculpture, replaced instead by a single sentence.

On the eighth day, the Mother loosens the bondage of death and receives the fallen from their graves.

Nayelle could feel her heart thumping in her chest. Her wimple was tight and heavy on her head, pressing painfully against her brow. Her feet were rooted to the spot, like one of the weeds from her garden burrowing deep into the soil.

Mother keep me.

The first step was the hardest as she forced herself to move closer to the font. She was still holding the medallion, and she squeezed it until the points of the triangle dug into her flesh. Two more steps. Three. Enough to bring her to the lip and see what was inside.

A liquid. Black as charcoal and thick as syrup. Nayelle could see her own panic-stricken face and wide doe eyes reflected in its slick surface. A mirror into the soul. An octagon of darkness so opaque that it made the font seem like the opening of a deep, unfathomable well.

Nayelle took a long, shuddering breath and plunged her hands into the inky substance. It was cold. Bitterly cold. A biting, freezing chill that tore at her flesh with fangs of ice. She stifled a scream. The sensation spread, slithering up her arms under her robes, and prickling her bare skin.

Her vision began to change. The spartan chamber faded, replaced by an unending field of pitch-black shadow. A starless, moonless sky devoid of light. But not sound. Things chittered and screeched deep within that darkness. Howled and cackled. Moaned and wailed. Nayelle could almost make them out; blurred forms on the very edge of her perception. Circling her. Like a predator stalking its prey.

Mother keep me.

"I am here," she said into the night, her voice a fearful whisper.

No sooner had the words left her lips than a faint, glowing halo flickered into existence, far away in the distance. The numbness in her fingers lessened slightly as if warmed by this new presence. Nayelle willed the apparition to come closer, but it fled her gaze, hovering like a firefly on the horizon. Something shimmered in its centre. Something golden. She caught a glimpse of shining hair.

My child.

A tidal wave of emotion crashed into her, and the scream she had been holding in exploded from her lungs. There was pain. Indescribable, raw pain. Disapproval. Frustration. Anger. Yet, there was also affection. There was love.

My child. Heed my desires.

Nayelle wept.

And listened.

ELEVEN
IRON AND BLOOD

"My initial calculations are distressing, to say the least. If they are correct, then the current cycle will reach its apotheosis far sooner than we originally thought. The only good news is that more and more of my fellow technologists have been drawn to my cause, as hopeless as it may seem. Some of the greatest minds of our age are working together in an attempt to change our fate. It is a beautiful thing to behold. Unfortunately, I fear it will not be enough."

First Technologist Arniel Sin, The Time Before

THE SQUARE BEFORE the Stables was wreathed in shadow, the sun hidden behind the monolithic majesty of Keselgraad's upper levels. Thane and his warden companion walked briskly to the archway leading to the central staircase and its iron elevator.

The thousands upon thousands of winding steps never failed to impress him. He placed both hands on the iron railing and leant out as far as he dared, admiring the way the concentric circles spiralled down into the blackness. He wondered how it would feel to pitch over the edge and tumble earthwards. To feel that single instant of weightlessness before falling, faster and faster, the surprised faces of those climbing and descending flashing by in a blur until the explosive finale, his bones cracking and flesh tearing as the Mother welcomed him home.

A fleet-footed messenger brushed past Thane's back, his muscular legs pumping as he bounded up the stairs two at a time to deliver some missive to the upper levels. The faster the messengers ran, the more jobs they could take on, and the more they could earn. The richest among them were the most reckless; sliding and jumping their way through the crowds to reach their destination as quickly as possible. It was a dangerous profession, even more so during the winter when the steps became wet and slippery, and when losing one's balance could lead to a broken leg or worse.

"My Lord." Devrard was waiting patiently by the elevator platform, his gloved hands clasped in front of him, his masked face unreadable. The flat tone of his voice had an unnerving quality that Thane couldn't quite place. He stepped away from the railing and approached a wizened old man sitting on a battered chair next to a score of ropes that ran down the entire length of the shaft. The white-haired operator wore a creased felt cap and a thick glass monocle that made one eye appear much larger than the other.

"Passengers?" he whined.

"Matellas Thane of House Quellion and Warden Devrard."

"Destination?"

"The artisan quarters on level five, then down into the Slums."

"Humpf." The man produced a sheet of vellum from his tunic and studied it carefully. "House Qarrel ... House

Quellion. Ah, yes. I trust your payments to the operator's guild are in order?"

Another fine example of Keselgraadian bureaucracy, Thane fumed. He tightened his grip on his cane and forced himself to smile.

"Indeed. As they were this morning when I descended from the top level."

"Perhaps. A lot of people pass through here, my Lord, and all must pay the tithe. It's the only thing that keeps the elevator going."

And probably what paid for that fine monocle, too.

"Both the warden and I have an annual agreement with the guild."

"That true? Very nice, very nice." He readjusted his lens and narrowed his eyes at the tightly packed script. "Humpf. My, my, we do get out and about, don't we, my Lord? Lots of ups and downs."

"I'm in rather a hurry, operator."

"Everyone always is, my Lord. Everyone always is." The old man swivelled round and placed his hands on the mass of ropes that hung together like the threads of a weaver's loom. "Fifth level. Humpf." He selected one and tugged. Somewhere far above their heads, a distant bell chimed.

Thick cables creaked. Metal screeched. On the far side of the shaft, an enormous counterweight whooshed past, passing inches from those toiling up and down the spiral stairs. Then, with a thundering rumble, the lift descended; a twenty-foot-square cage of rusting iron suspended from a host of pulleys and winches. It juddered to a halt before the operator, who stood with a disgruntled *Humpf,* swung a movable part of the iron railing aside, and pulled the lift door open with a clang.

Four black-clad wardens were waiting inside, their uniforms and masks so identical that it was impossible to tell them apart. Thane gave them a respectful nod as he stepped onto the metal-plated floor and wrapped his hand around one of the bars to steady himself. Going from solid ground to the swaying, shuddering lift always made him feel dizzy. Devrard entered behind him, showing no outward signs of discomfort. The operator slammed the door shut, ambled over to the ropes, and yanked on the fifth one from the right. Soon, the lift was moving again, continuing its ponderous journey down into the belly of Keselgraad.

Thane stared through the bars, watching the less fortunate citizens on the stairwell, most transporting goods or raw materials from one level to another. It would take them hours to reach their destination, whereas Thane would be there in minutes. It was regrettable, but such was the way of things. The lift was too small to be used by the entire population of Keselgraad so its access had to be gated. Besides, a brisk, daily walk was excellent for the lungs. Thane had, out of curiosity, taken the steps a few times himself and found it most invigorating.

The four wardens opposite him hadn't moved, displaying that stoic, solid discipline that Thane had always admired. They were not simple watchmen; they had evolved into something much greater. The largest, most proficient fighting force in all of Keselgraad. And they were under *his* command. He glanced across at Devrard who was standing apart from the others, his head once more cocked to the side as if in deep thought.

"Devrard," Thane said, his voice jittering with the vibrating movement of their descent.

"My Lord?"

"It was most perspicacious of you to send for reinforcements. You may need help with the harvest."

The warden turned. "I did no such thing, my Lord. I surmised that it was you who had sent word to the Den."

Thane saw a reflection in the glass eye-pieces of Devrard's mask. A gleam of steel. He ducked instinctively and felt something hiss past his head and clash against the iron bars. He lashed out and was rewarded with a surprised *oompf* as his boot connected with a leather-clad shin.

"Treachery!" he snarled, twisting the ball on the top of his cane. A gloved fist pounded into his shoulder before he could draw his blade free, and the weapon fell from his grasp, rolling across the plated floor out of reach. Thane cursed and wheeled to face his attacker. The warden had his stiletto-like knife out, and the ceramic of his curved beak was the colour of bleached bone. It made him appear cold and skeletal, a harbinger of death itself.

It was the first time that Thane had found himself on the other side of that expressionless stare. It was not a pleasant experience.

His fencing instructor's voice echoed in his head. Anticipation was the key to victory. A duel was akin to a game of cards; a slight flicker of the eyelids or a twitching of the nose could reveal the opponent's intent.

Except, of course, when your opponent is wearing a mask.

Thane dropped his gaze to the hand holding the blade,

ignoring a cry of pain from his right as Devrard scored a hit on one of the other wardens.

The man's elbow lowered. His wrist twisted. Thane side-stepped just seconds before his adversary lunged forwards, his thrust finding only empty air. With a triumphant shout, Thane grabbed the man's arm and slammed it as hard as he could against the bars of the lift. The dagger dropped through one of the gaps and plunged into the pitch black of the shaft.

The clash of steel had not gone unnoticed by those using the stairs, and most had abandoned their tiring ascent to crowd the railings, pointing and shouting as the lift trundled past.

"Get help!" Thane yelled furiously at them. "The Keeper of the Peace is under—" A bony knee crunched into his stomach, driving the air from his lungs in a gasping exhala-tion. He staggered, hooked his boot around the other man's ankle and pulled him off his feet.

The metal floor of the lift was already slick with blood. Devrard had eviscerated one of his foes who now lay slumped in the far corner with both hands pressed against the pulsat-ing mass of fat and viscera spilling forth from his stomach.

Thane looked down at his own opponent who was struggling to rise. He kicked the man hard in the ribs and rolled him onto his back.

"Who are you?" he shouted above the screeching of the lift and the moaning of the dying warden. There was no reply. No change in expression. Just that Mist-spawned, fea-tureless mask staring back at him.

Mocking him.

Thane stamped down hard. The ceramic fissured, then

shattered, peppering the bloody floor with white shards and revealing the face hidden beneath.

The path to becoming a warden was long and dangerous. It demanded sacrifice, both mental and physical. It brought about change. Irrevocable change. Thane had seen Devrard unmasked. He had seen … the cost.

The man lying at his feet had smooth, unblemished skin. His dark green eyes were clear. Whoever he was, he was not a warden.

"Your name," Thane ordered. An agonising shriek told him that Devrard had dispatched his final adversary. "Your name and the name of those who contracted you to kill me."

"I … cannot."

"What are you so afraid of? I am the Keeper of the Peace. I have an army at my command. I can protect you. Tell me."

"I … I am sorry." The man raised his right hand, revealing what it was holding. The remains of a curved ceramic beak.

Thane's eyes widened as he realised what was about to happen. "No!"

His opponent drove the sharp tip deep into his own left eye, popping the iris with a gelatinous squelch and continuing into his brain. His body jerked, his booted feet tapping a macabre rhythm on the metal floor panels. Thane recoiled in disgust. "Devrard!" he called. "I need one of them alive."

"That … may not be possible, my Lord."

The warden stood amid three blood-spattered corpses, his dual stilettos and waxed leather clothes caked in gore, his mask tarnished by a crimson smear under one eye.

By the Mother, Thane thought, *he's not even out of breath.* "Are you all right?"

Devrard bent to wipe his twin blades on a dead man's tunic. "Perfectly. They did not present much of a challenge. A confrontation with four real wardens would have been exponentially more complicated." He sheathed his daggers and tore the mask off one of the bodies. "Crude," he murmured as he squeezed it, cracking the ceramic. "And poorly made. A pale imitation."

"And yet, they managed to get the jump on you."

"Yes. Apologies. I was distracted by your news concerning the failing amethysts. I should have been more alert. It will not happen again."

The lift grated to a shuddering halt as it reached its destination. Thane could spy the shocked visage of another operator through the bars, his mouth opening and closing like a fish out of water. He half-fell out of his chair and tottered over to the railing.

"What … what happened here?"

Thane dismissed the four corpses with a wave of his hand. "Official warden business. Open the gate."

He turned away from the astonished operator and searched the floor of the lift for his fallen cane. It lay in the far corner next to the slouched form of the disembowelled assassin. Thane knelt in the muck of the man's viscera to retrieve it.

"Water."

It was a desperate, cracked whisper. The last wish of a condemned man. Thane shuddered and removed the mask. Two bloodshot eyes pleaded with him.

"It is too late for that," he said. "You must prepare yourself to meet the Mother. You must unburden yourself of all sin."

The dying man wheezed. "I—"

"You have been tricked, friend. Someone has deceived you into attacking the Keeper of the Peace. I am the only person who stands between the Mists and Keselgraad's destruction. Without me, the city will fall. Do you understand? You have committed heresy. You must atone."

"No ... I ..."

"Who sent you? Who conspires against the Mother herself? Free your troubled mind. Find your peace. Tell me."

The man gave a terrible, wracking cough. Fresh blood bubbled from his lips. His hand rose from the torn ruin of his gut to trace a familiar symbol in the filth.

Thane frowned. "Are you sure?"

The assassin could no longer answer. His slack jaw and dull gaze would reveal no more secrets.

"Devrard!"

"My Lord?"

Thane pointed at the bloody mark made by the dying man. "Does that constitute sufficient proof, do you think?"

The warden cocked his head. "Unlikely. It may well be seen as the delirious hysteria of a dying man."

"Hmmm. And if we could *produce* more evidence? A second conspirator, perhaps. A scapegoat. Someone with motive and a rebellious streak."

"That would indeed be more compelling, my Lord."

A plan was slowly forming in Thane's mind. A plan that would allow him to rid himself of two particularly annoying birds with one stone.

"Get the operator in here to witness this," he said. "Then head for the Slums."

Devrard bowed curtly and withdrew, leaving Thane to

watch the blood of the dead assassin slowly cover the markings traced on the metal panel.

A hammer and tongs.

Jeckle.

TWELVE
FIELDS OF GOLD

"Do you have any idea how much tilled land it takes to feed a family of four? I do. Two acres. The upper levels of Keselgraad were meant to supplement what was produced in the fields beyond the city walls, not replace it entirely. You're all worrying about how the Mists will kill us tomorrow. Starvation will kill us today."

Lord Potsworn, Keeper of the Fields, 829th Year of the Mother

ROE HURRIED THROUGH the streets of the Slums as fast as his long legs would carry him. The sole of one of his boots had become unstuck and flapped uselessly from his foot like a leather tongue, thwacking the dirty cobbles as he ran. His backside ached. His neck ached. His forearms ached. His head felt like it would explode at any moment, showering the passers-by with blood and brain matter. Yet, he pressed on, his arms pumping, a single name etched into his mind.

June.

Losing Ant had been terrible. Losing June would be unsurmountable.

A cracked sewage pipe leaked brown gunk from the higher levels. Roe splashed through it angrily. That was what the Slums had become; a dumping ground for the more fortunate. The merchant guilds and Noble Houses took what they needed – the minerals, the clay, the charcoal, the *people* – and gave back their unwanted waste.

The Collapse that had happened ten years ago had only further confirmed their complete disinterest in the Slums' plight. There had been a public outcry, of course. A day of mourning. Prayers and sermons. Condolences that had trickled down from the Noble Houses. All immaterial. Prayers would not fix the failing mirrors, prevent the undernourished families from dying of famine, or make the Mines safer. They would not stop the pipes from discharging piss and excrement onto the streets.

Roe reached the entrance to the Mines, a huge tunnel that resembled the gaping maw of a mythical beast, complete with stalactite teeth. Rickshaws were parked haphazardly in front of the opening, their drivers waiting for loads of raw ore for the smelters or clay for the kilns.

Spider staggered to a halt beside him and bent over double, panting.

"By the Mother, you move fast for a skinny, flat-nosed little runt."

"And you move slowly for a long-legged freak."

"I have rarely needed to run. Besides, I am still trying to wrap my head around what I've done."

"What *we* have done."

"I killed a man. *Me*, not you. I was holding the blade. And I did it in the most cowardly way possible; a dagger in the back while he was distracted and defenceless."

Roe fixed him with an incredulous stare. "He couldn't *defend* himself because he was busy choking me to death!"

"Krabbon may have had his faults, but he clothed and fed us ..."

"... whipped and beat us ..."

"... kept us from harm ..."

Roe threw up his arms in disgust. "Mists, Spider. Stop! Just stop. Have you already forgotten why we are here? He was *selling* us to the wardens! Like slaves! Krabbon was a sick, cold-hearted bastard who deserved far worse than a cut throat. If we hadn't been pressed for time, I would have pissed on his corpse and burnt his home down to the ground. You did the right thing. *We* did the right thing."

Spider was shaking his head. "And what will we do now? The orphanage is no longer safe. The other street gangs will soon learn of Krabbon's demise and retake control of what little territory we had left. How will we survive if we can no longer beg or steal? How will we find food? We may have buried one problem only to unearth another."

"We'll work something out. Our first priority is June." Roe began to walk towards the tunnel entrance, scratching at his blood-stained bandages. He spotted the foreman leaning against the wall a few feet inside, filling a crude pipe with some unrecognisable mix of dried leaves.

"Excuse me?"

The man looked up with a scowl. "You Mist-spawned roaches always seem to appear when I'm about to start my break. What does that bastard Krabbon want now?"

Roe coughed. "He sent us here to fetch June, Sir. She's needed elsewhere."

"Is she now?" the foreman's scowl deepened. "That's unfortunate. We discovered a new vein of iron ore this morning so we've started expanding the gallery. Little bug has been making sure the hewers are well-watered and the candles well-stocked. I'd hate to lose her."

Spider produced a bronze coin from his tunic and held it up between his thumb and forefinger. "For your trouble."

The man snatched it with a grimy hand and shoved it into one of the many pockets of his equally grimy overalls.

"Wait here," he grunted and wandered off deeper into the tunnel, pausing to light his pipe at a brazier riveted to the wall.

"Where in all the Mists did you find that?" Roe asked, impressed.

Spider took his arm and pulled him away from a group of rickshaw drivers. "Part of Krabbon's ill-gotten gains," he replied in a whisper, shaking his tunic to make it jingle. "I grabbed a couple of handfuls on the way out."

"That was … clever."

"Ah, so you finally admit it."

"I'm not admitting anything. Mother keep me, I cannot stand these bandages for a moment longer!" Roe tore at the dirty cloth covering his arms, ripping it from his skin. He used a length to tie the sole of his boot back on and threw the rest into the brazier where it burned with a greasy yellow flame.

The superficial cuts were already scabbing over, itching as they did so. Roe stared moodily into the fire as it danced and writhed. It reminded him of the Mists that churned against the base of the city wall a mere hundred feet from where he was standing. Before Ant's death, he had almost forgotten their menacing presence, much like the other inhabitants of the Slums. The fact that they were hidden from sight somehow made them fade from memory, like trying to remember a particularly horrific nightmare after waking up.

"Roe!"

June was caked in so much dirt that her mop of straw-coloured locks had turned a dusty grey. She was holding one of her mud dolls, six dried balls stuck together to resemble something vaguely human.

"Hello there, little June Bug."

She skipped towards him with a crooked-tooth grin and wrapped her tiny arms around his waist.

"Ow!" Roe said, ruffling the girl's hair affectionately. "Careful."

June stepped back, taking in his bloody tunic and bruised neck. "By the Mother, what happened to you?"

"Krabbon."

"Oh no, did he beat you again? You have to stop making him mad, Roe. One of these days he'll go too far, and you'll be feeding the fields."

"I don't think that will happen," Spider replied cautiously, his eyes on the foreman who was clumping back up the tunnel, his head wreathed in smoke from his pipe.

"Why is that?"

"Because I killed him."

June's grin slipped. "Oh no," she said quietly. "Mother keep me … Mother keep all of us. What have you *done*?"

"Saved your life," Spider replied with a hint of annoyance. "Now, perhaps we should leave, unless you still want to be here when the warden comes to cart you off to Mother-knows-where."

Her bottom lip trembled. "W … what?"

"Stop it, you're scaring her," Roe said, taking June's hand in his.

"Good! She should be scared! She's wanted by the most terrifying group of killers in all of Keselgraad!"

"We just need to find a place to hide."

"Hide? In the Slums? Without Krabbon's protection, we won't last more than two minutes. Mists, half the people down here would turn her in for a bronze coin or a loaf of bread."

"Then, we find somewhere else. On one of the other levels."

"Where?"

"I don't know!" Roe shouted back, drawing curious stares from the rickshaw drivers. He felt June squeeze his fingers with her own.

"Mrs Pattyworth will help us."

"Mrs ... who?"

"Mrs Pattyworth, the wheatwatcher. I sometimes used to take her messages from the granaries or the pig farms. Before Krabbon started sending me to the Mines every day. She always invited me in for a bowl of kernel soup or mixed grain salad. I think she's lonely."

Roe glanced down at his disintegrating boots and June's threadbare sandals, with her scratched ankles and chipped toenails. "The wheat and corn fields are just below the Noble Quarters," he said. "That's a two-hour climb. Are you sure you can— Ow!"

June had kicked him playfully in the shins. "Don't be silly. I've been up and down those stairs more than you. You'll be the one trying to keep up."

"And if this ... Mrs Pattyworth turns us away? It will

be dark by the time we get there." Roe glanced up at the sky, but the sun was either hidden behind the upper levels or obscured by the thick black smog. "Spider, what do you think?"

The older boy was attempting to rearrange his crow-black hair. He shrugged. "It's as good a plan as any."

Roe sighed. "A ringing endorsement. Fine. Lead on, June."

The entrance to the central stairwell was nearby; a huge vaulted archway that must have once been magnificent to behold, before the smoke from the furnaces had sullied the stone, and various disgruntled residents of the Slums had covered the crumbling surface with crude graffiti. A crowd of people surrounded the lift platform just inside, blocking it from sight. There was the faintest scent of blood.

"What's going on?" Roe asked a burly carrier, his wicker basket filled with rye bread from the upper-level bakeries.

"The Keeper of the Peace was attacked," the man replied. "Supposedly fought off a half-dozen wardens single-handedly."

"Wardens? Why would wardens want to murder Lord Thane? I thought he was their leader?"

"Dunno. Perhaps he wasn't paying them enough." The carrier cackled at his own joke and turned away. Roe spied a few crumpled bodies and what appeared to be the remains of a ceramic mask.

"Can we go, please?" June pleaded in a small voice. "I don't like it here."

Roe nodded, and they began their arduous climb up the thousands of steep spiralling steps. Spider spent the first few levels explaining to June what they had found in Krabbon's throne; the vellum with the names of those who had disappeared. Then, as the afternoon dragged on, the conversation became sparser as each of them concentrated on putting one tired foot in front of the other.

The evening brought more weary travellers. Soot-stained workers from the kilns and furnaces. Tanners, their aprons smelling of smoke and urine. A trio of city watchmen with their bronze breastplates and coned helmets. A mirrorman. Two lamplighters. Four wimple-clad members of the Mater Sorores. A constant ebb and flow of exhausted citizens, hundreds of boots resonating off the stone like a funeral march.

Roe and his companions kept close to the outer wall with their heads bowed, trying to draw as little attention as possible to the blood on their clothes. They needn't have bothered; most of those they met coming the other way barely spared them a second glance.

Spider bought them three cups of water and a bowl of soup to share from one of the vendors squeezed into an alcove near a residential-level archway. The water, like most liquid in Keselgraad, came from the same place: rain collected in buckets and other containers and then filtered through clay. The resulting taste was muddy and brackish but drinkable.

"How much further to the fields?" Roe asked, forced to raise his voice over the hubbub of the evening crowds.

"Four or five levels, I think," June said. She fished a piece of what was hopefully pig meat from the steaming bowl and popped it into her mouth with a satisfied smack of her lips. The central cables shuddered and then began to move.

"Lift is fixed," Spider remarked, wetting the sleeve of his tunic and dabbing at the blood on his face.

"Mist-spawned wardens," Roe grumbled.

"Perhaps they are."

"Are what?"

"Mist-spawned. You know they are sent out beyond the walls as part of their initiation, right? Officially, it's supposed to be to test the resilience of the suits, but maybe there's more to it than that."

"Stupid men and their stupid bird masks," June added, spitting out a morsel of gristle. "They don't scare me."

"They're not meant to. The masks are designed for protection, just like their waxed coats and gloves. The beaks are stuffed with herbs from the Church of the Mother to ward off the poisonous air of the Mists."

Roe drained the last of the soup from the bowl and belched. "But, in that case, why do they still wear all that stuff *inside* Keselgraad? We're safe here. How come no one has ever seen a warden without his mask?"

"No idea. Krabbon didn't tell me. Honestly, between his constant brooding and bouts of inebriety, I'm surprised he managed to share as much as he did. Shall we move on?"

Steps. So many steps, subtly changing the higher they climbed. Gas lamps were now set into the archways of each level and the lift platforms. The stairs themselves showed signs of being cleaned and the rust scrubbed from the railings.

"Why … are … these Mist-spawned fields … so … far up?" Roe groused in between loud exhalations. "When everyone who eats bread is so far *down*."

"Not everyone," Spider corrected. "There are still plenty of mouths to feed on the upper levels. The crops need the sunlight, too. It would cost a fortune in mirrors if they were lower down. Not to mention the smog from the furnaces."

"We're here," June said breathlessly.

Roe had only seen the fields three or four times and never just before the harvest. He stepped through the archway and stopped, awestruck. The sun was setting, painting the sky in hues of red and orange. Rippling waves of green and gold filled his vision, much like the rolling clouds of the Mists, but instead of fear, he felt a comforting sense of tranquillity wash over him, leaching some of the exhaustion from his tired frame.

The Mists were death. This was *life*. Growth. Birth and rebirth, the swaying stalks feeding off the bodies of the dead citizens of Keselgraad who had been buried in the soil, serving the city one final time. All would end up here or on another of the agricultural levels. Rich and poor, good and evil. Decaying corpses sucked dry by the hungry roots of the fields.

Rainwater cisterns sprouted out of the maize and wheat like huge mushrooms, and on the horizon, as close to the edge as possible, five windmills turned lazily, their sails casting long shadows. To the left, the grandiose peak of the city rose towards the heavens. Roe could see more levels brimming with rapeseed and barley, the gleaming marble mansions of the Noble Houses, and, shining over them all, the Church of the Mother, the amethysts on its spire flashing as they caught the last of the sun's rays.

He felt a tear trickle down his cheek. It was easy to forget, when down in the muck and squalor of the Slums, that beauty could still be found within the walls of Keselgraad.

That there was still … peace.

"Mother keep me," Spider murmured beside him, his

customary bored expression replaced by one of wonder. "It's a paradise."

"Mrs Pattyworth's house is right there," June said happily, pointing to a squat little cottage nestled on the edge of one of the corn fields. She skipped away, humming a tune that Roe didn't recognise.

"Wait!" he shouted after her. "We should scout out the area! Make sure it's safe!"

But she was already knocking on the door. It swung open to reveal a smiling, chubby-faced woman with a body shaped like an apple and short, stubby arms and legs.

"My little bug!" she exclaimed, sweeping June up into the air and pressing her against her ample bosom. "What in the Mother are you doing here at this time of day? You'll never make it back down to the Slums before nightfall!" Her gaze landed on Spider's tunic, which, despite his best efforts, was still stained crimson. "And who might you two strapping young lads be?"

"They're my friends," came June's muffled reply.

"I see." The smile faltered. "Not come here to rob a poor old woman, have you, boys? My man is still out in the fields, but I expect him back very soon."

"No, Ma'am," Roe said. "We're … we need a place to stay."

Mrs Pattyworth set June down and held up the medallion she was wearing. An x-shaped cross surrounded by a triangle. "Do you believe in the Mother, boy?"

"Y … yes. I mean, of course."

"It is only by her good grace that we survive here. It is through her generosity and sacrifice that Keselgraad still stands." The smile returned, splitting the woman's face in two. "We are all part of her flock. All part of her family. It would be my honour to welcome you into my home."

Roe breathed a sigh of relief. "Thank you."

"No need. No need. Come along." Mrs Pattyworth ushered them inside. The living room was small and cosy, its floor covered with two luxurious cowhide rugs. A cast iron pot bubbled merrily over the firepit in one corner.

"I was just about to prepare dinner," she said. "But it can wait. There's a washbasin in the bedroom. How about I fill it with hot water and you can clean yourselves up?"

June went first, returning shortly afterwards, rosy-skinned and grinning. "There's soap," she squeaked. "Tallow soap!"

Mrs Pattyworth smoothed down the little girl's unruly straw hair. "A gift from my brother-in-law," she said. "He works at the slaughterhouse. Did you wash behind your ears?"

"Oh, yes. It was wonderful!"

"Good. Now help me grind the wheat grain while your two friends make themselves presentable."

Roe followed Spider into the other room. He shrugged off his tunic, splashed some of the warm water on his face, and scrubbed furiously at it with a linen cloth, his mood improving with every layer of grime he scraped away.

"I'm done," Spider said a couple of minutes later, getting dressed again.

"Already?"

"You're too slow. I'll go help June. Your arse still looks terrible, by the way."

"Thanks. Oh, wait a minute, I think you missed a spot."

"Where?"

Roe cupped a handful of tepid water from the bowl and threw it in Spider's face. "There."

"You … you *bastard*!"

"It'll dry."

Spider made an obscene gesture and left, wiping at his dripping nose. Roe took his time, running the cloth over his aching body, allowing the warmth to seep into his muscles. When he finally returned to the living room, the table had been set with five wooden plates and bowls. Mrs Pattyworth was showing June how to stir the pot while Spider lounged in one of the chairs, attempting to balance Krabbon's dagger on his middle finger.

"Ah, there you are, dearie," Mrs Pattyworth said. "You were in there so long we were beginning to think you'd been swallowed by the Mists."

"Apologies."

"It's no trouble. Would you be so kind as to—"

She was interrupted by a series of sharp knocks.

"Ah, that'll be my husband. Always likes to announce himself. Be a dear and open it for me, would you? My hands are tied."

Roe nodded and went to pull the door open. A figure stood waiting patiently on the other side. Dressed in black, his features hidden by a shining ceramic mask, the smooth surface marred by a splash of red on one cheek. The flames from the firepit were reflected in two eye-slits of thick glass.

"Good evening," said Warden Devrard.

And drew his blade.

THIRTEEN
AMETHYST SHARDS

"Today, we celebrate. For we have found it. After months of sleepless nights and innumerable failed hypotheses. The solution, in the end, was disarmingly simple. The key to our salvation lies all around us. It infuses the very air we breathe. The water we drink. The ground beneath our feet. The world we live in is brimming with raw, intrinsic energy waiting to be used. We just need to develop a way to harness it."

First Technologist Arniel Sin, The Time Before

"Hurry it up, Pine!"

Always the same dream. The same nightmare. Forced to relive those Mist-spawned events over and over again.

"Coming!"

He watched his younger self creep down the torchlit tunnel, a pitcher of water in one hand and three large round loaves of bread in the other. Pine and his fellow miners had been down in this part of the Depths for over two weeks now, long enough for him to forget the feel of the sun's warmth on his skin. Or to breathe in air that didn't taste of dust.

The sound of falling pebbles from one of the second-ary galleries made him stop abruptly. There were scores of shafts, caves, pits, and passages down here; hundreds, even. A disorientating warren that stretched for miles under the surface, rivalling the streets and alleyways of the residential levels. And not all of the tunnels were natural. Some were ancient, crumbling structures that Gamin believed predated Keselgraad itself. Uncharted territory, unknown and unexplored, a veritable treasure trove of secrets for those brave or foolish enough to venture into the darkness.

"Aldin M. Pine, if I have to come and get you, I can promise you will regret it!"

He quickened his pace, reaching the end of the tunnel where a young woman was waiting for him with her hands on her hips, a couple of dark curls straying from a crimson bandana tied over her head.

Run! Pine wanted to scream at her. *Get out now!*

But his younger self only smiled. "Apologies, Bera. I was ambushed by a half-dozen children as soon as I arrived at the camp. You know how they get when left unattended. I was lucky to escape with my life."

She tried unsuccessfully to frown at him. "Unattended? Gamin's there, isn't he? Besides, most of them barely reach your thigh; you shouldn't have had any trouble fending them off. Now, hurry it up. Hale's getting hungry, which means he's getting crotchety, and I've no inclination to listen to him whine all afternoon."

Pine allowed himself to be dragged into the chamber behind Bera where the other miners were waiting, their grimy faces illuminated by a soft purple light. At the very centre, upon an iron pedestal, sat the largest gemstone that Pine had ever seen; an amethyst taller than a man and twice as wide, its pulsating glow so bright that he found it difficult to look at for more than a few brief moments.

"Aldin!" one of the miners exclaimed. "You were gone so long we thought you had been devoured by a denizen of the Depths! How is my son?"

"Food first. Questions later," another grumbled, his bushy eyebrows scrunched together into a scowl that forbade any discussion.

"Of course, Hale," Pine replied amiably, tossing him a loaf of rye bread. "Everyone back at camp is doing fine. A bit restless, perhaps. Jumping at shadows."

"That's your fault," Hale retorted, munching vigorously. "Scaring them with wild tales of missing tools and strange noises."

"I was only telling the truth."

"Sometimes, it's better to say nothing at all. How's Gamin holding up?"

"His arm is healing. Slowly. He's already talking about coming back down here."

"To do what? Use his pick-axe one-handed? Old geezer needs to get it through his thick skull that he'll never work here again."

"Leave it alone, Hale," Bera admonished. "I'm sure deep down he knows that. Let him come to terms with it in his own time." She ran her tongue over her dry lips. "Mist-spawned dust in these tunnels makes me thirstier than a drunkard in a wine cellar. Someone give me some water, would you?"

Pine handed her the pewter jug. She paused before raising it to her lips.

"Fate and fortune." The words were echoed back to her

by the rest of the miners, loud and sonorous in the cramped confines of the chamber.

"We should probably leave some for the second group," Pine advised. "They haven't returned yet."

"Lazy bastards," Hale muttered, the purple light twisting his features. "Mapping out the underground passages while we have to haul this thing back to the surface. They get all the easy jobs."

"Perhaps, but we get all the *important* ones. You heard what Lord Thane said. This relic has been requisitioned by the Keeper of the Faith herself. A gift from the Mother, she called it. A way to save us from the Mists."

"May her name be praised," a skinny miner warbled, taking an effigy of the goddess from his tunic pocket and kissing its hair.

"Bollocks," Hale retorted, swallowing. "This thing is as mystical as my arse. The Sister Superior doesn't want it because it's a relic; she wants it because it's worth its weight in gold."

The other miner struggled to his feet. "Heresy!"

"Shut up, Lyle, or I'll break your jaw. What I mean is …" Hale glanced back down the torchlit tunnel. "Maybe we get a bit … you know … lost on the way back to camp. Or rather, the jewel gets lost. Perhaps we're, um, ambushed by whatever is making all these noises down here, and we're forced to flee to safety."

"Bad idea," Pine warned. "Lord Thane is waiting for us with a couple of wardens. Rumour has it they can sniff out a lie at a hundred paces."

"Lord … Mists take you, lad, why didn't you tell me?"

"You were so busy rambling on and on, I couldn't get a word in edgeways!"

Hale growled and bunched his hands into fists. Pine stared back at him defiantly. The big miner held his gaze for a moment, then snorted and looked away. "One of these days, something bad is going to happen to you, Pine, and when it does, I hope I'm around to see it."

Run! All of you! Get out while you still can!

But no one could hear him. He had dreamt this moment a hundred times, and no matter how much he screamed and ranted, they never listened. He could only watch as they finished their meal of bread and water, slotted long metal poles into the grooves set along the side of the pedestal, and hoisted the jewel up onto the shoulders of the eight strongest miners like a makeshift palanquin.

Every time the scene played out in his mind, Pine noticed new small details. The way Lyle gave the idol of the Mother one final kiss. The way the amethyst seemed to glow even more brightly as if relishing its impending freedom. The way Bera brushed her fingertips against the back of his hand before taking up her position among the rear guard. The last time he would feel her touch.

Pine pleaded as the group set off up the tunnel. He tossed and turned in his bed, drenched in sweat, his fists beating against the mattress. The pebble was in the same place as it always was, a mere hundred feet away from their base camp. His younger self walked over it without even noticing, focusing instead on the dark openings of the branching side passages. A dozen paces behind came Hale, gritting his teeth with exertion, his face beetroot-red. One booted foot landed on the tiny stone, enough to make it slip sideways.

And make the big miner lose his balance.

Time slowed to a trickle. Hale stumbled, pulling his pole with him. The amethyst teetered on the edge of its pedestal. Helplessly, Pine willed for it to stay upright. It would not, of course. This was not just a dream. It was a memory. The past cannot be changed.

The jewel fell, tumbling over and over, shining brighter than the torches lining the tunnel. Brighter than the sun. Pine caught a glimpse of his own horrified face reflected in one of the crystal facets before the amethyst hit the rock floor and shattered with an echoing crack that would forever be etched into his soul.

Thousands upon thousands of tiny, needle-like shards peppered Pine's face and hands like the barbed stingers of a merciless swarm of bees. The pain was so intense that, for a moment, he thought his skin had been set aflame. Blood dribbled down into his eyes from a myriad of cuts on his forehead, turning his vision red.

"Bera," he croaked.

The dusty air was infused with glittering purple motes. Like falling violet snow. At least five of the miners were already dead, their lacerated corpses littering the ground, surrounded by chunks of crystal that pulsed with an inner light. The jewels were humming. A soft chorus. A portent.

Somewhere deeper down the tunnel, a female voice was screaming.

"Bera!"

Hale was standing a few feet away with his head bowed. Pine ran over and tapped him on the shoulder.

"Bera! Have you seen Bera?"

The big miner turned slowly. His face was a mass of pulped flesh; a glistening slab of meat that had been tenderised with a hammer. Gelatinous tears ran in rivulets from empty eye sockets. Pieces of amethyst sparkled within the exposed muscle.

"See?" Hale repeated. He tried to grin, his teeth a white scar. "No. I can no longer see. Lyle was right. I am a heretic. A blasphemer. This is my penance. My punishment."

His manic laugh was smothered by the growing thrum of the amethysts. Pine stepped back in disgust, his foot squelching on something soft. He looked down to see a severed hand wrapped around a decapitated effigy of the Mother, the fingers still twitching. Sluggish fluid leaked from the torn remains of a skinny wrist.

Lyle.

"Mists take me," Pine whispered, tasting blood on his lips. "Mists take us all."

"Aldin!"

He recognised her voice, shrill with fear and worry, piercing the swelling vibrations. He wiped at his eyes with his palms and searched the darkness beyond the purple halo.

"Bera?"

"Aldin!"

There! Thirty feet away, her face covered in cuts, her bandana repurposed into a sling for her right arm. She was wounded and afraid, but she was alive.

Hope drove the clogging fog of madness from Pine's mind. Nothing mattered now. Nothing except Bera. He had to get her out. Keep her safe.

He took a step towards her just as the throbbing sound

reached its paroxysm. It was no longer a hum; it was a scream. A wailing shriek that bounced off the walls again and again until it became a hundred disconsolate cries. Until the pent-up energy could no longer be contained.

The tunnel exploded.

Pine was thrown through the air like a ragdoll, pieces of amethyst whistling past him in a hail of deadly missiles. One slammed into his shoulder, snapping his collarbone as if it were a twig and adding to the pain that already wracked his battered body. He crashed to the ground as the roof of the tunnel collapsed around him. A wooden beam crunched into his chest, driving the air from his lungs and pinning him in place. Rocks pummelled his legs and stomach. He fought to raise his arms over his head to protect his face. He could hear distant screams as the surviving miners were crushed under piles of falling rubble.

"Bera," he tried to say, but it came out as a rasping cough. The entire tunnel was now choked with glittering purple dust, and some of it found its way down his throat to tear at his insides. The torches had long since gone out, leaving only a faint violet luminescence to highlight the gruesome tableau of twisted limbs and broken bones.

Pine didn't know how long he had lain there in the dirt, listening to his friends die. It could have been minutes. Or hours. Listening as each suffering voice fell silent. Until he was alone with his thoughts and the beating of his heart. Perhaps Hale had not been so mad after all. They had strayed from the Mother's light. They did not deserve to return to the surface. He did not deserve to see Bera again.

Pine dropped his arms to his sides, closed his eyes, and let the pain wash over him. At least the children would be safe. And Gamin, too. Far away from the blast. Maybe his own death would serve as a warning to those tempted by the secrets of the Depths.

Some things are best left hidden.

"Get up."

Two words, clipped and authoritative. Sharp enough to cut through the cloying blanket of hurt that was threatening to drag him deeper into the darkness.

"Leave me alone," he mumbled as fresh blood trickled into his mouth.

He heard booted feet crunching on fallen gravel and shattered crystal. The beam across his chest shuddered then was lifted away. Suddenly, he could breathe again. Pine opened a weary eyelid and stared up at his saviour. Hard grey eyes flecked with gold glowered back at him from the depths of a gaunt, chiselled face.

"I cannot leave you alone," the man said, examining his cut palms. "I am in need of answers, and you appear to be the only one capable of giving them to me." He gestured irritably down the tunnel, and Pine turned his aching neck to see an impenetrable wall of broken beams and rubble. A pale arm protruded from halfway up the debris, its stiff fingers curled into a claw as if the unfortunate miner had attempted to dig his way out.

"The … only one?"

"They are dead, Pine. Dead and buried. All of them."

"Thane … you are Lord Thane."

"Yes. And you are the one who has doomed all of Keselgraad. The jewel was the only thing keeping us safe. You have sent us down a path towards our own inevitable destruction. A path from which we cannot escape. Unless …"

The Keeper of the Peace bent down and picked something up from the ground. A splintered shard of amethyst the size of his forearm, still emitting a soft luminescence.

"Diminished but not quite empty," he mused, half to himself. "Perhaps this will suffice. Perhaps there is still hope. With more resources. More men to excavate the cave-in. The Council will have to approve, of course, although that should not be an issue. Fear is a powerful motivator."

Thane stood, still clutching the crystal, and moved away, leaving Pine on his back in the dirt, tears trickling through the blood on his cheeks as he mourned the loss of his friends.

⌘

Ten years later he awoke, covered in sweat, his damp hair plastered to his forehead. He stumbled over to the wash basin and splashed some cold rainwater onto his face. No matter how many times the memory returned, the pain was always the same. Pain tinged with guilt at having survived when so many had perished. They were still down there, the bodies of the fallen, their flesh and muscle stripped away by the passage of time to leave empty, dry husks. He should be with them, instead of trying to hide behind the bronze breastplate and shining sword of the City Watch. He was a fraud.

A cowardly, hollow fraud.

A shutter banged against its frame in the other room, each wooden thunderclap accompanied by a squeal of rusty hinges. Pine wiped at his scarred face and shuffled across the straw-covered floor of his living quarters to the only window. Moonlight streamed through the opening, illuminating a lopsided table, a scratched clothes cupboard, and a hefty metal-banded chest. His discarded weapons and uniform lay where he had left them, tracing a wobbly trail between the front door and his sweat-stained mattress.

"How did you spring open, you Mist-spawned thing?" Pine grumbled to himself, pulling both shutters inwards and latching them shut. The cold night air had seeped into the room, and he shivered involuntarily, goosebumps springing to life along his naked arms. The tunic he was wearing was sodden with his perspiration, sticking uncomfortably to his skin. Pine tugged it over his head and went to open the clothes cupboard. The door was ajar.

"I keep you locked," he muttered. "Always locked. Something's wrong."

The three shelves inside were stacked with a variety of tunics, breeches, hose, shirts, and jackets. All surprisingly neat and tidy, considering the state of the rest of the apartment. Apart from one pile, near the bottom, slightly askew. A garment that Pine had never seen before had been placed on top. Black, waxed leather.

Before he could investigate further, there was an insistent knocking at the front door.

"Who is it?" he called, selecting a tunic at random.

"Watchman Selene, Captain!"

"At this time of night?"

"It's important, Sir."

There was a slight edge to her voice that Pine had never heard before. He pulled the deadbolt back with a frown and yanked on the handle to reveal Selene's unsmiling face. Two more watchmen lurked behind her, their bronze helmets gleaming in the moonlight.

"What in the Mists is going on?"

"You are under arrest, Sir."

He blinked. This was another dream. It had to be.

"Arrest? For what?"

"Conspiracy to murder."

Pine blinked again. Slowly. "Watchman, I am very, very tired. Be more specific. Conspiracy to murder whom?"

Selene glared back at him, her gaze resentful.

"Lord Matellas Thane, Keeper of the Peace."

FOURTEEN
DISCOVERED

"Many believe that it was the Keeper of the Peace who invented the wardens. Nothing could be further from the truth. The Mother, in her eternal Grace, visited the Sister Superior in a dream and urged her to unravel the mysteries of the Mists. The Council were sceptical at first, but once the Sister had assured them that she could prepare the necessary herbs and philtres to dull the poisonous air and repel the ravenous tendrils, they relented. A few short months later, the first masked volunteers were sent beyond the walls. And, much to the surprise of the Council, most of them returned."

Sister Nayelle, Keeper of the Faith, 822nd Year of the Mother

THE HOLLOW CLICK as Devrard closed the cottage door behind him hit Roe like a punch to the chest. His eyes darted around the enclosed space, looking for an exit. A weapon. Anything.

"I believe this is the only way out," the warden said to him calmly. "Apologies for interrupting you just before supper."

He breathed in deeply through the slits in his beak mask, testing the air. "Nothing. Not even a wisp of cooked wheat. These herbs mask even the strongest of scents. It is one of the things I miss the most."

June started to cry as Roe's search grew more frantic. The ceramic bowls and wooden spoons on the table would be of little use, nor would the pestle and mortar used to grind the grain. That left the piping hot gruel, still bubbling over the firepit. If he could get closer and somehow manage to lift the heavy iron without burning his hands … he doubted even a warden could survive a face full of boiling liquid.

"How did you find us?" he asked, taking a step towards the firepit.

"With some difficulty," Devrard admitted. "The rickshaw drivers saw you heading towards the stairs, but I was unsure of your final destination. Thankfully, I could count on the Mother's blessing to show me the way."

Roe managed to catch Spider's gaze and flicked his eyes in the direction of the boiling pot. The other boy frowned and shook his head.

"The soup vendor overheard you," the warden continued. "He was initially reluctant to reveal the contents of your conversation, but once I reminded him of the penalty for impeding an agent of the Keeper of the Peace, he managed to find his tongue."

Roe took another minute step. "And now you've found your prey, whose throat will you slit first?"

June gave a tiny moan. Mrs Pattyworth gathered her close. "Stop it," she said, her usual bubbly tone replaced by one of quiet terror. "You're scaring the little one."

"She should be scared. We found a list. Krabbon was selling us to the wardens. He's been doing so for years. Murdering the very people he was supposed to be protecting."

There was a sound like a dog barking, and it took a moment for Roe to realise that Devrard was laughing. "So young, so sure of yourself. And so wrong. Murdering. Why in the Mother would we want to do that?"

"Scarab. Moth. Dragonfly," Spider said, speaking for the first time. "None of them ever returned. Whatever's left of their corpses is probably close by, feeding the wheat."

The warden cocked his head. "A fascinating hypothesis. You believe that Lord Thane would spend copious amounts of his own fortune to build an orphanage dedicated to helping the progeny of those lost to the Collapse, only to then have them killed a decade later?"

Roe faltered. "But all the secretive meetings. The *list*."

"It is because you are special. All of you. Your presence—" Devrard paused. "I know you, don't I? I have been trying to place you ever since I walked in. Where have I seen you before?"

"No idea."

"Hmm. I think … the marketplace. Yes, I remember now. I must apologise for that unpleasant situation. You were simply in the wrong place at the wrong time."

Roe felt a visceral anger stir in his belly. "Ant … the Mists … that was *you*?"

"Unfortunately. I was working in an unofficial capacity, and any witnesses could have led to unwanted questions. I only intended to scare you."

"You killed him!"

"No, your companion died through his own carelessness. He is the only one responsible. The ramparts are off-limits for a reason. You were foolish to attempt to scale the city walls."

Roe hesitated. He was five feet away from the steaming pot of gruel. Five feet away from a means to avenge his friend and free Ant's screaming visage from his thoughts. He inched closer.

Devrard let out a long sigh that was transformed into a muffled wheeze by the curved protuberance of his herb-stuffed mask. "Please do not insult my intelligence by continuing to shuffle your way towards the firepit."

Roe froze.

"Boiling water would not hurt me as much as you think, and I have already sent a runner to the Den to request reinforcements. Even if by some miracle you managed to incapacitate me, my companions would certainly not allow you to leave the fields." The warden gestured with his blade. "Sit."

I could leap over the table. Try and claw the mask off. Get my nails into his eyes.

"Sit, little one. I will not ask again."

Roe gave an acknowledging grunt of defeat and slid into a seat next to Spider.

"Thank you. Now, where was I? Ah, yes. You are *special.* You see, all of Keselgraad only talks about the collapse of the *Mines*, but that was triggered by a detonation that happened far below, in a place known as the Depths. A powerful relic was shattered, creating a cloud of dust that affected all those nearby. Including the children. Your bodies—"

Spider's dagger whistled across the room, lightning-fast. It punched through the warden's right eye-slit in a tinkling of broken glass, embedding itself up to the hilt in his skull. Devrard staggered backwards and crashed against the door, sliding down the wooden frame to collapse onto the cowhide rug. One hand reached feebly towards his face. Two fingers closed around the rounded pommel, and for a horrible instant, Roe thought the warden would manage to pull the dagger from his head. Then the arm flapped limply to his side.

"You talk too much," Spider said, unable to hide the tremor in his voice.

"A warden," Mrs Pattyworth whispered. "You killed a *warden*. No one has ever done that before."

"He was threatening June."

"He … he is an agent of the Keeper of the Peace."

"That doesn't mean he can do what he wants."

"Actually, under the statutes set down by the Keepers Council, a—"

"Enough!" Roe interrupted. "Spider is right. I'm tired of people telling us what is and isn't acceptable. If the Council's laws only lead to pain and suffering, then perhaps there is something wrong with *them*, not us."

Mrs Pattyworth was wringing her hands. "But you murdered him. In cold blood. There is no way to justify this. You will be taken to the crosses and gifted to the Mists. All of you. And I will be strung up right alongside you."

"They'll have to catch us first," Spider said, retrieving Devrard's fallen stiletto and tucking it into his belt.

"Then, let's stop wasting time," Roe agreed. "He sent a runner to the Den. That means the central stairwell will be blocked."

"All levels have another way out. Don't they, Mrs Pattyworth?"

The older woman was staring at the crumpled form of the warden with a faraway expression on her face. "My husband warned me not to show kindness to strangers. I should have listened."

June stood up on tiptoes and kissed her on the cheek. "I'm really sorry. I didn't want any of this to happen."

Some focus returned to those kind eyes. "I know you didn't, poppet. I suppose this is the path that the Mother set me on, for better or for worse." Mrs Pattyworth sighed. "Inside the rightmost windmill, there's a length of rope hidden in a sack of grain near the back. It'll take you down to an abandoned house on the level below that has a shutter you can open from the outside."

"Thank you!" June clapped her hands together and smiled.

"No need. Your visits always brought me joy, dearie. It can get quite lonely out here, what with the husband out in the fields all day and no children of my own. You were my little ray of sunshine. Time for me to repay the favour." She patted June on the head and stood with a cracking of tired knees. "Off you go, then. Straight through the stalks towards the setting sun. Oh, and Roe, there's a pair of my leather boots in the corner. You might as well have them. Even if they don't quite fit, they'll be better than what you're wearing."

Roe nodded gratefully and exchanged his torn, floppy boots for the old woman's.

"When the wardens arrive, tell them we forced you to help us," Spider advised, nudging the door open carefully and peering outside. "We put a knife to your throat and made you tell us about the windmill."

"They'll know I'm lying."

"You have to try. Roe. June. Come on, we—"

A gloved hand snaked out and wrapped around his ankle. Spider yelled out in surprise and tugged his boot free. The distorted form of Devrard shuddered. Floundering arms found the cowhide rug and pushed the shaking body up into a sitting position.

"Mists take me," Roe murmured aghast as the gleaming ceramic mask turned in his direction, the dagger still embedded in the right eye-slit.

"I told you that you were special," the warden said in his bland voice. "So am I. The Mists change us. The Mists change us *all*."

He rose onto one knee and wrenched Spider's dagger free in a spray of black blood. A boiling pot of wheat gruel hit him on the shoulder and knocked him prone again.

"Run!" Mrs Pattyworth shouted, grimacing with pain as her hands turned red. "RUN!"

Devrard was already rising again as steaming liquid dripped from the wide brim of his hat and ran down his waxed leather coat. Roe grabbed June by the arm and crashed through the door out into the twilight where Spider was waiting for them. To the east, gas lamps lit the entrance to the central staircase, its opening crowded with dark figures. To the west, tall stalks of corn swayed, cold and uninviting.

Roe took a deep breath and plunged into the field. A shrill scream echoed behind him, ending abruptly. Thick stems surrounded him, row upon row of dense foliage packed as closely together as possible to use every available inch of soil. He pressed on, dragging the sobbing June behind him, stray leaves cutting at his face and neck.

To Roe's tired mind, the corn became a crowd of silent skeletal watchers, jostling and pushing in an attempt to reach him and pull him down into the soft earth to join the worm-riddled bodies of the dead. He tripped on a loose rock and fell, grazing both his knees and biting down on his tongue. He cried out from the pain.

"Quiet!" Spider hissed. "Devrard is out there, somewhere, searching for us. And make June shut up, too, or I'll leave you both here."

Roe brushed the dirt from his tunic and turned to June who was shaking with fear, her face covered in scratches. She had somehow managed to keep hold of her sausage-limbed mud doll and was clutching it close to her chest like a shield.

"We're nearly there. Just a bit further," he said as kindly as he could. "You can do this."

"He was dead," she sniffled. "I *saw* it. He wasn't breathing. Mother keep us. Mother keep us from these monsters."

"I know. But we are so close now, June. You have to be strong. And brave."

"Like you?"

Roe laughed. "Me? I'm scared out of my mind! As soon as we find somewhere to rest, I'm going to dissolve into a blubbering mess."

"Really?"

"Really. Fear is like every other emotion; you cannot control it. You cannot tame it. All you can do is embrace it and make it a part of you."

June wiped at her nose. "I … I'll try." She held out her hand, and he took it again, feeling the softness of her skin against his.

They hurried on; the sound of their footsteps muffled by the rustling of the corn. Roe's head whipped left and right as he scanned the forest of dark stems, expecting Devrard to spring from the shadows at any moment, his blood-spattered mask askew, his dagger raised high to sink into Roe's chest. Every ominous creak of the soaring stalks caused fresh dread to crackle through his pounding heart until he thought it might burst.

Mother keep us.

Were they even going the right way? Perhaps they were running round and round in circles, or worse, heading back towards the cottage and the central staircase where the wardens would be waiting to haul them away. He looked up. The bulbous ears of corn formed a near-impenetrable canopy above his head, obscuring the upper levels and the Church of the Mother. All he could see were blotchy patches of sky stained an ugly red by the setting sun as if the heavens themselves were bleeding.

"This way," Spider called softly from somewhere up ahead. Roe followed the sound of his voice and breathed a sigh of relief when the first of the creamy-white rectangular sails came into view, turning languidly in the evening breeze. He pushed through the last row of cloying corn and let go of June's hand.

The squat, domed windmills were perched precariously on the very edge of the level, just before the vertiginous drop into one of the residential areas below. Roe walked as close to the lip of the cliff as he dared and gazed earthwards, taking in the dozens of circular tiers that made up the lower part of Keselgraad, stacked one on top of the other like a pile of different-sized plates. He could just make out the blast furnaces, the smoke belching from their chimneys seemingly mixing with the cold white monochrome of the Mists.

Roe had never seen the Mists from this height before.

At this distance, they appeared calm and peaceful; inviting almost, shimmering and still. He wondered what it would be like to plunge into that milky lake, to leap off the side and plummet to the ground. No more running from the wardens. No more begging and stealing. No more blistered feet and aching body. Just a quick moment of pain, then eternal oblivion. Unless he survived the fall long enough to feel the snakelike tendrils tear him apart.

"Don't look at them for too long," Spider said, coming to stand beside him. "They can draw you in, play games with your mind. Mist-crazed, they call it. It's one of the reasons that the Keepers Council stopped regular patrols along the city walls. They were losing too many men."

Roe glanced over at his companion. His scratched face was as pale as ever, the lines around his eyes and mouth etched deep by the twilight shadows. It made him appear older than his years.

"How did all of this even happen?"

"All of what?" Spider replied absently.

"The Mists? The lands around Keselgraad weren't always like this. Where did they come from?"

The older boy tapped the pommel of the stiletto on his belt. "Another mystery. One we will not solve today. Come on, let's find that rope and get as far away from the wardens as we can before it becomes too dark to see."

Before Roe could reply, a familiar voice cut through the whispering of the corn. "I fear it is a little late for that."

They surged from the depths of the field like obsidian phantoms, a trio of mask-wearing demons whose humanity had long been lost to the Mists. Devrard led them, his remaining stiletto unsheathed, droplets of black sludge still dribbling from the shattered eye-slit like gruesome tears.

"You have led us on a merry chase," he observed. "We have not been tested like this for some time. I had almost forgotten what it felt like. The … exhilaration."

Spider let out a terror-filled yell and charged at the wardens in panic. Devrard waited patiently, dodged a clumsy thrust to the belly, and kicked his opponent in the ankle, knocking him off balance. A second kick crunched into Spider's face, silencing him.

"Find the girl," the warden ordered before turning his attention back to Roe.

"I wish you wouldn't make this so difficult. You should be overjoyed at the chance to serve the Mother. The fact that you were so close to the amethyst that day. The fact that you survived the blast. These things cannot be simple circumstance. They are all part of her plan."

The sun had vanished from the horizon now. Everything was blurred and hazy. Roe could feel the edge of the cliff at his back, a half-dozen feet away. If he turned and ran, Devrard would not be able to catch him before he jumped. He would be free.

The door to the closest windmill banged open, and one of the wardens reappeared, hauling a crying June out by her hair.

He would be free. But the others would not. They still needed him.

"Very well," he said bitterly. "I'll come with you. If you promise that June will be safe."

"June? The little one? Of course. She is perhaps the most blessed of you all. Now, come closer."

Devrard produced a pewter receptacle from the fold of his waxed leather coat and removed the cork. "A sleeping draught. If you would be so kind as to take a sip. Our final destination must be kept secret."

Roe reluctantly allowed a drop of acrid liquid to splash onto his tongue. He swallowed with difficulty. Suddenly, the tiredness he had been feeling ever since leaving the orphanage was magnified tenfold. His legs became weak and rubbery, unable to hold his weight. Roe sank to his knees, his eyes closing, his thoughts unravelling like twine. The last thing he saw before surrendering to the darkness was Devrard's mask, shining cold and white.

Like the Mists.

⌘

He awoke strapped to a chair of cushioned leather with tight strips wrapped around his wrists, ankles, chest, and fore-head. He couldn't move.

Paralysed.

His eyelids itched terribly as if a colony of ants was crawling around inside the sockets. He tried in vain to close them but they had been wedged open; held in place by some sort of metallic contraption that had been slipped under the skin, cupping his eyeballs like eggs.

He began to panic now, straining against the bonds that tied him to the chair, shouting into the foul-smelling gag that had been wrapped around his mouth.

Mother keep me. Mother keep me. Mother keep me.

Figures stirred at the edge of his vision. Others like him. Prisoners.

A soft luminescence flickered to life nearby.

A shaft of sunlight, perhaps, or the flame of a candle.

No. The colour was different. A deep purple, growing steadily brighter.

Bright enough to reveal where he was and who he was with.

The final pieces of the puzzle slotted into place.

And Roe began to scream.

FIFTEEN
TRIAL

"We serve Keselgraad in death as we do in life. That is our honour. Our bodies become one with the city itself. With the city, and with its citizens. For the food we eat is grown from the corpses of those who came before. A tiny piece of them lives on in us and will continue to live on in our children and grandchildren. We are immortal, in a way. We are special. That is why being gifted to the Mists is the worst form of punishment. They leave nothing behind. They devour all."

Sister Nayelle, Keeper of the Faith, 833rd Year of the Mother

YOU HAVE FAILED **me.**

The voice flowed through the icy black liquid that covered Nayelle's hands and arms to tear at her heart. The weight behind those words was soul-crushing. She started to weep.

"I … I am sorry, my Lady. So sorry."

The golden light flickered. Another surge of emotion enveloped Nayelle, warmer this time, like a glass of hot wine on a cold winter night. It rippled out from her fraught mind, trickling down to thaw her frozen fingertips. She smiled through her tears.

No. It is I who am sorry. I should not have entrusted such an important task to you.

The halo dimmed, and for a moment, Nayelle thought her goddess had abandoned her. Then it returned, more brilliant than ever, blazing with a radiance that burned stronger than any fire.

I will take care of this myself.

⌘

The holding cells on the ground floor of the Stables were familiar to Pine, although this was the first time that he had found himself *inside* one of them. The reconverted equestrian stalls measured five by ten feet with walls that were half wooden planks and half metal grille, their floors covered with slowly decomposing straw.

Pine paced moodily around in a circle, carefully avoiding the foul-smelling bucket that had been dumped in one corner. Selene had been uncharacteristically tight-lipped while escorting him back to the Watch House and had refused to answer any of his questions. All he knew was that he had been accused of a crime that he had most certainly not committed. Which meant that someone was trying to frame him. But who? And why?

He had made his fair share of enemies during his long tenure as watchman, increasingly so since rising to the rank of Captain. Conversely, most of them were petty thieves and drunkards who could barely string a series of words together to form a coherent sentence, let alone conceive a stratagem to implicate Pine in a plot to murder the Keeper of the Peace.

"You'll wear the soles of your boots out."

He looked up to see Selene staring at him through the grille of the stall. Her crumpled clothes and the heavy bags under her eyes told Pine that she probably hadn't slept much more than he had.

"I hope you're here to bring me my breakfast," he said in what he hoped was a sarcastic tone.

"No. Council summons have arrived. I'm here to bring you to them."

"For what? My trial? Already? But it's barely dawn! You've made arrests, Selene, you know how it works. It takes days or weeks for prisoners to be judged. Not *hours*. Doesn't that seem at all suspicious to you?"

She took a ring of keys from a peg on the wall behind her and inserted one into the sliding door of the stall. "Stop trying to influence me. I'm being asked to testify too. I shouldn't even be talking to you." She held up a pair of manacles and raised one tired eyebrow. "Now, do I need to use these?"

Pine considered his options. He was stronger than her. More experienced. And she had come to fetch him alone. He could probably overpower her, take her sword and armour, and escape down into the lower levels where he still knew a few people who could help him disappear. However, fleeing now would be a clear admission of guilt. There would be no need for a trial; the wardens would have free rein to hunt him down and kill him on sight.

Then there was Selene. Coming here by herself meant that she didn't consider him a threat. It meant that she still trusted him.

Pine locked his fingers together and pushed them away from his body to make his shoulders crack.

"No," he said. "I'll come quietly. If you answer a couple of questions along the way."

"I'm not supposed to—"

"Please, Selene."

She hesitated. "Fine. But not here. Come on."

She led him through the Stables. A dozen or so men were scattered along the benches in the main hall, polishing their breastplates, scratching patrol reports onto tiny sheets of ageing vellum, or playing knucklebones. The low hubbub of conversation trailed off into an uneasy silence as Pine came out of his cell. He passed among them with his head held high, ignoring their stares. The only thing worse than a corrupt citizen of Keselgraad was a corrupt *watchman* of Keselgraad; someone who had sworn an oath to protect the city and its inhabitants only to break it for a handful of coins.

If Pine managed to prove his innocence, he would be welcomed back into the fold with open arms, but for the moment, he was no longer their captain. He was a pariah to be shunned.

He followed Selene outside and across the cobbled courtyard under the metallic glare of the mounted cavalryman. The Council chambers were several levels higher than the Stables, close to the walled mansions of the Keepers. Pine waited until they had reached the central stairwell before trying again.

"So, when did this so-called attempted murder happen?"

Selene had donned her coned helmet. She answered without looking at him. "Shortly after we met with Lord Thane, he was ambushed by a group of assassins dressed as wardens. They were waiting for him in the lift."

He scratched his scarred cheek. "They knew he was coming."

"Yes. Someone must have tipped them off."

They passed a wide landing where a pair of lamplighters were extinguishing the gas lanterns. It was still early, and the traffic up and down the steps was a slow trickle of bleary-eyed merchants and carriers.

"Well, it can't have been me, can it?" protested Pine. "We were together the whole time."

"Not quite. Lord Thane sent us home, remember? After you threatened him."

"I wasn't … I didn't *threaten* him. I questioned him."

"Forcibly."

"I prefer insistently."

"And then you went home."

"Of course."

"Who, exactly, can attest to this apart from yourself?"

Pine stopped abruptly and put his hand on her arm. She turned her head and fixed him with a cold stare until he removed it.

"You know I live alone," he said. "So, you know I can't prove it. How about instead of trying to gift me to the Mists you turn your keen inquisitive mind to *why* I would want the Keeper of the Peace dead?"

The lift screamed past in a mass of rusting iron and twitching cables; the pale faces of its passengers sliced into thin strips by the bars of the cage.

"I'm not sure," Selene admitted, watching it rattle off down towards the lower levels. Her familiar pout returned, twisting her freckles.

"Motive is important, Watchman."

"As is tangible evidence. We found a set of waxed leather robes in your clothes cupboard."

Pine rolled his eyes in disbelief. "Oh, well no need for a trial, then. I was *obviously* involved. My shutters were open, Selene. I'd bet my weight in paper that I closed them before going to bed. Someone managed to unlatch them from the outside—"

"You live on the second floor."

"Someone *dextrous* managed to unlatch them from the outside and plant the warden's garb in my closet."

"That's not all. We found something else. A letter."

"Vellum? I'm not paid well enough to have my own supply, let alone the ink. What did it say?"

She looked uncomfortable. "I'm not supposed to say."

"Never mind. I'm about to find out, aren't I? We're nearly there. Just … just promise me one thing."

"I … I can't help you, Captain."

"No, nothing like that. Promise me that if I'm sentenced to the cross, you won't come."

"I think I owe it to you to—"

"You don't. Have you ever seen someone gifted to the Mists before?"

"No."

"It's excruciating. I don't want you to remember me like that."

"I …"

"Please, Selene."

"It's just that—"

Selene stopped. They had reached another landing, its archway etched in gold and silver. Two scantily clad maidens had been carved directly into the stone columns on either side, their arms raised above their heads as if supporting the vault with their palms. A squad of armed men was stationed just inside the entrance, their shield-adorned purple cassocks denoting them as members of House Quellion's honour guard.

"Stand to attention, boys," their leader sneered, doffing his plumed felt hat. "Dead man walking."

Pine squared his shoulders. "Unless Keselgraad's system of justice has changed overnight, I am an innocent man going to trial, not a condemned prisoner being led to the cross."

"If that's what you want to keep telling yourself, Captain. Although I must warn you that both the Keeper of the Peace and the Keeper of the Anvil are in a particularly foul mood this morning. I doubt you will find them in a very lenient state of mind." The officer's gaze dropped to Pine's unbound wrists. "Where are your cuffs?"

"I did not think them necessary," Selene interceded smoothly. "The Captain has given me his word that he will not attempt anything unpleasant."

"Hmmm," the man said, the sneer transforming into an equally insufferable leer. "Didn't realise they were letting women into the Watch, now. How come I haven't seen you around before?"

"Probably because I've never visited Ruby Red's brothel," she replied with a sweet smile. "Or that pox doctor down on Butcher Street. The one that specialises in the *really* itchy rashes."

Another of the honour guard sniggered before being glared into submission by his superior. "The Keepers

Council are waiting," the officer said flatly. "Let's not make them angrier than they already are, eh?"

Pine was ushered through the archway. He paused for a moment on the other side to take in the view. No matter how many times he visited the Noble Quarters, it still managed to take his breath away. The place was just so … *clean*. Well-swept pavements lined mud-free avenues bordered by magnificent, multi-storeyed mansions, perfectly designed to follow the natural curve of the level's circular structure. Wrought-iron gas lamps interspaced with tall oak trees provided light at night and shade during the day. Pale-faced women in tight corsets and billowing gowns strolled leisurely along these spotless streets of iron and stone, fanning their rouge-tinted cheeks and tittering like giddy schoolchildren.

It was as if Pine was no longer in Keselgraad but had somehow found himself transported to another world, one untroubled by hunger or disease. One that didn't need mirrors to profit from the sun's light. Where the air wasn't polluted by the constant stench of animal carcasses left to rot in the gutter and the smell of charcoal from the kilns and furnaces. A society more concerned with the stiffness of their starched collars and the frills of their lace dresses than how they were going to afford their next meal. The rich and pampered, blissfully unaware that they owed their perfect lives to a thousand lesser citizens, toiling down in the muck and grime to provide the bread for their tables and the leather for their overcoats.

Pine looked over at Selene and was surprised to see that she appeared just as awestruck as he was, her eyes wide and searching.

"I suppose it never grows stale, does it?" he asked her.

She blinked. "Sorry?"

"The view. I mean, you must have seen it hundreds of times growing up. Either here or on one of the higher levels. I would have thought you'd be bored with it by now."

"Oh … um, I guess you're right. It still packs a punch." She smiled briefly. "Besides, my family home is not nearly as luxurious as some of these."

"Really?"

"Only a dozen rooms and five servants. Paupers compared to this lot. Why, my father sometimes had to lace up his own boots. An absolute travesty."

Pine caught the familiar twinkle in her eye. "Mists, you nearly had me. I—"

The butt of a halberd poked him in the kidney. "Enough reminiscing, Captain, you are only delaying the inevitable."

The Council chambers were just a short walk away, the marble columns that lined their entranceway a simple yet effective display of the Keepers' riches. Marble could no longer be mined since the arrival of the Mists and had consequently become a finite commodity; as precious as gold, jewels, or paper.

Pine's scruffy tunic and Selene's shining bronze helmet drew a host of curious stares while overly dressed women tightened their grip on the arms of their chaperones as if fearing that Pine would suddenly try to murder them. He kept moving, his head bowed, and breathed a silent prayer of thanks to the Mother when his escort finally ushered him up a short flight of steps and through a set of imposing double doors into the tiled vestibule of the Council chambers.

"Down the hall," the officer commanded, motioning for two of his men to stand guard near the entrance.

The corridor led to the court of law; a semi-circular room dominated by a crescent-shaped raised dais upon which stood five carved wooden chairs. Four of these were occupied. Lord Matellas Thane had taken the central seat, his back ramrod straight, the raised collar of his overcoat brushing against the bottom of his angular jaw. Eyes the colour of granite bored into Pine as if he were some sort of insect.

To Thane's right, Lord Potsworn was squeezed uncomfortably into his own chair, his pudgy fingers clutching the armrests. Rumour had it that the Keeper of the Fields' increasing obesity was due to the fact that he took it upon himself to sample every crate of food that passed through his warehouses. Whether that was true or not, there was no denying that the man was losing the battle with his own clothing, the silver buttons of his canary-yellow doublet visibly buckling under the pressure of his considerable girth.

Next to Potsworn, Lord Jeckle, the Keeper of the Anvil, stifled a bored yawn and scratched at the frilled ruff that sprouted from his neck like a dahlia. And lastly, on the opposite side of the dais, Lady Hellington, Keeper of the Coin, her half-moon spectacles perched precariously on the end of her nose, her steel-grey hair pulled back into a bun so tight that it tugged at the skin of her forehead.

"Greetings, Captain," Lord Thane said in a regretful tone. "It is unfortunate that we meet again in such unpleasant circumstances."

"My Lord—"

"We were discussing your *temperament* while waiting for you to arrive. I informed my fellow Keepers that you have, in recent months, become more and more disillusioned with your position."

Pine's eyebrows shot up in surprise. "I don't think that's accurate."

"Watchman Selene has testified to me that you were dissatisfied with the way the Watch was being run."

"I may have occasionally expressed my displeasure at—"

"A problematic flaw when combined with your frequent insubordination and uncontrollable temper."

"Will you allow me to speak?" Pine asked hotly.

"Raising your voice to me only proves my point. As does yesterday's altercation when you went as far as to imply that I myself may have somehow been involved in this travesty of a murder investigation."

"Preposterous!" Lord Potsworn sputtered, his double chin wagging.

"Indeed."

The door behind Pine banged open, and Sister Superior Nayelle hurried in, her hands hidden in the folds of her clerical robes, the skin of her face tinged with an unhealthy waxy sheen. "Apologies," she mumbled, almost tripping as she stepped up onto the dais.

"Keeper of the Faith, are you all right?" Lady Hellington asked in concern. "You look terrible!"

"I have had a … difficult few days," Nayelle replied in a quiet voice. "There are many burdens that weigh heavily on my mind."

Lord Thane reached over to pat her arm. "Then, we shall strive to expedite matters here as quickly as possible, Sister. We have already discussed the Captain's questionable character. Which, in itself, is not a crime. However, a runner arrived at the Watch House last night bearing a message claiming that Captain Pine was part of a group plotting to assassinate the Keeper of the Peace and that the failed attempt in the central lift yesterday afternoon was only the first of many."

"That's absolutely ridiculous," Pine fumed. "A man cannot be judged simply on his temper and an anonymous accusation."

"I could not agree more," Thane said. "Which is why the Watch performed a thorough search of your quarters. What exactly did you find there, Watchman Selene?"

"We …" she shook her head in reluctance. "We found a black leather cloak and hat, which appeared to have been designed to imitate those worn by the wardens, and several sheets of vellum detailing—"

"I have them here," Thane interrupted. "My schedule, the names of my servants, the various routes I take during the day, the members of my honour guard who would be susceptible to corruption or intimidation … my entire *life*."

"Unacceptable," Lord Potsworn roared, hammering on his armrest hard enough to crack the wood. "An example must be made, Thane! The citizens of Keselgraad must be shown that any threat to the Keepers Council will *not* be tolerated. This man and any who assist him should be gifted to the Mists!"

"Agreed," Lord Jeckle added, stroking his worm-like moustache. "And I will contribute whatever aid is necessary to see that his co-conspirators are brought to justice."

"Then, by unanimous vote, we find Captain Aldin M. Pine guilty of conspiracy to murder. May the Mother forgive him."

What just happened? Pine thought in shock. *That wasn't a trial! Since when is the defendant given no opportunity to defend himself?*

He opened his mouth to reply, but Lord Thane beat him to it. "There is one more crucial piece of evidence," the Keeper of the Peace said, handing out the sheets of vellum to the other members of the Council. "Every page bears a wax seal made by a signet ring." He paused. "A hammer and tongs."

"What?" Lord Jeckle exploded, lifting the parchment to his face and staring at the bottom of the page in disbelief. "This is … a trick! A conspiracy!"

Thane frowned. "The signet rings we bear are unique, are they not, Lady Hellington?"

"Y … yes," the Keeper of the Coin admitted, dabbing at the corner of her lips with a lace handkerchief. "How could you do this, Jeckle? How *could* you?"

"It was you," the Keeper of the Anvil snarled, pointing a shaky finger at Thane. "*You* did this. I don't know how, but I am going to find out."

"I think not. The punishment for treason is the same, no matter who you are. Gifted to the Mists."

Jeckle's eyes bulged from his sockets. "Ridiculous!" He looked around wildly, searching for allies. "My fellow Keepers, surely you aren't gullible enough to fall for this poorly disguised attempt at victimisation?"

"All those times you told us that Lord Thane was stealing from you," Lady Hellington said. "I could tell you didn't like him but *murder*? Over a few misplaced bars of iron?"

"A vote!" Lord Jeckle shouted, his voice shrill. "I demand a vote, as is my right!"

"Very well," Thane agreed. "Your part in this is clear and plain to me, Keeper. I vote guilty."

"As do I," Lady Hellington said. "These are signed with *your* ring, Jeckle. A Keeper's seal is impossible to forge. I am sure of it. And you have sufficient motive. I'm sorry."

Lord Potsworn squirmed in his seat. "The evidence is there, certainly … yet, I have known the Keeper of the Anvil for years. I consider him a friend. There must be something we are missing. Not guilty."

"A tie," Jeckle grinned.

"Sister Nayelle has not yet voted," Thane countered, turning his head to fix her with his steely gaze. "Who will you support, my Lady? Who do you … trust to keep the city safe?"

She looked back at him for a long time. Her right hand slipped from the confines of her robes. The fingers were stained black. Finally, her lips moved.

"We cannot hear you," Thane said.

A whisper. "Guilty."

"NO!" Jeckle shrieked as men in purple livery invaded the dais. "You're making a mistake. You'll regret this. You'll all regret this."

"Captain Pine. Lord Jeckle," Thane intoned, rising from his chair. "The Council has spoken. Tomorrow, at first light, you will be taken to the gatehouse roof, tied to the cross …" his gaze found Pine and a smile flashed across his face, there and gone again in the blink of an eye.

"… and gifted to the Mists."

SIXTEEN
CONFESSIONS OF THE CONDEMNED

"Time, once again, works against us. We have found a means to break the chains of fate. The crystal is close to completion. Another day and it will begin syphoning the energy we desperately need to keep us safe. Yet, the scouts have returned. The Mists have been sighted. In a matter of months, they will be scratching at our door, searching for a way in. My daughter looks at me with love in her eyes and asks me if everything is going to be all right. My heart breaks for I do not know what to tell her. I cannot reveal the truth. Her hope is all I have left."

First Technologist Arniel Sin, The Time Before

AFTER SPENDING A day and a night locked in a prison cell with Lord Jeckle, Pine was almost looking forward to his execution. The former Keeper of the Anvil had devolved into a frazzled mess, alternating between angry diatribes and unhinged accusations at a pace that left no room for respite or, more importantly, sleep.

"He must be bribing them somehow," Jeckle repeated for the umpteenth time, the twin prongs of his dyed moustache swinging like a pair of dead cats' tails as he gesticulated. "Did you see how the Sister Superior refused to even look at him? He's exploiting his position and his pet wardens to unearth all our secrets then using them against us."

"The wardens?" Pine asked tiredly, scratching at the patchy stubble that was beginning to form on his chin in between the scars.

"Of course! Keep up, will you? There's not a jeweller in Keselgraad with enough skill to replicate my signet ring, which means that he must have had it stolen from my chambers. Only a warden could get in and out of there undetected."

"He seems to be going to a lot of trouble to murder two innocent men."

Jeckle's mouth slammed shut for the first time in several hours. He slumped down into the corner of the cell and picked moodily at his ruff. Pine felt a growing sense of unease prickle along his bare arms.

"You … you *are* innocent, are you not, my Lord?"

"You don't understand," Jeckle replied, looking more than ever like a contrite child. "He stole from me, Pine. Not just from me. From the city of Keselgraad. Where I come from, if a man is robbed and does nothing in return, it is seen as a sign of weakness. He will pillage and plunder again and again until there is nothing left. I could not let that happen. I had to retaliate."

"The lift …" Pine muttered incredulously. "That was you? Mists take me, you really *are* guilty! You have condemned us both! What were you thinking? The Keeper of the Peace appropriates some of your resources and you reply with attempted murder?"

"It's been going on for months. And not just me. Potsworn has had shipments mysteriously disappear, too.

Whenever either of us tried to confront that bastard Thane, he laughed in our faces. What other course of action did I have? He controls the Watch. He controls the wardens. Even combining both our honour guards would not be sufficient."

"You could have voted him off the Council."

"Ostracism? Don't you think we tried? He's got Faith and Coin so wrapped around his finger that we couldn't pry them loose."

"Hmmm." Pine rubbed at his temples and strained to think. Two nights with little to no sleep was playing havoc with his mind. "What did he take?"

"How is that important?"

"Humour me."

"Mists, Pine, I don't know. Glass, ore, precious metals, leather, pork intestines … Why does it matter?"

"Because it's now obvious to me why *you* are in here, but I still don't quite understand why *I* am."

Jeckle gave a mirthless laugh. "He doesn't seem to like you very much."

"That's not new. He's been harbouring a grudge against me ever since the Collapse. It's like he blames me for it, somehow. I didn't realise it at the time, but I'm fairly certain he only offered me a place in the City Watch so that he could keep an eye on me."

"Why would the Collapse be your fault?"

Jeckle was looking at him intensely.

Of course, Pine thought. *He wasn't Keeper of the Anvil at the time. He doesn't know. Well, I suppose there's no point in keeping secrets from the condemned.*

"The cave-ins that happened in the Mines were triggered by an explosion further underground, in—"

"The Depths," Jeckle finished. "I'm not a complete fool. I wouldn't have lasted long in the Slums if I was. So, you were there when the amethyst shattered. Interesting."

"Yes … when my friends died," Pine stared at his feet. "Their bodies are still down there, somewhere, buried under several tonnes of rubble, never to be recovered."

Jeckle laughed again. It was a decidedly unpleasant sound, like the chittering squeal of a large rodent. "Never recovered? Then, you don't know."

"Don't know what?"

"Yours wasn't the last expedition into the Depths. After the Collapse, Lord Thane rattled off a host of heartfelt speeches and made a great show of condemning the entrance to the lower levels of the Mines, but about four or five years later, the Keepers Council gave him authority to go back."

Pine felt a cold chill ripple down his spine. "Go back? Are you mad? Why in the Mists did you agree to such a thing?"

Jeckle squirmed uncomfortably.

"For a share in the profits. Why else?"

"But … the manpower you would need to reopen the collapsed tunnels … How did Thane manage to keep it a secret?"

"He uses the wardens. At night. Bastards don't even need lanterns to see down there. They cleared the rubble away in a week."

"Mother keep me. Your greed might get us all killed."

"Or save us. What if the wardens find another amethyst?"

"They won't. They'll only find …" Pine trailed off as the penny dropped. "Mists, the drawings we found in Spritt's atelier. I was under the misguided assumption that they were a decade old, but maybe they're not. Maybe they were discovered recently. Very recently."

Jeckle sat up, suddenly alert. "That must be it, Pine! You saw something that bastard Thane didn't want you to see."

"Sent to the cross for laying eyes on a piece of metal resembling a pair of tongs," Pine replied with a wry smile. "I still can't quite believe it."

"It *must* be significant," Jeckle continued animatedly, his eyes gleaming. "What did this man … Spritt have to say?"

"Not much. He's dead. I took the drawings to an old acquaintance of mine, one of the few other miners who survived the Collapse. He recognised where they came from and even offered to take me there, but of course, that will be quite impossible now."

"There you go again, Pine, taking me for a fool. I still have friends. Allies. My accomplices have been informed of my current predicament. Trust me, they'll free us before we set foot on the gatehouse roof. And once we are free, I can use your testimony to convince the other Keepers just how conniving that rat Thane is. We'll exclude him from the Council and close off the Depths for good."

Jeckle was still in good spirits when a priestess of the Mater Sorores arrived a half-hour later, holding a stone effigy of the Mother in one hand and a sheet of vellum in the other.

"Penitent souls," she crooned from under her wimple. "Those who will soon find themselves at the feet of our most beloved goddess. May you go to her unburdened by your past transgressions. By liberating yourselves of your sins, so too do you unshackle your hearts from the darkness that threatens to consume us all."

Pine winced as her high-pitched voice rattled around his

skull. "Answer me this, Sister. Can the Mother bring back the friends I have lost?"

The nun's devout expression faltered. "If you pray …"

"I tried that. In fact, I tried asking her many things. Most of my questions revolved around why I survived while everyone I'd ever known and loved died."

"A miracle! You are blessed."

"Ten long years of constant nightmares and gut-wrenching guilt is not a blessing, Sister, believe me. I have said all I need to say to the Mother. She knows where to find me if, one day, she wishes to reply."

"I … very well. And you, Lord Jeckle?"

The Keeper of the Anvil was attempting to make himself presentable by removing bits of straw from his green doublet and smoothing down his moustache. "You did not bring enough vellum to record all I would need to confess, Sister," he said, somewhat regretfully. "I will go to the Mother with my sins laid bare for all to see. She will judge me as I am, warts and all."

"R … right. Then, may she have mercy on both your souls. I will inform the guard that you are ready. The crosses await."

⌘

The gatehouse was another reminder of Keselgraad's glorious past; a rectangular crenellated buttress that protected two huge banded doors, which hadn't been opened in almost a century. And, as with many buildings, what had once been one of the most important edifices in the entire city had since been reconverted into something else entirely.

Two x-shaped wooden crosses, weathered by the elements and stained with dried blood, now adorned the crumbling battlements. Hinges fixed to the bottoms of each cross allowed them to be swung down from a vertical to a horizontal position, effectively tipping them over the edge to bring them – and anything strapped to them – closer to the seething terror of the Mists.

This sadistic but practical means of execution had seen the light of day shortly after the revolt that had led to the downfall of the last King of Keselgraad and the instauration of the Keepers Council. In the following days, thousands of loyalists were swiftly found guilty and sentenced to death, far too many for the city's single gallows. Several alternative methods were considered, including burying them alive in the fields of wheat and corn, but in the end, it was decided that the easiest solution was simply to throw them off the wall into the Mists.

This solved one problem while creating another. The condemned fell without a sound, swallowed by the churning white clouds, their fate left unseen and unheard. This displeased the then Keeper of the Peace, who argued that the point of an execution was not only to punish the enemies of the Council but also to serve as a warning; a glimpse of the fate that would befall any other potential dissidents. And so, the crosses were invented; near enough to the Mists to be fatal to those tied to them and close enough to the ramparts to provide an unforgettable spectacle to all those contemplating a second revolution.

Executions were rarer now, yet they still drew enormous crowds, scrunched tightly into every inch of free space offered by the gatehouse and spilling down into the streets of the Slums to line the path between the entrance to the central staircase and the much shorter flight of steps up to the flat roof and wooden crosses.

Pine and Jeckle emerged shortly before midday, having spent several hours descending the score of levels that separated the Watch House from the Slums. The Keeper of the Anvil had become increasingly despondent on their trip down, and Pine surmised that the various contingency plans that Jeckle had hoped for were failing one after the other which, considering Lord Thane's spider-like web of informants, was not surprising. What *was* surprising, however, was how little Pine was affected by the prospect of his impending death.

This is what the Mother intended for me all along, he thought, oblivious to the jeers and insults that accompanied his last hundred feet to the gatehouse. *The fact that I survived the Collapse was all part of her design. My suffering is finally at an end.*

Pine felt a huge weight lift from his shoulders. All that guilt that he had been burdened with. That pressure to do something with the life he had been given. It had all been a charade. He was no better than Bera or Hale or any of the others who had been crushed by falling rocks. His punishment had simply been delayed.

"Why are you smiling?" one of the purple-clad honour guard asked him suspiciously. Pine recognised the same officer who had escorted him to the Council chambers the previous day.

"It's a beautiful day," he replied.

The other man scowled and glanced up at the sky where

dark grey clouds were brewing ominously. "Mists take you," he muttered.

Pine was fully aware of the irony behind those words. His smile broadened.

The steps up to the gatehouse roof loomed. Lord Jeckle became agitated at the sight of them, his frantic gaze scanning the crowds for a familiar face. He had to be half-dragged the rest of the way while his feeble attempts to bribe the six members of Thane's honour guard were met with dismissive laughs.

The Keeper of the Peace himself was waiting for them at the top wearing his immaculate silver-buttoned greatcoat and flanked by Lord Potsworn and Lady Hellington. Behind the trio, silhouetted against the shimmering white Mists, were the two crosses, their hinges oiled and straps tested.

Jeckle's eyes bulged, and he bucked like a cornered deer, shouldering aside one of the guards and running for the stairs. A dark figure materialised out of the throng of bystanders and drove its fist into the little man's gut.

"I advise you to go to the Mother with decency and honour," a cold voice intoned. A waxed leather glove closed around Jeckle's ruff and hauled him back towards the crosses.

"Dev … Devrard," Jeckle spluttered. "I remember you before you became a warden. You were a brave man. A … *good* man. Surely you can see that what is happening here today is wrong?"

The ceramic mask swivelled in his direction. The right eye-slit was broken, yet the inscrutable dark abyss revealed beneath somehow made Devrard appear even more terrifying.

"You are not entirely incorrect," he admitted in his usual

monotone. "Lord Thane's methods have once again proved to be somewhat unconventional."

He lifted the prisoner into the air effortlessly and began to tighten the straps around his wrists.

"Yes, yes!" Jeckle stammered, pointedly avoiding looking over the edge into the Mists. "You are blindly taking orders from a man who has a blatant disregard for human life! You must … you must listen to me! I am only the first to fall to his relentless ambition. Potsworn, Nayelle, and Hellington will suffer the same fate. He will not stop until he is crowned King of Keselgraad. Is that what you want? Another tyrant?"

Devrard finished securing the prisoner's legs. He leant close and spoke in a hushed voice that only Jeckle and Pine could hear. "You are incorrect on one important point. Lord Thane holds no power over me. We both simply walk the same paths, and it is easier to let him believe he is the one pulling the strings. He is just another puppet. Like us all. Puppets of the Mother, to be shaped and moulded as she sees fit. Besides, soon she will have no further use for Lord Thane."

The tip of the beaked mask brushed against Jeckle's cheek. "For what good is a Keeper of the Peace … if there is no peace left to keep?"

SEVENTEEN
THE PARTING OF THE MISTS

"Mother is beauty,

Mother is grace,

May the Mother keep me,

In her embrace.

Mother is fury,

Mother is rage,

May her enemies suffer,

Under her gaze."

Prayer to the Mother

JECKLE WHIMPERED AS the last of his defiance dissolved into fear. Devrard stepped away from the quivering man and motioned to Pine. "Captain, I regret to inform you that I must also secure your straps."

"Of course," Pine answered absently, rubbing at his hands. He allowed himself to be led to the second cross and raised his arms.

"This will be an interesting experiment," the warden

said, tightening the leather. "I have never seen one of the cursed like yourself be gifted to the Mists. I am most curious to see what the reaction will be."

"What … what are you talking about?"

Devrard paused. "Apologies. I did not mean to be cryptic. The scars on your skin. Traces of the shattered crystal. All who were present that day were affected. Affected by that *blight*."

"Affected?"

"Changed. Cursed."

Pine tried to make some sense of what he was hearing. "I thought … the amethysts, are they not a blessing from the Mother?"

Devrard cocked his head. "Is that what you believe? Interesting. Then, you did not find the archives. It's probably for the best."

"I … I don't understand. What archives? What curse? If I had been changed somehow, it would have manifested itself by now."

The warden tied the final knot. "Perhaps it already has. I … I must apologise again, Captain. I am … uncomfortable in sending a man like yourself to meet the Mother so soon, but you are far too dangerous to be left alive. You must believe me when I say that it is for the good of the city. Always the city. Keselgraad is paramount."

"Finished, Devrard?" Thane called, tapping his cane impatiently. "The day is not getting any longer."

"Yes, my Lord."

"Excellent." The Keeper of the Peace motioned to his honour guard who then hammered the butts of their halberds into the stone roof until the murmurings of the gathered onlookers faded into an expectant silence.

"People of Keselgraad! The traitors you see before you are guilty of the most heinous of crimes. They sought to end the life of a member of the Keepers Council; those who toil tirelessly day and night to ensure your protection! Imagine a world without the City Watch patrolling your streets. Without the wardens to keep you safe. Without the mirror-men to bring light to your homes. Without the carpenters and stone masons to keep these very walls maintained!"

The silence became angry and brooding.

"Keselgraad is a wonderful place. A beautiful place. One I am proud to call home. Yet, it is fragile, balanced on a knife's edge. A single failed harvest is all it would take for us to starve. An untreated case of the pox could ravage entire levels. Our city is both majestic and delicate. We survive because of the five pillars. Peace, Faith, Fields, Anvil, and Coin. Working in harmony for the benefit of all."

Thane stabbed at the wooden crosses with his cane. "This is what these two traitors wanted to shatter! All that we have strived for! All that defines us! Broken!"

"KILL THEM!" someone in the crowd yelled, his cry echoing off the great cliff-like walls.

Thane raised a placating hand. "Every soul that the city loses is a tragedy. You have all seen the empty homes and deserted squares. Our population dwindles. Each death is a cut to the heart of Keselgraad. These men shall be gifted to the Mists. Yet, we shall not rejoice. We shall not gloat. For even now, at the very end, they continue to make us weak. Warden. Begin."

Devrard placed himself behind Jeckle where a circular

crank enabled a spool of rope to be unwound. He turned the handle, and with a jittering shudder, the cross started to move.

"Wait!" the Keeper of the Anvil shouted shrilly. "I have information. There are things the Council have been hiding from you. All of you! Secrets! I will tell you everything."

The cross continued its inexorable descent. The Mists swirled.

"Money! I have money! I am one of the richest men in all of Keselgraad. A hundred gold coins for the man who cuts me free! Enough for a lifetime of luxury!"

No one moved. Thane and his wardens had done their job well, weeding out the last of Jeckle's supporters and making sure that all of his sycophants would be as far from the city walls as possible. Too far away to intervene.

"Please! You don't understand! I don't deserve this!"

The cross was nearly horizontal, suspending him three feet over the Mists. A single inquisitive strand, as thin as a rose stem, spiralled out of the white veil and tugged playfully at Jeckle's boot. He moaned in fear. A dark patch appeared on the front of his breeches, and Pine could smell the stench of hot urine.

"Mother preserve us," he murmured as more writhing tendrils latched onto the wailing man, exploring, searching, uninterested in the gaudy green doublet or the mud-stained ruff. It was skin they were after. And what lay beneath. Then the first of the feelers brushed Jeckle's cheek, and the screaming began.

Pine found himself unable to look away. Eight or nine years ago, still a young watchman, he had been assigned to a missing person's case down by the slaughterhouses. It had taken him two days to locate the young woman, and by that time, the rats had found her first, burrowing, gnawing, and clawing into her decaying corpse; making it spasm as if it were alive.

This is what the Mists reminded him of now; a pack of ravenous, insatiable rodents, tearing at every inch of exposed flesh. Digging and digging until they reached the bone.

Jeckle was no longer screaming, his face mercifully hidden by seething fog, his small body bouncing and jerking on the cross as he was devoured from within. The demeanour of those watching had changed. Anger and excitement had become horror and disgust. Many averted their gaze or clapped their hands over their ears. A green-faced adolescent vomited noisily onto the paving. Others simply fled the rooftop, running down the steps back to the streets below where the execution could only be heard and not seen.

Lady Hellington was weeping openly, her handkerchief pressed tightly to her lips. Potsworn's normally ruddy cheeks were whiter than chalk. The Keeper of the Fields winced at every agonising sound and occasionally squeezed his eyes shut as if doing so would make the nightmare end. Only Lord Thane showed no outer signs of discomfort, his right hand tightly gripping the brass pommel of his cane.

The Mists chewed slowly through Jeckle's lifeless hands and wrists until his corpse slipped free of the leather straps and fell, disappearing into the swell.

Devrard reversed his grip on the crank, raising the cross back into an upright position, and came to stand behind Pine.

"No!" a woman in the waning crowd cried. "Mercy!"

Her pleas were taken up by a dozen more cracked voices, made raw and hoarse by what they had just witnessed.

Lord Thane didn't answer, only looked at Devrard and nodded.

Pine felt the cross start to move. He craned his neck over his shoulder as far as he could and saw a fresh face. Amber curls framed emerald eyes that shimmered with tears.

Selene.

"Mist-spawned girl," he whispered. "She never listens."

He offered her a rueful smile, and she smiled back, removing something from her pocket and holding it up for him to see. A scrap of paper. Taken from him by Lord Thane. She had retrieved it somehow. Which meant …

The Depths.

No, he mouthed at her, but it was too late, the cross was already pitching over the side, and she was lost from sight. Now all he could see were the Mists. White and pure, like a field of snow. Pristine. As hypnotically beautiful as they were deadly.

Everything else faded away.

There was only Pine and the Mists.

He watched with a strange detachment as the first of the tentacles rose from the fog, twisting and turning as if it were dancing.

Bera. Hale. Lyle. Just a little longer. One more moment of mind-numbing pain, then he would see them again.

Fate and fortune.

The strand of the Mists drew closer, sniffing the air. He felt the faintest of touches against his leg before it travelled higher, creeping over his breeches, his belt, his tunic.

It slithered over his cheek in a soft caress.

Come on, Pine willed. *Come on, damn you! What are you waiting for? Get it over with!*

The tendril lingered, resting against his skin. He sensed its lightness. Its hesitation.

The moment stretched. Sounds filtered through into Pine's tired mind. Shouting. Yelling. Voices raised in exaltation. He struggled to raise his head. Something was happening.

There on the horizon. What had once been a tranquil plain of smooth fog was now tarnished by an unnatural disturbance. A tear in the fabric. Boiling. *Rippling.* As if some unseen entity was pushing the veil aside like a curtain. It surged closer, creating miniature waves that rolled out from its epicentre to lap against the city walls.

The Mists spiralled around it. It became a whirlpool, the tear widening, the fog spinning. Lightning crackled, turning the white pall a cerulean blue wherever it kissed the surface. Pine could taste metal on his tongue. The air was charged with it. Thick and heavy like before a storm.

The thing advanced, and the Mists retreated before it like a frightened child. The tentacles encircling Pine unravelled. His skin prickled. He could almost see into the centre of the raging tornado where broken, pulsating clouds fought to escape whatever lay beneath.

The wind whipped through his hair, drowning the noise of the crowds. It was as if the Mists themselves were screaming.

An earth-shattering roar. Louder than thunder. Pine cried out. Blood trickled from his nose. The wind was a constant, deafening wail. His skull thrummed. Something had to give or his mind would explode.

Mother keep me.

A crescendo of light and chaos; screeching and calling and buzzing and screaming as it reached its final, desperate paroxysm.

A blinding radiance.

The birth of a new sun.

The sound of reality tearing itself apart.

And the Mists parted.

At last, Pine saw what lay beneath. He had expected a charred, blackened wasteland but could not have been more wrong. Lush green grass swayed peacefully, dotted with a kaleidoscope of colourful flowers. A woman was walking towards him, her bare feet leaving the softest of traces, her lithe frame covered in a flowing pale tunic. Her long hair, the colour of burnished gold, fell in a cascade of scintillating curls, their aurelean glow suffusing the cloudy skies.

She stopped before his cross and looked up.

Her eyes met Pine's.

Twin pools of blue ice enveloped him. He fell helplessly into their cold depths, their flickering irises stripping away layer after layer of his weary psyche to reveal his raw, unde-fended core. His lies, his secrets, his wants, his dreams, all laid bare. Indescribable power flooded every part of him. He was a candle in an ocean, to be snuffed out without a second thought.

Beyond that smothering gaze, Pine could just detect the extremity of something larger. Something ancient and primal, a being who had lived a thousand lives and would live a thousand more, who had seen the rise and fall of civili-sations. Who had been the first to walk upon the earth and would be the last to leave it. Warm and loving. Cold and uncompromising. Everything.

And nothing.

Pine screamed at last, torn between terror and ecstasy. Hate and love. His guilt, rage, anguish, and pain sprang free from their prison to ravage his mind.

And below his writhing form …

The Mother smiled.

PART TWO

EIGHTEEN
MASKS AND MADNESS

"People speak of sacrifice without understanding the symbolism behind the word. It has come to mean losing something important for the sake of a better cause, but there is another, older signification: an oblation. A gift to the Holy Mother. This is the trial the wardens must face. This is the sacrifice they must make. An offering. Freely given. Body, mind, and soul."

Sister Nayelle, Keeper of the Faith, 831st Year of the Mother

"YOU HAVE BEEN chosen." Lord Matellas Thane's authoritative voice carried easily to all four edges of the courtyard, cracking like a whip. "Not because you are the strongest. Or the bravest. But because you are *resilient*. You are *survivors*. You have stood tall and proud against the storm when so many others have been shattered."

Henely Chroll straightened his back and lifted his head to proudly display the burn marks on his right cheek. He had earned them five years ago, during a routine inspection of one of the lower-level bakeries that had turned sour. Apparently, the man's apprentice had been using dough to smuggle uncut gems up from the Mines, and the ensuing kerfuffle had set the entire place on fire. The two watchmen accompanying Chroll had died when the rafters collapsed while he had endured, half-buried by rubble, the flesh seared from his face. A miracle, the Mater Sorores had called it. A gift from the Mother. And he was not alone.

A dozen watchmen had been summoned by Thane to the yard behind the Stables, all bearing their fair share of scars. Chroll recognised some of them: Croucher, stabbed three times in the chest by a startled burglar; Heintz, his ear torn off with a broken pewter tankard during a particularly nasty bar fight; Mienhaffen, the veteran, already old when Chroll had first been sworn in, his wrinkled skin marred by uncountable run-ins with Keselgraad's petty criminals.

A watchman's job was not for the faint-hearted. Dangerous. Stressful. Long hours, poor pay, and little to no recognition. Until now. The Keeper of the Peace had finally deemed them worthy of the highest possible honour.

"What I offer you is not fame," Lord Thane continued, his steely eyes fixing each of them in turn. "It is not glory. You will be further from the light than you have ever been before. You will be … among the shadows."

The excitement amid those listening was palpable. The drumming in Chroll's chest increased its joyous cadence.

"Perhaps you think I do not know you. Yet, I do. For you are like me. You love this city. You love its people. And you are prepared to do anything to keep them safe."

"Praise the Mother!" Mienhaffen yelled, an exultant grin plastered on his ancient face.

"Praise her, indeed. It is through her strength that Keselgraad still stands. Although her enemies circle her like buzzards. Waiting for a moment of weakness. The baseless heretics who strive to disrupt the fragile peace that we have earned with the sweat from our brows. She cannot face the darkness alone. She is in need of guardians. Protectors. *Wardens*. Will you answer the call? Are you ready to give your lives for your goddess? For Keselgraad?"

"KESELGRAAD!" the assembled watchmen bellowed as one, and Chroll felt his heart swell. He had never married. Never had the time for it. The City Watch was his family, and these men were his brothers.

Lord Thane let the moment linger. "Then, it is decided," he said. A strange expression flashed across his face. There and gone again in an instant. Something Chroll could not quite place. Something akin to regret.

"You stand now on the threshold of greatness," the Keeper of the Peace went on, one hand gripping the top of his cane. "There is but one more trial to overcome. You must face our greatest enemy. You must face the *Mists*."

Chroll's good humour drained away faster than a tankard of cool ale to be replaced by a sinking sense of trepidation. He had seen prisoners gifted to the Mists. He had seen what that white horror could do to a man's flesh.

"You will report to the Den to be clothed in protective garments and masks. The wax on the leather coats will prevent the demons from attaching themselves to your skin, and the herbal mixture prepared by the Mater Sorores will keep the poison from entering your lungs. The only true way to vanquish fear is to face it head-on."

Chroll almost laughed out loud with relief. He was about to receive the most wondrous of gifts. And with it, he would be invincible. He followed the other watchmen out of the courtyard, pausing only to remove his worn bronze breastplate and helm. They had served him well against bolt and blade but would be useless in the Mists.

The Den was two levels above the Stables, tucked away at the end of a nondescript alleyway. A multi-storeyed house, much like any other, with a plain wooden door and tightly latched shutters. Most of Keselgraad's citizens would walk by the featureless facade with barely a second glance, which was exactly what the wardens wanted. Only a small plaque next to the knocker revealed its true identity: the shield emblem of the Keeper of the Peace.

The watchmen milled around uncertainly on the street in front of the building until Chroll summoned his courage and gave the knocker a couple of resonant taps. Hinges creaked in reply. A flat, wide-brimmed hat emerged from the darkness beyond. White ceramic glinted underneath.

"Enter," the warden ordered, standing aside to let them pass.

The interior was darker than a disused mine shaft. Chroll paused in the entranceway, waiting for his eyes to adjust to the gloom. Motes of fine dust glittered in the cloying air, catching what little light filtered through the panelled shutters. All the furniture in the room was hidden under dirty covers, and the fireplace set into the far wall looked like it hadn't been used in an age.

"Do not climb the stairs," the masked warden cautioned, pointing with a gloved finger at the curving staircase that disappeared through the ceiling. "We are very particular about our privacy."

He led the watchmen through a series of unused rooms, including a kitchen with rows of rusty pots and an iron cauldron half-filled with something that smelt as bad as it looked. Chroll began to wonder where everyone else was. Resting on the second floor, perhaps? Far from prying eyes?

Finally, they entered what seemed to be a vestibule. Black waxed garments hung neatly from a line of pegs, complete with elbow-length gloves, high boots, and flat-topped hats. Before the pegs, placed reverently on a wooden table, a dozen beak-shaped masks gleamed. Chroll studied the glass eye-slits, breathing fast. How many times when a warden had passed him by had he wondered how the world would appear through those thick lenses? And now, he would find out for himself.

"Please select a suitable attire," their host said. "The boots first. As tight as possible against your breeches. Then the hooded robe, ensuring the neck, ears, and scalp are fully concealed. Finally, the gloves."

"And the mask?" Chroll asked, selecting a pair of boots.

"I will assist you. The mask is the most important item of all. It must be perfectly attached to avoid any risk of contamination by the miasma."

The former watchmen dressed quickly, exchanging pieces of clothing and helping each other find the right sizes in a series of hushed whispers. The warden waited patiently until they had finished. Chroll flexed his fingers. The fabric used to make the gloves was significantly lighter and more flexible than he had initially expected, almost as if he wasn't wearing them at all.

"These masks have already been filled for you," the warden said, lifting the first one and coming to stand before Chroll. "Although in time, you will be taught how to make your own herbal concoction and how to stuff the beak efficiently."

"What ingredients do you use?" Chroll enquired, detecting a faint floral aroma.

"Lavender, mint, and cloves to dull the stench of our sweat. Vinegar and resin to stop the Mists from entering our nostrils."

"Our … sweat?"

"The demons cannot see us, Watchman. But they can smell us. The greater our fear, the easier we are to detect. You will need a strong heart and a calm mind to resist. This you will learn. Among many other things."

The warden raised the mask. "You must only remove it if you are alone, in the presence of others like yourself, or if the Keeper of the Peace demands it."

Chroll felt a flicker of doubt. "Why? If they were conceived to offer us protection against the Mists, surely there is no need to keep them on inside Keselgraad?"

The backhanded slap came so fast that it took him completely by surprise, cracking across his jaw and splitting his lip.

"I sympathise with your curiosity, Watchman," the warden said calmly as if nothing had happened. "But we do not tolerate stupidity among our members. What is our creed?"

Chroll could taste blood in his mouth. "The protection of Keselgraad."

"Yes. Lord Thane must have told you that the city is under attack from threats both without and *within*. A man's identity is a weapon to be used against him, just like any other. You were chosen not only for your endurance but also for your celibacy. No … unwanted baggage that could be turned into leverage. Anonymity is like a shield. Do you understand?"

"Yes … Sir."

The warden placed a hand on the watchman's shoulder. "I am not your superior. I am your brother. We are all your brothers. Are you ready?"

Chroll nodded. He inhaled slowly as the mask was placed on his face, covering the only patch of skin still visible, from forehead to chin. Apart from a slight loss of peripheral vision, the eye-slits were surprisingly clear so that the dim confines of the vestibule were tinged with the barest of blurry sheens. He felt firm hands tighten the straps across the back of his head. The herbal aroma was both flowery and sweet. It was intoxicating. He breathed deeply, shivering with pleasure as the scented air entered his lungs, the mint and cloves purifying and cleansing. It was …

"Wonderful," he murmured in delight. Intoxicating was the wrong word. It was *invigorating* as if his brain had been awoken from a dreary slumber. He was thinking clearly for the first time in his life.

Of course, the wardens would choose to keep their masks on at all times. Why in the Mother would they ever want to remove them? And be deprived of this … rapture.

"You are ready," their host said, an undercurrent of pride in his usually bland voice. He was still standing among the former guardsmen, but now it appeared that he had replicated himself. Twelve identical masked figures.

Brothers.

"You are ready," the warden repeated. "Only one last thing separates you from the gift of the blade. You must leave the confines of this haven. You must pass the trial of the Mists."

⌘

Nearly all Keselgraad's citizens believed that the only way out of the city was through the now-condemned gatehouse. This was far from the truth, however. On the contrary, it would have been very foolish indeed for those who had engineered the construction of the great wall that ringed the Slums not to have conceived several alternative exits.

A great many of these had been forgotten. Yet, at least three had been preserved, their locations known only to the wardens and the Keeper of the Peace. Chroll followed his guide through the winding stalls of the marketplace, down past a row of chop shops – where meat traders bought and sold whatever the higher-level butchers had left behind – all the way to a crumbling storehouse leaning tiredly against the city wall.

Chroll revelled in the wide-eyed stares and respectful awe that his new status afforded him. Watchmen were neither feared nor respected. A warden was both. People stood aside to let him pass or even crossed the street to get out of his way. He saw one devout woman make the sign of the Mother and bow her head. He was, at last, being seen. Seen without being recognised. The perfect compromise.

Two more of his warden-brothers ushered him inside the storehouse and through another door into a tiny yard at the back. The wall rose high overhead, a colossal block of hard, impenetrable stone. Chroll peered more closely. There. A hairline crack, six feet long, running vertically from a spot in front of him to the base. Without his mask, he would have missed it entirely, but everything seemed so much easier now. Despite the constrictive view of the eye-slits, his mind was so … *clear*.

"A postern gate," one of the wardens said, scraping away

a patch of moss to reveal a keyhole. "One that only unlocks from this side, for obvious reasons." He slid a key into the lock. It turned with little effort.

"Your objective is simple. You are to walk a hundred paces into the Mists. *Walk*, not run. Then simply turn around and come back again."

Mienhaffen, the veteran, cackled. "That's all?"

"Yes. Please proceed."

The hidden door swung open to reveal an undulating wall of fog, pushing against some invisible barrier. Chroll's heightened senses meant that he could see each individual strand, thousands upon thousands of threads all woven together to make up an enormous tapestry. He had often gazed upon the Mists from afar, but he had never been this close.

And he was about to get closer.

A single step took him across the threshold. The ground was soft and spongy underfoot. Another step. A blurry figure passed him on his left. One of his companions, unrecognisable in his robes and mask.

Twenty paces. Chroll glanced back over his shoulder. The open door was the faintest of silhouettes. Soon, it would be swallowed by the white pall, and he would have to rely on his own sense of direction to find his way home.

Fifty paces. He felt a slight prickling along his forearms and looked down to see tentacular filaments wrapping around his gloves. They couldn't penetrate the leather. He was protected. He was … *invincible*.

Chroll murmured a brief thanks to the Mother. She had chosen him, and he would make her proud. He would make all of Keselgraad proud.

Eighty paces. The tingling itch had reached his face, an admittedly unpleasant sensation, especially on the patches of burnt skin that were still raw and tender. He pushed on.

There. A hundred paces. He was surprised to feel a flood of relief. But why? What was there to fear? Was he not invincible?

He turned. Through the soft blur of his glass eye-slits, the view remained the same. Bright and cold. As if he hadn't moved at all.

We all think that we are afraid of the dark. But it is not the darkness we fear. It is the blindness that comes with it. It is the way our imagination creates nightmares from the things we hear but cannot see.

It took every ounce of Chroll's courage not to run. The prickling on his face was unbearable. He wanted to tear off his gloves and mask so that he could scratch at it.

Twenty pa … or was that thirty? Or ten? He wasn't sure.

"Mienhaffen? Croucher?"

His voice was muffled by the herbs. They no longer smelt so sweet.

His cheek was on fire. It brought back memories of being trapped in the burning bakery, the half-finished loaves roasting until their crusts were dry and black. Roasting and steaming as the flames ate away at his skin.

He coughed. Wet and sticky. His hands were pure agony within his gloves. More wetness. More blood.

It is a lie, Chroll realised in mounting panic. *The mask. The clothes. They do not work. The Mists are flaying me alive.*

Something small and hard slithered over his tongue. A tooth, dislodged from weeping gums. He whimpered in despair.

Another stumbling step. Fluid clogged his throat. He tried to swallow. Drowning. He was drowning in his own blood.

A trio of figures appeared suddenly from within the white horror. Chroll looked upon their bird-like masks and screamed.

"This one has survived," one of them stated calmly. "Take him to her."

Chroll blacked out and then came to again with a surge of fresh pain. He was being carried. Metal shrieked. Cogs whirred. The lift. He had somehow been brought back inside Keselgraad. Inside the lift.

He faded in and out of consciousness. A flash of sunlight. Marble steps. Dour statues fixing him with their disapproving gaze. The buzzing of bees.

"Remove his mask." A soft female voice, like a waft of cool spring air. He moaned. Gloved hands fumbled at the leather straps. His ceramic prison slid from his face, its interior caked with gore and pieces of torn skin.

The woman leant over him. A medallion hung from her neck. An x-shaped cross contained within a perfect triangle. "You are dying," she whispered mournfully. "I am sorry. The Mother tests us all. We are bound to her in pain. Our oaths sworn in our final moments, signed with the last drops of our weeping blood. You have a choice. The ultimate choice. I can leave you to die. Your body will be laid to rest in the fields to help others grow. The agony you now feel will end."

She produced a glass vial. Something dark glistened inside. Something terrible.

"Or you can live. The pain will continue. You will learn to master it, but it will never leave. In return, you will become a true warden. An agent of her will. Unbreakable. Unstoppable. The question is simple. It is the same one I ask myself every morning. The same one I ask my congregation. Do you have faith?"

Chroll forced his right hand to move. Whatever slushed and squelched in his gloves was no longer flesh and bone, yet he somehow managed to wrap his fingers around the vial and take it from Sister Nayelle's unresisting grasp.

"Mother keep me," he replied simply, tipping the contents into his mouth.

And in doing so, was reborn.

NINETEEN
RIGHTING WRONGS

"The crystal is filling with agonising slowness. One drop a week, sometimes even less. All while the Mists continue their inexorable advance. At last, our military leaders understand that we have failed. They are attempting their own futile counterattacks. A hundred cavalry lost in a single, desperate charge. Horse-powered windmills overrun. And now, they have set the fields on fire. Acres of farmland put to the torch. I can see the great curtain of flame from the ramparts, an orange tear between earth and sky. It will not stop the Mists. Nothing can."

First Technologist Arniel Sin, The Time Before

P**INE WAS HAVING** another nightmare. Bound to a cross. Suspended over a sea of churning white. Fighting to free himself from the leather straps that dug into his wrists and ankles as tentacular strands slowly encircled his struggling body in their cold embrace. A flash of golden locks. Two piercing blue eyes. He opened his mouth to scream.

The dream changed. He was somewhere else. Underground. A passageway as old as the city itself. A chamber, empty save for an octagonal font filled with a liquid darker than the night. A woman, strangely familiar, stood with her back to him, her arms outstretched. Black tar dripped from her fingers.

Run.

He tried to reply. It was as if his lips were sewn shut. He reached out. She shuddered at his touch.

Run.

The surface began to boil. Something was coming. Something that meant to tear him limb from limb. He had to get out. He had to—

"Pine."

His eyes snapped open, and the familiar sight of the Stables prison cell swam into focus, complete with festering straw and a half-full slop bucket. He groaned.

"I know you're awake, Pine."

He rolled onto his back and immediately regretted it. His arms felt like they had been pulled from their sockets and then reattached. His head pounded with the thrumming rhythm of a man who has consumed too much of Fletch's ale, although he was, unfortunately, completely sober.

"Mists," he grumbled, raising his hands to his face. Pinpricks of dried blood had joined the network of decade-old scars, and the skin around his wrists had been rubbed raw. He pulled himself up into a sitting position and looked through the bars to see Selene gazing back at him, her expression a curious mix of worry and annoyance.

"The cross. It wasn't a dream, was it?" Pine asked, taking in her tired eyes and haggard complexion.

"I am afraid not."

"Then ..." he struggled to say it. "The Mother is ... real? She has ... returned to us?"

Selene crossed her arms over her breastplate. "Walked

right out of the Mists as if she was coming back from an afternoon stroll. You should have seen the look on Lord Thane's face."

"I remember her stare. So *cold*. Like an icicle plunged into my chest."

"We all felt it. Lady Hellington went down on her knees, and the rest of us followed suit. We would probably still be there if the nuns of the Mater Sorores hadn't appeared and ordered us to open the gates."

"Those rusted old things haven't been used in a hundred years!"

"They took a bit of persuading, but once the wardens lent their strength to the task, the hinges relented."

Pine ran his fingers through his greasy grey hair, dislodging several pieces of straw. He would kill for a basin of water, a bar of tallow soap, some clean clothes, and enough alcohol to numb the various aches and pains that pervaded his body. "So, the Mother has entered the city?"

Selene nodded. "Strode straight through the crowds without a word and ascended the central stairwell all the way up to the Church, with the Mater Sorores and the wardens trailing after her like a flock of sheep following their shepherdess."

"No one tried to speak to her?"

"I ..." she gnawed at her bottom lip. "I think everyone was just in a state of utter shock. I was on the gatehouse roof, further away than most, and even there I sensed her presence. Her ... *aura*. She never looked at me, yet I could somehow feel her touch my mind. It's ... it's stupid."

"No," Pine countered, recalling the way he had shrivelled

under the Mother's gaze like vines in winter. "No, it's not. Did you follow her?"

"Lord Thane was the first to come to his senses. He rounded up his honour guard and set off after the wardens. The lift wasn't working so they had to climb the entire central staircase. It took them the rest of the day and a good part of the evening. By the time they reached the top, the Mother and her sycophants had disappeared into the Church … and the doors were firmly shut."

Pine rolled his shoulders, wincing as something cracked. "Thane must not have been happy."

"There wasn't much he could do. From what I heard, he pleaded and cajoled for a time, then retreated to the Council chambers and summoned the other Keepers to join him. They've been in there ever since. Leaving the Watch to clean up the mess. We've been out on patrol more or less non-stop since the Mother reappeared. The city is growing restless."

"Hmmm." A tired question shuffled its way to the forefront of Pine's mind. "Didn't you promise me not to come to the execution?"

She gave an embarrassed cough. "No. You *asked* me not to come. And after careful consideration, I decided to disagree."

"Yes, you have a habit of doing that, don't you? Following orders only when it suits you. I imagine that's why you appear to be the only watchman still here while everyone else is out keeping the peace."

"Look, I …" A lock of auburn hair fell in front of her freckled face, and she brushed it away. "I need you to listen. Closely. Because I am only going to say this once."

Pine spread his arms wide to draw her attention to the cramped prison cell. "It's not like I can go anywhere, is it?"

"You – damn the Mists – I think you were *right*."

He smiled. "Well, that confirms it. I'm obviously still dreaming."

"Shut up."

"Right about what?"

"This whole thing being a set-up. Everything slotting into place a little *too* conveniently. While you were lounging around in here—"

"*Lounging?*"

"Yes. While you were lounging around, I took it upon myself to follow up on some of the threads that make up this sorry tapestry. I started with the runner. The one that tipped us off."

"Good idea. What did he have to say?"

"I don't know. I couldn't find him."

Pine raised an eyebrow. "The messenger's guild has to keep records of all of its members, Selene."

"I'm not an idiot. Whoever this man was, he wasn't part of the guild."

"I see. It would have been helpful to have had that information *before* the trial."

"There was no time."

Pine tutted in frustration. "Which is exactly what I told you. They never schedule a trial hours after an arrest. It's too soon. Unless your entire case is as flimsy as a rotten plank of wood. What else did you find?"

She came closer to the bars. "Not much. I went back to your apartment. No discernible footprints on the floor or on the street below your window. There *were* some scratches on the outside of your shutters, which could have been made by a knife."

"Half the mortar in that wall has crumbled away. A blind, one-armed child could scale it without breaking a sweat."

"Perhaps. Although that still means that someone managed to enter your living quarters and walk around without waking you."

Bera. Hale. Lyle.

Amethyst shards covered in blood.

"I'm … I'm a heavy sleeper."

"You must be. Very. That left the question of motive. I went to see Gamin. He told me certain things."

Pine felt an ugly anger boil in his belly. "You had no right to—"

"No right to what? Prove your innocence? It was obvious from the scars on your hands that you were part of the Collapse, but why didn't you tell me that it was Thane who pulled you from the wreckage? That he paid for you to be nursed back to health? That he set up an *orphanage* for the children of all those who died?"

"Because we're not friends," he said, regretting the words as soon as they left his mouth.

A rosy flush crept up her cheeks. "Of course, Mother *forbid* you let anyone get close to you. Keep running away from everything and everyone. Never mind that Gamin was grieving too and could have used a shoulder to cry on. Never mind that a score of scared children suddenly found themselves without mothers and fathers. Out of heart and out of mind, eh? That's the brave way out."

Pine leapt to his feet. "Is that what you think? I didn't do it for me. I did it for *them*. Everyone died down there, Selene, do you get that? *Everyone*. They weren't just my friends; they were my family. I was the only one who survived. Every time those orphans saw my face, they would be reminded of those they had lost. I couldn't do much, but I could at least spare them that. And make sure it would never happen again. You could never understand."

"HOW DO YOU KNOW?" Selene slammed her hand against the bars hard enough to make the metal ring. Pine recoiled in shock.

"Wha …"

"You sanctimonious bastard! How can you even begin to fathom what I do and do not understand? You have no *idea* who I am and why I am here. Because you never thought to ask."

"Watchmen don't pry into each other's pasts," Pine said meekly.

"Mists! Is that all I am to you? A watchman?"

"No, I—"

"I have given up more than you could imagine. Sacrificed more than …" she trailed off, panting, seemingly realising that she had gone too far. "Just … just forget about it, all right?"

"Selene …"

"The motive," she said firmly. "It doesn't fit. You are impatient, impolite, and insubordinate—"

"Thank you."

"—but I've only seen you kill when you have to. You take no pleasure in it. And you're certainly not the sort of man to murder someone who saved your life. Perhaps you *are* innocent after all."

Pine gave a weary exhalation. "It feels nice to hear someone other than me say it. Although none of this brings us any closer to why anyone would go to all that trouble to have me framed. A knife to the back would have been significantly easier."

"And would've raised a whole lot of questions. There's one more thing I haven't told you. It's why I was late to your execution. I was dealing with Spritt."

"The corpse in the morgue? Why? Did the physician find more conclusive evidence of poisoning?"

"No, not Jethro Spritt. *Bendel* Spritt. The jeweller. His body was found in his workshop the day before last."

"Mists!" Pine clapped his hands together. "Cause of death?"

"Unknown. No signs of struggle. Slight bruising around the lips…"

"Oh, come on, it's poison again, Selene, it has to be! It's all linked, isn't it? That contraption that Jethro was working on. The sketches of the relic. We were getting close to something, something important. A secret that should have remained buried. Buried in the Depths." Pine stopped, suddenly remembering what he had seen in her hand when hanging from his cross over the Mists. "You stole the piece of paper back from Thane. You're going down there, aren't you?"

She wrapped her fingers around the bars and stared resolutely into his eyes. "Yes. Gamin will show me the way."

Pine could feel his entire body shiver. That Mist-spawned place would eat her alive. Or worse; drag her even deeper into the darkness to tear her soul apart. But why should he care? She was nothing to him. A watchman. A bored courtesan with a new plaything.

"Don't go," he heard himself say in a small voice.

She reached through and touched his scarred hand. "I have to."

"What if I ordered you to—"

"You've already forgotten that I only follow orders when I want to. I need to find out what's going on, Aldin. It's important."

Her use of his first name caught him off guard. "Then … if your mind is made up, at least promise me you'll listen to Gamin. He knows more about the Depths than anyone I have ever met."

"I will."

"I hope you find what you're looking for. Goodbye. And good luck."

Selene laughed. Pine wasn't sure he had ever heard her do so before. A joyous sound that banished some of the darkness wrapped around his heart.

"I'm glad you find my imprisonment and impending death so amusing," he huffed. "You do realise that as soon as this city comes to its senses, I'll be back on that cross?"

She wiped at the tears of mirth rolling down her cheeks. "By the Mother, Pine, for someone usually so perceptive you really are blind to what's going on, aren't you?"

Selene stepped away from the cage, removed the keychain from the peg on the wall and jingled them suggestively. "I've come to let you out."

"Are … are you mad?" Pine sputtered. "Releasing a prisoner? That's punishable by death. You'll be strung up beside me and gifted to the Mists."

"Mother keep me … you're impossible!" she shot back, raising her eyes to the heavens. "Fine! Do it yourself." She threw the keys through the bars. They landed with a metallic clunk in the straw at Pine's feet.

It would be safer for him to stay here. Safer for everyone. He was tired. He deserved some rest. A long, peaceful rest.

Keep running away from everything and everyone.

Perhaps … perhaps that was why he was so tired. Because he was always running. Had been for ten years. And he had never asked himself what would happen if he stopped.

Pine bent down and picked up the keychain, selected the right key and reached through to unlock the cell door from the other side. Selene watched him silently, her hands playing with the links of her silver necklace.

"I'll say I overpowered you," he said to her. "I forced you to let me out. That should spare you the cross. But you'll still be punished. Manual labour of some sort, I would imagine. And … you'll be discharged from the City Watch. That much is certain. They'll send you back to House Eckelston in disgrace. I'm sorry."

He expected sadness. Or regret. Instead, Selene smiled.

And in that moment, she was beautiful.

"My dear Captain Pine. Now that we are partners in crime, I believe I can let you in on a little secret. I didn't come here to join the City Watch."

She leant closer, her emerald eyes filled with an intensity he had never seen before.

"I came here to find *you*."

TWENTY
THE NEVER-ENDING CYCLE

"The Mists have reached the walls. We are desperate now. Anything we can do to increase the absorptive properties of the crystal must be considered. I have an idea, although fear makes me loath to share it. There is a source of energy that we have not yet plundered. Untapped and waiting to be harvested. That source . . . is us."

First Technologist Arniel Sin, The Time Before

THANE HELD THE decanter up to the light and tipped it slightly so that he could admire the amber liquid inside. The glass itself was unbelievably expensive, but its value paled in comparison to that of its contents. A measure of whisky from one of the last surviving casks in all of Keselgraad.

Before the Mists, when the city had been surrounded by farmland, acres of healthy soil had been devoted to growing barley; the grains were dried, steeped, and germinated in huge malthouses to be used to brew beer or distilled to make spirits. It was something that both fascinated and horrified Thane; so much valuable space squandered to produce an inessential luxury. Kilns and stills, kettles and vats, barrels and casks … a ludicrous amount of time and equipment, all for this. This golden-coloured nectar.

Thane leant back in his chair and stared up at the portrait of his great-grandfather that hung over his desk. The resemblance was obvious; same sharp cheekbones and jaw, same hard eyes and close-cropped hair. His military doublet was perfectly tailored, braided in red and black with gold thistle buttons. Three gleaming medals were expertly pinned to the left breast.

His ancestor had been a leader. A general of an army that no longer existed. Fighting wars against enemies who had since disappeared. Thane envied him in a way. His opponents would have been other men like himself. Soldiers who could be understood. Battlefields that could be studied. Strategies and tactics that could be tested and refined. To his ancestor, victory would have been obtained simply by … winning.

And now, hundreds of years later, Thane was also fighting a war. Although this time, it was different. His enemies were intangible. Victory unobtainable. Thane could never win; it was objectively impossible. He could only strive for the next best thing.

He could try not to *lose*.

The Mists were relentless in their assault on Keselgraad. They did not need to pause to eat or sleep. There was no negotiation. No ceasefire. No feasible way to distract, bribe, confuse, or betray. A continual, unstoppable onslaught that could only be countered by a continual, unbreakable defence.

And therein lay the crux of Thane's problems. He did not consider himself a power-hungry man per se but rather a pragmatic one, and it was undeniably apparent that the democratic principles so proudly championed by the Keepers Council were woefully unsuited to combatting the ever-looming threat of the Mists. Every single strategy had to be debated and voted on. Every requisition of materials carefully recorded, right down to the very last nail. It had reached the point where Thane half-expected someone to be waiting outside his privy to weigh and categorise his morning stool. It was … infuriating. And paradoxically, in wanting to ensure the city's survival, the Keepers Council was condemning it to a slow and painful death.

Thane put down his glass and looked at the chequered black-and-white board that covered his desk, complete with its carved wooden pieces. He picked up the largest one with its crowned dome.

The king.

The monarchs of Keselgraad had, by all accounts, been insufferable bastards. Yet, there must have been some merit in not having every single decision bogged down by trivial arguments and rolls of scratched vellum.

He ran his fingers over the other figures. The horse. The tower. The nun with her mitre-shaped headpiece.

Thane scowled.

The Mater Sorores. Another thorn in his side. Their insistence on removing the amethyst from its pedestal in the Depths had set another cascade of unfortunate events in motion. Thane had fought long and hard to delay its transport until they had had ample time to study its properties or explore the surrounding chambers for further clues as to how it managed to keep the Mists at bay. Yet, his logical arguments were overruled by the other Keepers, desperate for some positive recognition after untold years of dwindling grain stores and several successive underwhelming harvests.

And so, the amethyst had shattered, and suddenly, food supplies had become the least of their problems. As the Keepers floundered in confusion, Lord Thane had become their saviour. The terrible failure of the destroyed gemstone became the Collapse: a fictitious tragedy conceived to bind the inhabitants of the Slums together in solidarity. The shards had been set into the Church steeple to provide the hope sorely needed by the city. And Thane, under the mandate of investigating the calamity, had finally obtained the authority to explore the Depths unchallenged.

It had taken a decade – ten, long, arduous years – for Thane to consolidate his grip on the Keepers Council. Lord Jeckle had been the last hurdle. His demise should have been a cause for celebration; Thane's ascension to becoming the unchallenged ruler of Keselgraad. Until the unthinkable had happened, and the impossible had become possible.

His index finger tapped the piece on the board that he despised the most. The black queen. Wearing her own crown. Standing nearly as tall as the king. His equal.

There had never been a Queen of Keselgraad, but Thane had no doubt as to whom the figure symbolised.

The Mother.

At first, Lord Thane had thought that her sudden appearance must be a trick. That Lord Jeckle had somehow orchestrated an elaborate diversion to stave off his execution. But the way the Mists had refused to touch her … Thane knew what those ravenous tendrils could do to a man. He had seen the wardens without their masks. No one in all of Keselgraad was immune.

The only logical explanation was that whoever was now residing deep within the Church was either the Mother or, at the very least, a similar god-like entity with the power to resist the enemy that Thane had been fighting against for so long.

It was a question that would soon be answered. In the middle of the chequered board in front of Thane, carefully placed between the rows of black and white figures, was a small scrap of vellum that had been delivered to his mansion that morning, stamped with Nayelle's seal and containing two simple words: *She calls.*

Thane retrieved his whisky and lifted it in an unspoken toast to the portrait of his ancestor before downing it in a single gulp. He felt it slither down his throat to warm his belly. To his surprise, the hand holding the empty glass was shaking slightly. Was he sensing some sort of … trepidation?

Ridiculous, he thought, standing up so abruptly that the wooden pieces on the board shook. He glowered one final time at the black queen before leaving the study. His servant was waiting for him as usual with his coat, gloves, and cane. Thane accepted them wordlessly and drew several inches of steel from the hidden scabbard. It had been sharpened and oiled to his precise specifications. He allowed himself a thin smile of approval.

"Any news from Lady Hellington or Lord Potsworn?" he asked, buttoning his greatcoat up to the lip of his starched collar.

"They are still hiding – ahem – *recuperating* in their respective mansions after the ordeal, my Lord. The men you ordered to watch their houses have not reported any runners this morning, so I would surmise that you are the first and perhaps the only Keeper to be summoned into her presence."

"Hmmm. Save for Sister Superior Nayelle, of course."

"Indeed, my Lord."

Thane covered the brief distance between his mansion and the Church with brisk, rhythmic strides, pausing only to ensure that the crenellated walls of his domain were manned by double the usual number of guardsmen, as per his request.

The flight of steps leading up to Keselgraad's jewelled apex seemed longer than usual or perhaps he was unconsciously slowing his pace as he drew closer to the arched entrance. More unfounded apprehension. He had done nothing wrong. Quite the opposite, in fact. The Mother probably wanted to congratulate him for all the sacrifices he had made to keep the city safe. Or perhaps she wished to give him her blessing; to officially endorse him as the new ruler of Keselgraad.

His confidence returned as he strode across the immaculate patch of grass and rapped the brass pommel of his cane against the right-hand door. "Lord Matellas Thane of House Quellion."

On his third knock, it swung open of its own accord to reveal row upon row of empty pews. At the very end of the central aisle, a throne of carved stone had been placed before the altar. And there, under the stained-glass window made in her image, sat the Mother.

"Approach."

Thane wasn't sure if she had actually spoken or if her voice had appeared directly in his mind, heavily distorted by an accent he couldn't quite recognise. His feet began to move, almost involuntarily, dragging him inexorably towards the lithe, golden-haired form of the woman who claimed to be his goddess.

A second figure was kneeling at the Mother's bare feet, her crumpled wimple stained with some sort of glistening black liquid. Sister Superior Nayelle looked up as he approached. Her haunted eyes met his from the depths of cavernous sockets. Her cheeks were pale and distended, her neck bloated, her chin sagging. Fat lips moved incessantly, whispering something that Thane couldn't hear.

She's afraid, Thane thought, gripping the pommel of his cane tightly. *Perhaps—*

Then, it hit him. An aura of power so overwhelming that he was forced down onto one knee. It pressed against him with the strength of a dozen men, and he needed all of his mental fortitude not to be pushed flat onto his belly. He bowed his head, yet could still feel her gaze impaling him to the stone floor of the Church. A part of him knew that if he raised his eyes to challenge her stare, he would be well and truly lost.

"My Lady," he murmured in a subdued tone. How could he have ever believed that this was some sort of deception? Her mind encircled his like a hand around a glass. All she needed to do was tighten her grip, and his sanity would shatter.

"Lord Thane of House Quellion." The words brought a comforting warmth with them, and suddenly, he was no longer afraid. "A proud and noble lineage."

She shifted her posture, and he saw her bare feet at the edge of his vision, smooth and pale like marble. There was something strange about them. The nails perhaps.

"I remember your ancestor," the goddess continued. "I

remember him standing almost where you are now, watching as the last of the coloured glass was set in place. He was a good man. A devout man. I am hoping that you will be the same."

The pressure lifted from Thane's shoulders, yet he remained kneeling, basking in the light of her undivided attention. "I … I am, my Lady."

"Prepared to do anything for the good of Keselgraad. Sacrifice everything."

"Yes … of course, my Lady. The city is paramount."

"It is." She paused. Thane sensed a rippling undercurrent in the wave of adulation that consumed him. Something cold. And angry.

"I fear you have been deceived, Lord Thane."

"My Lady?"

"You have wasted valuable time and energy fighting the wrong battles."

Sister Nayelle gave a soft whimper. Thane could barely think straight. He fought to free himself from the Mother's radiance. "I don't understand."

"The Mists are not your enemy, Keeper of the Peace. They are your *salvation*. They are the only thing that can prevent Keselgraad's fall into chaos."

"How … how can you know?"

It was obvious how. Yet, he needed to hear her say it.

"Because I created them."

Thane squeezed his eyes shut as if the darkness would erase the words from his mind. But he couldn't stop the memories from resurfacing. Lord Jeckle on the cross, his blood-spattered body jerking like a tree in the wind as he was torn apart. Devrard removing his mask to reveal the horror that lay beneath. All those deaths. All that suffering. The Mother was responsible for it all.

"You believe me to be a monster," the goddess murmured. "And perhaps I am, although you must understand that I feel the loss of every one of my children. Every soul that leaves this place is a cut to my flesh. They remind me of my failure, do you see? Of all the times I have failed before."

Thane felt her palm on the back of his bowed head. The skin was soft, yet he had no doubt she could crack his skull open with little effort. "I will tell you a story," she said quietly. "And then you will have a decision to make. A decision that will shape the future of Keselgraad."

She knelt opposite him with a swish of her sky-blue tunic. He could detect the faintest of scents. Deep and earthy. It reminded him of tilled soil and old rock. Ancient and strong.

"I was not born here," the Mother said. "Nor was I born alone. Three sisters we were. Three *Mothers*. Bound by blood. Each of us was gifted a world to rule. Mine was this one, and you were my first creation. My *children*. I guided you as any mother would, allowing you the freedom to discover this place. To expand and evolve. To proliferate under my watchful gaze. Your boundless creativity led to things of such beauty. Cities ten times the size of Keselgraad, filled with wondrous works of art. Great fortresses built into the very mountains, impregnable bastions of iron and stone. Ships dominated the oceans, enabling you to explore beyond the boundaries of this land. It was a Golden Age. A paradise. Until you began to change."

Thane risked a glance at Nayelle. The Sister Superior was trembling, her pallid cheeks wet with tears.

"This world corrupted you," the Mother said. "There is a poison here. It is everywhere. In the ground you walk upon. The water you drink. The air you breathe. It took hold of you before I realised exactly what was happening. It made you into … *abominations*."

The last word was spoken with such hatred that it made Thane recoil in shock. The Church grew colder as if the sun was setting and leaching the heat from the stone.

"Some of you gained the ability to project your thoughts across great distances. Others bent the elements to their will, spouting fire from their fingertips or sculpting the earth into whatever they desired. Your petty wars were then fought with hurricanes, tsunamis, and walls of incandescent flame. It was chaos. And yet, I swore not to intervene. Until … until you dared to challenge ME!"

Thane cried out as her anger hammered into him. Vessels burst in his nose, sending a stream of blood to spatter his gloves. Several bright red droplets speckled the Mother's bare feet. She paid them no mind.

"The arrogance. The *stupidity*. Turning on the very hand that fed them. Matricide. The most heinous of crimes. I tried reasoning with them, only for them to laugh in my face. Laugh at *me*. That was when I realised that there was no saving them. The Mists were a terrible but necessary solution. To scour the land clean of all but the greatest of my children. The cities and fields would endure, ready to welcome a new generation, untouched by the taint of this world."

"The Rapture," Nayelle squeaked shrilly, her black-stained hands raised in supplication. "Praise the Mother."

Thane could still not bring himself to lift his head. Countless questions rushed around his mind in a continual whirlwind. He latched onto one. "So, you started anew. We are the second generation of your creations?"

There was a long silence, punctuated by Nayelle's heavy breathing.

"No," the Mother admitted. "Despite my best efforts, the corruption always returns. Every thousand years, it takes hold of my children. And every thousand years, I have no choice but to unleash the Mists."

"How … how many times?"

"I do not know. It is a never-ending cycle. Each subsequent civilisation is built on the ashes of the one that came before."

"The Depths …" Thane realised suddenly. "That was Keselgraad. Or rather, Keselgraad from another age."

"Precisely. And it worked, for a time. Unfortunately, there was something I did not foresee. Generations began to hide warnings in what they left behind. Research on the Mists. Ideas on how to stop them from spreading. Most of it was useless, of course. The wardens and their suits. The wall around Keselgraad. They only delayed the inevitable. Until, through a mix of good luck and pure stubbornness, they found something that worked. They harnessed the taint of this world. Captured it and concentrated it in a glass prism."

At last, Thane looked up past the kneeling goddess, high above the altar where the spire began its vertiginous ascent. "The amethyst," he whispered.

"The shards alone are not a problem; their potency fades with time. But you have found a way to repair them, despite Nayelle's best efforts to sabotage your contraption. You must put a stop to it. Can you see that? For the good of Keselgraad."

"For the good of …"

The hand returned to his head. He could feel it resting there. Waiting.

"Yes. For the city is paramount, is it not? Your own words. This, now, is the decision you must make. Are you truly the Keeper of the Peace? Are you the protector of the *people* or the protector of the *city*? Choose. Now."

Thane knew with absolute certainty that there was only one answer that would allow him to leave the Church alive.

"The city."

"Excellent. Then, please descend to the Depths immediately and put an end to that heretical apparatus." She paused. "And to those that fuel it."

"My Lady," Thane acquiesced, retrieving his cane and using it to push himself upright. He turned and walked swiftly down the aisle without looking back, the heavy door of the narthex shutting behind him with a sonorous clang.

The Mother waited for several more minutes to pass before regaining her seat on the throne. Nayelle brought a basin of rainwater and began wiping the specks of Thane's blood from the goddess's feet.

"What did you glean from his mind, my child?"

"He fears you."

"He does," the Mother agreed. "Although not quite enough. He tried to hide his true thoughts from me. A feeble attempt. And he showed no surprise when I revealed the truth."

"He already suspected."

"He has found the archives. The knowledge left there. It has tarnished him. Even worse, I sensed a flicker of uncertainty buried deep under all that admiration. A pity. He would have made a good seed for the next cycle."

She sighed. "Summon the wardens. There is a new dawn rising, but Lord Thane is blind to it. We will have to ensure that he remains down there in the dark. Where he belongs."

TWENTY-ONE
RETURN TO THE DEPTHS

"The city has been completely overrun. We have fled deep into the underground passageways in a feeble attempt to buy ourselves a few more desperate days. Deep, yet not deep enough. I can hear the screams of those still trapped above. I can hear their terrible wailing as the Mists tear them apart. It filters down through the cracks in the rock to remind me of my failure."

First Technologist Arniel Sin, The Time Before

"WHY ME?" PINE asked for the hundredth time as he and Selene descended the central stairwell towards the Slums. They had raided the Stables' armoury and both were now equipped with ill-fitting breastplates and helmets, crimson cloaks, and straight-edged officer swords.

"Now is not the time or the place," she hissed back at him. "And keep your head down. If anyone recognises you, we'll both be gifted to the Mists."

Pine pulled his cone-shaped helm down as far as it would go, fuming silently. Damned woman and her damned secrets. He realised just how little he knew about his auburn-haired companion. The city was always in need of more watchmen, which meant that almost anyone could be sworn into the ranks provided that their criminal record wasn't too egregious. Selene had produced a letter of recommendation stamped with the seal of House Eckelston and had taken the oath an hour later.

Was she even *from* one of the Noble Houses? And if not, why fabricate some ridiculous backstory to join the City Watch, one of the only professions that didn't care where you came from or where you were going? Not to mention spending six months in one of the worst jobs in all of Keselgraad just to get close to him? It sounded utterly ludicrous. Yet, the more Pine thought about it, the more he picked up on certain things about her that didn't quite fit.

For example, the way she had handled herself in the skirmish against those back-alley thugs. A far too competent display of swordsmanship from someone who had supposedly spent their days strolling in the parks and attending the various social gatherings synonymous with the upper levels. Then there was her reaction to the wide, gaslit boulevards of the Noble Quarters. That look of awe on her face had been genuine, he was sure of it. And the Mines, the Collapse … the Depths. She had known about the Depths.

"Oi! You!"

Pine was pulled from his ruminations by a sweaty carrier, his wicker basket full of chopped wood, his cheeks beetroot-red from the climb.

"Do I know you?" the man asked, wiping the perspiration from his forehead.

"I don't think so. What level are you from? Perhaps my patrol route has taken me there?"

"Nah. Nah. Those scars … you're that captain, aren't

you? The one that tried to murder our Keeper of the Peace?" The crimson flush grew darker.

"You must be—"

"Why d'ya do it, eh?" The carrier removed his pack. His booming voice bounced off the cramped confines of the stairwell, drawing a few inquisitive stares.

"I didn't—"

Selene stepped in between the two, her hand on her weapon. She only reached the red-faced man's chest, yet there was such fury in her eyes that he was forced to take a step back.

"Is there a problem here?" she barked.

The carrier jabbed at Pine with a thick finger. "This bastard—"

"Has been absolved of his sins by the Mother herself."

"He … what?"

"She wishes her return among us to be remembered as a day of joy and celebration, not one of death. Lord Thane himself was present at this man's absolution, as was the Keeper of the Faith."

"But how—"

"Of course, if you doubt my words, perhaps it would be best for me to escort you to the Church of the Mother so that you can take up your grievances with her directly?"

The carrier deflated slightly, his once rosy cheeks now a sickly shade of green.

"That … um … no, that will not be necessary, Watchman. I … um … Mother keep you."

"Praise her name," Selene agreed with a thin smile. She took hold of Pine's elbow and guided him on down the steps.

"Smoothly done," he said in admiration.

"Don't flatter me."

"I'm not. Although, I am wondering where exactly you learnt to be so glib. It can't have been something that was taught at the prestigious Noble schoolhouse. Somewhere else, perhaps."

"Perhaps."

"So why—"

"Stop talking! You've drawn enough attention to us as it is!"

"You didn't learn your insubordination from the upper levels, either," he grumbled.

"No, I got that from you. And I can't be insubordinate because you are no longer a captain, are you? Mists, you're not even a watchman!"

Damned woman and her damned secrets.

"Can you at least tell me where we're meeting Gamin?"

"Where do you think?"

Pine uttered a dejected sigh.

The Dripping Bucket.

⌘

If Fletch was surprised to see them, he didn't show it. The barkeep was scrubbing the inside of a pewter tankard with an undisguised vigour that sent rivulets of sweat running through what remained of his thinning hair.

"Nothing sticks harder than dried beer," he spat, setting the cup down with a frown. "What can I get you?"

"We're here for Gamin," Selene said, looking around the empty tavern.

"By the Mother, is it you who are responsible for the

way he's been acting? Scheming and muttering. He's barely touched a drink in the last few days. Bad for business."

"Bad for business but good for him," Pine countered. "Old man needed to feel useful again."

Fletch's frown deepened. "You're going back down *there*, aren't you? Despite what happened last time."

"It's not what you think. Thane reopened the Depths shortly after the Collapse. There have been more expeditions. Led by wardens."

"Wardens? Those bastards aren't normal people. One of 'em came in here a couple of years ago. Didn't order anything. Just stood in the doorway staring at my patrons with that Mist-spawned mask of his. Like a hawk studying its prey. Then he left without another word. Who knows if it's even safe in those tunnels anymore? What about the monsters?"

"Rumours and superstition," Selene sniffed dismissively, making her freckles dance.

"I listen to a lot of stories from a lot of different people," Fletch insisted. "Part of the job. A score of 'em have heard the voices. How can they all be wrong?"

"Probably half-drunk on whatever passes for ale in this fine establishment."

"Hey, no need to be cruel. Just want you to be careful, that's all."

"We will be," Pine reassured the barkeep. "How about a pitcher while we are waiting? Could be the last thing we ever drink."

Fletch gave a curt nod and found a couple of cups. They had only taken the tiniest of sips before they were interrupted by a clamorous clattering from the doorway. It was Gamin; a rusty breastplate hung from his scarecrow-like frame, a pick-axe slung over one shoulder, and a short-handled shovel over the other. A small lantern was tied to a belt already sagging under the weight of a half-dozen bulging pouches.

"Aldin!" he cried with genuine pleasure. "Selene told me the Mists had spared you, but I didn't want to believe her. I'm very happy to have been proven wrong."

"So am I," Pine said with feeling. "The Mists had nothing to do with it, though. It was the Mother."

Gamin cackled. "Not you, too! The Bucket was buzzing with crazy rumours last night about some sort of madwoman who had somehow survived those bastard tentacles."

"It was her. I'm sure of it. When she turned and looked at me, it was … it was as if she was peeling my mind like an onion. I felt something in return." Pine suppressed a shudder. "Something ancient. Something monstrous."

Gamin stared at him for a moment then burst out laughing. "Oh, my boy. My poor, poor boy. You nearly had me there, you really did! Unfortunately for you, I've had my leg pulled enough times to recognise a tall tale when I hear one."

"But—"

"Do you have the paper? We've got a long journey ahead of us; the sooner we get our arses down to those Mist-spawned Depths, the sooner we can come back here again." Gamin reached past Aldin to filch Selene's cup and downed her ale with a flourish. "Fate and fortune."

"Fate and fortune," Pine echoed, draining his own drink. "Fletch. Can you spare us a few strips of dried meat and a skin of filtered rainwater? We may be gone for a while."

The barkeep considered it. "Who's paying?"

"I … how about you just put it on my tab?"

"You haven't had a tab here for ten years, Aldin, and you never even settled the last one."

"Ah, yes, but *this* time you have my word—"

A trio of silver coins rolled across the sticky surface of the pockmarked wooden plank that served as a bar. Selene slipped her pouch back under her breastplate and raised an eyebrow. "Sufficient?"

Fletch beamed at her. "Indeed, it is, my Lady. Let me prepare a few victuals for you. I'll let you decide whether you share them with your skint companions or not."

He disappeared back into the kitchen and re-emerged moments later with a canvas sack, which he gave to Selene. She glanced inside, nodded, and dumped it unceremoniously into Pine's arms. "Here. If you're not going to pay for it, you can at least carry it."

Gamin gave a hearty snort, clearly enjoying himself. "I like her. Reminds me of Bera. Hand me that paper, girl."

"I'm not your girl."

"Aye, you're right about that. Now, do you want my help or not?"

She sighed and passed it over. Gamin produced a pair of cracked spectacles from one of his pouches and peered closely at the numbers. "Aye, no doubt about it. Ninth level."

"So, how do we get there?" Pine asked. "The Depths are officially closed."

"One of my old miner friends is foreman now. Couple of years ago, he was ordered to remove his men from a certain stretch of tunnel."

"Ordered by the Keeper of the Peace."

"Aye. Which means that that's where we're most likely to find a shaft leading right to the Depths. Ready to go?"

"As ready as I'll ever be," Pine said, trying not to look at his scarred hands. He felt nervous. More nervous than he ever had before, even when Devrard was strapping him to the cross.

Come on, you stupid, cowardly man, he thought as he followed Gamin outside. *There's nothing to fear down there. Nothing but regret and bad memories.*

The entrance to the Mines was a stone's throw away from the Dripping Bucket, its maw-like tunnel waiting to swallow him whole. The two watchmen waited by a pedestal supporting one of the massive light mirrors while Gamin went to find the foreman. Pine kept his gaze fixed on the dark opening, shifting impatiently from one foot to the other.

"Keep still," Selene hissed, shoving as much of her copper hair under her helmet as she could. "You're drawing attention to us again."

"Good. They can take me back to my nice, comfy prison cell."

She gave him an exasperated look. "Stop being such a grump. I know that you want to get to the bottom of this just as much as I do."

"Really? What makes you say that?"

"Because you're a watchman." Selene waved an arm at his breastplate and crimson cloak. "You help people. It's in your blood."

Pine scowled. "I've already told you that it was Thane who got me the job. Probably half out of guilt and half because he wanted to keep an eye on me."

"Sure, he made you a watchman, but he didn't make you *stay* a watchman, did he? Ten years! You could have left whenever you wanted. So, why didn't you?"

"I … can't answer that."

"That's what's so contradictory about you, Aldin. You spend all your time analysing other people, yet you never try to analyse yourself."

"You make me sound like a fool."

He felt a soft touch on the back of his scarred hand and looked down to see her fingers resting there. "Oh, I don't know about that," Selene replied with a gentle smile. "I find it rather endearing."

Gamin returned before Pine could reply, accompanied by another man nearly as old as he was, his silvery-white hair half-obscured by a cloud of foul-smelling smoke that sputtered forth from the pipe clamped between his lips.

"Watchmen?" the foreman growled. "You never said they were watchmen. Bloody lapdogs. Barking and growling on the orders of that bastard Thane."

Pine lifted his helmet slightly. "Not quite."

Pupils grown large from lack of sunlight squinted at him through the haze. "You're the idiot that tried to kill 'im. Good idea, though. Setting up an ambush in the lift. We raised a glass to you that night, we did. Pity you missed."

"I didn't—"

"I don't care. I'll make sure my men stay quiet about it. No one will stop you." The foreman sucked on his pipe and exhaled into Pine's face. "But no one will help you, either. You're not one of us. Not anymore."

"Fair enough."

"Fourth gallery on the left. Bastard wardens threw us out. That's where you'll find your way down. Mother keep you."

Pine grasped the man's wrist in thanks and motioned for

his two companions to follow him into the dark. In a matter of minutes, the constant drone of the Slums had faded to a dull whisper, smothered by new sounds: the creaking of overloaded minecarts and the rhythmic ringing of pick-axe on stone. They passed grimy workers, unrecognisable under the dirt that caked their clothes and faces, strips of fabric tied across their noses and mouths to protect against the dust-filled air that scorched their lungs. Many carried lanterns with candles burnt down to the wick, sputtering feebly as they consumed the last of the tallow.

Gamin soon paused to light his own, passing a flint and firestone to Selene. She drew sparks on her first try, bringing a yellow flame to life.

"Something else you learnt as a member of House Eckelston, I'm sure," Pine remarked sarcastically. "In between the poetry and painting classes, probably."

"Shut up."

The further they ventured into the tunnel, the more deserted it became. "The veins in the upper galleries are worked out," Gamin explained. "Have been for years. Every year they have to dig deeper. And work longer. Look."

He pointed at a mark scratched into the rock near one of the numerous branching passageways. A shield.

"Must be the way to the fourth gallery."

"No guard?" Pine asked

"To do what? Stop people going down into the Depths? Mists, boy, everyone I know hated that place. And that was *before* the Collapse. You won't find a soul in Keselgraad willing to go there now."

"Except the wardens," Selene added, peering into the dark.

Pine recalled Devrard's cracked mask. "Let's hope we don't run into one of them."

"They followed the Mother up to the Church, remember? I think we're safe for now. Onwards?"

"Fate and fortune," Gamin muttered, holding the lantern high and taking a few tentative steps into the gallery. It ended rather abruptly after fifty feet. A rope had been coiled around a single pulley bolted into the ceiling, both ends disappearing into a hole that spanned the width of the passageway like the opening to a deep well.

"We used the same sort of thing when exploring the Depths," Pine said. "People down below can pull the rope to hoist things up, and those up top can send things down. Gamin, perhaps Selene and I should go first, then we can lower—"

"By the Mother, boy, I'm not completely useless! Give me that sack of food and take my lantern." He grabbed the nearest rope with one hand and began his descent, crossing his ankles to control his speed. Pine shook his head in bemusement and turned to Selene.

"The trick is to—"

She flashed him a smile and brushed past him. "I think I can handle it."

He watched her vanish down the shaft after Gamin, then attached the lantern to his belt and swung out over the hole, feeling a brief jolt of exhilaration as his feet left the ground. He lowered himself slowly, taking care not to bump into the sides or burn his hands on the rope. Selene's helmet flashed and glinted below him, on the edge of the light. Beyond that, nothing but pitch black.

"Anything?" he called down to Gamin.

"Rocks and worms."

Pine fell silent and concentrated on trying to calculate the distance they had travelled from the gallery. He lost track somewhere after three hundred feet, just before Gamin's surprised grunt echoed up the shaft.

"I've reached the bottom."

"What is it? A cave? A tunnel?"

"I … I think it's *stairs*."

TWENTY-TWO
THE CITY OF MIST AND TEARS

"We will be remembered for our accomplishments, not for the actions we took to achieve them. Dozens died building the steeple of the Church of the Mother, yet they are long forgotten while its beauty remains. I will be known as the man who stopped the Mists and brought order to Keselgraad. The names of those sacrificed along the way will fade from memory, like shadows banished by the light of dawn."

Lord Matellas Thane, 833rd Year of the Mother

PINE SLID DOWN the last short length of rope. The lantern revealed a large stairwell similar to the one that ran through the heart of Keselgraad, spiralling away into the darkness.

"By the Mother," Pine said with an appreciative whistle. "It's enormous. Did you know anything like this existed, Gamin?"

The old miner shook his head. "No, but I'm not sure we ever made it this deep. We sunk our shafts blindly, hoping to hit something interesting. This looks like the wardens knew exactly what they were aiming for."

Selene pointed to a strange symbol etched into the outer wall of the staircase, one Pine didn't recognise. "We're still too high up. Another three levels before we reach the room marked on the paper."

"No more rope," Gamin stated.

She squatted and peered at the steps. "Footprints in the dust. I bet the stairs are still sturdy enough to carry our weight."

"You *bet*?"

"It's either that or we go back."

Gamin gave a shrug of his bony shoulders that made his pick-axe and shovel rattle, then held his hand out for the lantern. "I'll go first."

He set off with purpose, the light bobbing up and down. Pine followed warily, flexing his aching fingers. Something was nagging at him. Something important.

They passed two more levels, denoted by similar indecipherable scribbles. As they reached the third, Gamin stopped and set down the lantern so that he could fish out the scrap of paper from one of his pouches. He squinted at the sequence of symbols and checked the marking on the wall. "They're the same," he confirmed. "This passageway should lead us to what we are looking for. Be prepared for anything."

Pine drew the sword stolen from the Stables' armoury. Its grip was strange and unfamiliar, but it seemed sharp and well-balanced, its weight comforting in his hand.

They pressed on into the tunnel. Pine had taken only a half-dozen paces when he suddenly understood what his brain had been trying to tell him for the last few minutes.

"Selene," he murmured slowly. "When we found those schematics in Spritt's workshop, you said you had never seen the symbols before."

"Yes?"

"So, how did you know what level we were on?"

She stopped so abruptly that Pine almost ran into the back of her. "Ah."

"Ah?"

"I can explain. Once we find the room, I—"

"No. Enough. Who are you? Some sort of spy for Thane? Or one of the other Keepers? You're obviously not a Noble; that much is painfully clear."

Her emerald eyes fled his gaze. "It's complicated, I need time to—"

"NO!" He shouted the word, his grip tightening on his sword. "This ends now, Selene. We're not going another step until I get some answers."

Her hand moved very slightly towards her own blade, and for a heart-pounding moment, Pine thought she was going to draw it free, but then her arm dropped to her side, and her shoulders slumped in defeat.

"Fine. I knew you were going to find out eventually. I just hoped I wouldn't have to explain things to you at sword-point."

"Start at the beginning."

"ALDIN!" Gamin's voice echoed up the passageway, fearful and urgent.

"Not now!"

"I've found the room. There are … there are people here that need our help."

Pine cursed. "Damn it! Damn the Mists and damn you, Selene! This isn't over!" He turned on his heel and hurried down the tunnel towards a distant opening illuminated by the soft yellow glow of the lantern … and another, fainter

light. Purple. He had seen that colour before. He knew what
it was.

Someone screamed.

"Gamin!" Pine's worn boots pounded along the dusty
stone.

Bera. Hale. Lyle. All gone.

He wouldn't let anyone else suffer.

Pine burst through the doorway and staggered to a halt,
a cry of horror escaping his lips. Gamin stood a mere few
feet away, a warden's leather-clad arm wrapped around his
neck, a needle-thin stiletto pressed against his cheek.

Behind him, a circle of eleven high-backed chairs surrounded a central pedestal similar to the one Pine had tried
to remove from the Depths all those years ago. Into each
chair was strapped a young child, strips of leather wrapped
around their arms and legs. They were gagged, and more
restraints had been pulled tight across their foreheads to
immobilise their heads and necks. Their violet-flecked eyes
were being forced open by a pair of pronged, metallic tongs
that Pine instantly recognised as the contraptions that Jethro
Spritt had been working on.

And the children were *weeping*.

Thick, globular tears dribbled down emaciated cheeks to
be caught and filtered into a series of tubes made from pork
intestine, which ran down the side of the chairs and snaked
across the floor to deposit their salty liquid into the convex
bowl of the pedestal. Pine didn't need to be any closer to see
what the bowl contained; the shimmering purple halo made
it obvious enough.

An amethyst.

This is what that bastard Thane had been doing. Using

this … torture device to extract, no to *harvest* something from the bodies of these children in order to repair the weakened shards of the crystal that had shattered a decade ago.

Before Pine could react, Selene arrived, unsheathing her sword with a shriek of metal, her eyes blazing with undisguised fury.

"Let them go," she spat at the warden.

"I am afraid I cannot do that," the masked man replied. "Lord Thane was quite specific in his instructions. Please lower your weapons or I will be forced to puncture the jugular of your companion here." He applied pressure to the dagger held against Gamin's throat, enough to break the skin. Crimson blood dribbled down the blade.

One of the children, a dark-haired adolescent with a flat nose and wide forehead, had noticed their presence and began to moan at them through his gag, straining against the straps that bound him to the chair.

Pine placed a cautious hand on the tip of Selene's sword and pushed slightly to make her lower it. "This doesn't have to end in bloodshed." He took a tentative half-step, his eyes fixed on the warden. "The prisoners you are guarding look tired and unfed. When did they last eat?"

"Lord Thane dictates the schedule."

"You must see that they are starving."

"Lord Thane—"

"*Fine*. Then, explain to me how what you are doing here can be seen as anything other than torture. Wardens are supposed to protect this city and its inhabitants, not cause them pain and suffering."

The black-clad man was silent for a moment. "The

Mother demands sacrifices from us all. Better that some die so that many can live."

"They … they are only *children*."

"No, they are orphans. Without families. Their contribution to the economy of the city is minimal. This is the best way that they can serve."

Orphans. Pine's world came crashing down as he finally understood. The poor, starving things strapped to the chairs were the sons and daughters of those who had perished in these same cold, dark tunnels all those years ago. The … sons and daughters of his fellow miners. Of his … friends.

Fate and fortune.

A thick fog obscured his sight, swirling like the Mists but a bright, violent red. The ringing in his ears was louder than ever, high-pitched and screaming. Pine sprang forwards with a primal roar, his helmet tumbling from his head with a clatter. He slammed into the warden and tackled him to the ground. His opponent tried to raise his stiletto, but Pine batted it aside with an angry growl and began pummelling his fists into the ceramic mask. The beak-like nose was the first to crack, then the left cheekbone.

Slender fingers touched Pine's shoulder. He lashed out, pushing them away. A piece of the mask fell away to reveal an eye without lashes, brow, or lid, its pupil blacker than pitch. Somehow, half-buried among the shrieking whine and crashing crimson waves, Pine could still hear the warden laughing at him.

"Shut up!" he screamed in a voice he barely recognised. Scarred hands wrapped around the dark leather covering the warden's neck. After all this time, he finally had a target for all the guilt and self-loathing that poisoned his soul.

Pine squeezed. He squeezed until his shoulders ached, and his wrists grew numb. He squeezed until tears ran down his cheeks. He squeezed until the banging, raging, ear-shattering bloody haze faded away, leaving him shaking and crying on top of the body of the dead warden.

"Aldin." It was Selene, her voice soft and soothing.

"Leave me alone."

"The children. We can't leave them like this."

Pine nodded wearily. He stumbled to his feet, wiping at his cheeks. "Let's set them free." The closest orphan was the broad-nosed adolescent who had moaned at him earlier. Pine removed the eye-pincers and gag, then began to cut away the straps.

"Thank you." The words came out as a dry rasp.

"Think nothing of it. What's your name?"

"Roe."

"How long have you been down here, Roe?"

"I … I don't know. Days and days. Some of the others much longer."

"Have you eaten?"

The boy shook his head.

"Gamin!" Pine called over his shoulder. "Bring some water. And Fletch's supplies. We'll share what we can."

He moved on to the next prisoner, a young girl with a mop of sandy hair. Her eyes contained significantly more amethyst flecks than the others, so much so that both her pupils appeared almost violet.

"Gamin!"

There was no reply. Pine turned to see the old miner on his knees. A stiletto had been thrust expertly through the rusty iron of his breastplate, leaving only the hilt to protrude from his scrawny belly. He wore the confused expression of someone who didn't understand what was happening. His remaining hand reached out and touched the knife as if trying to confirm it was really there. Then his disbelieving gaze found Pine and widened in sudden shock.

"Watch ou—"

A black whirlwind careened into Pine and threw him off the young girl with enough strength to send him flying through the air. He crashed into the central pedestal with a bone-jarring crunch, dislodging the bowl and the amethyst inside.

What in the Mists?

He tried to rise, but the warden was already there, impossibly fast. A boot connected with his stomach, slamming him into the pedestal once more. Selene charged to his side, and Pine heard a metallic clang as her blade was caught by the warden's second dagger. She pulled back too late to avoid a whistling punch that clipped her on the jaw and snapped her head back.

A single lidless eye the colour of obsidian fixed Pine intently through the cracked mask. The stiletto rose and fell.

"No!" Pine yelled, raising his hand instinctively. He felt a surge of white-hot pain as the tip bored through the soft flesh of his palm and exploded out the other side, showering him with his own blood.

"Mists take you," he cried in pain as the warden pulled his blade free. "You're dead. I felt your pulse stop. How are you still alive?"

"We are the Mother's angels," the mask-clad man replied. "We can never die."

The knife was raised for one final blow.

Pine scrabbled around in the dirt for a weapon, his hand a throbbing mass of agony. Bloody fingers closed around something long and sharp.

Something *glowing*.

Pine hammered the amethyst into the warden's thigh as hard as he could, shouting with satisfaction as he managed to pierce the thick leather robes to penetrate the muscle beneath.

The warden *screamed*.

The sound was barely human, merged with a bestial howl that set Pine's teeth on edge. Limbs twisted at strange, unnatural angles. The neck cracked to one side. The howl became a heaving cough. Pine turned his head just as a sickly stream of black liquid was vomited forth from behind the confines of the ceramic mask, drenching his tunic and pattering off his breastplate like rain. He fought off his own rising nausea and pushed himself away with his hands and heels, grimacing every time his bloodied palm touched the dirt.

The warden retched again, then collapsed into a pool of viscous slime.

Pine lay there in the dirt for a time, drawing long, ragged breaths to try and calm the incessant drumming of his heart. When he finally gathered the courage to move, the first things he saw were Gamin's dead eyes staring at him accusingly.

"I'm sorry," Pine muttered, pressing one palm against the other to try and staunch the flow of blood. "I'm so, so sorry."

"It wasn't your fault." Selene was sporting a large purplish bruise on the left side of her face but appeared otherwise unharmed. "That … thing suddenly jerked awake. There was no way we could have anticipated that."

"Cursed."

"What?"

"That's what Devrard called me. Cursed. It's the name the wardens give to those who survived the Collapse. I should have realised what was going on. The orphanage. Thane. Damn the Mists."

Pine tore a scrap of black fabric from the vomit-covered corpse and used it to bandage his hand, then bent to pick up his sword. "Selene. The other prisoners. Help me."

She didn't move, fingering the silver chain around her neck. He frowned at her hesitation. "What is it?"

"I … It's just … Did you hear what the warden said? If we stop this, then the crystals will no longer be repaired. Keselgraad will fall prey to the Mists."

"Look at them, Selene."

"That—"

"Please. Just *look* at them."

Pine took her arm and guided her to the sandy-haired girl with violet eyes. She couldn't have been more than eleven years old. Too young to have any memories of her parents. The orphanage would have been her entire life, the other children her sole family. He pulled the tong-like devices away and removed her gag gently. "What is your name, little one?"

She coughed. "June. My eyes, they hurt."

"I know." He turned to Selene.

"It doesn't matter who you are or why you are really here. Just ask yourself, what is Keselgraad's safety worth?

What cost are you willing to pay? How many lives are you prepared to sacrifice?"

She didn't answer, only bent to wipe the last few tears from June's cheeks before moving away to release the others.

In minutes, all the children were free, huddled in a circle around Fletch's supplies. Pine dragged Gamin's body into one corner and covered it with his crimson cloak.

"I recognise him."

It was the boy named Roe who had spoken, his jaw moving as he chewed on a tough piece of dried meat.

"You do?"

"I think so. I remember a scruffy beard that scratched my face and the way his eyebrows knitted together like a hairy worm when he was angry. Who was he?"

"A miner like your parents. He looked after you while they explored the Depths." Pine took a deep breath. "I was part of all this too."

"I …" the boy scrunched his brow in frustration. "I don't remember you. I can't recall anything else. The Depths? This is where we are now, isn't it? This is where the wardens took us. Far below Keselgraad."

"Yes."

"And you're just going to leave him here?"

Pine sighed. "There's no way for me to carry his body out. We're too far from the surface. Besides, this might be a better place for him. Among friends."

"My parents, you mean. I know they died in these tunnels. Did you know them?"

Pine studied the boy's lightly tanned features. "Maybe. Apologies, but it was a long time ago and … well, to be honest, I always thought that you children were more of a hindrance than anything else." He peered closer. "Mother keep me, I'm not sure, you all looked so alike. What's your name again?"

"Roe."

"I don't … wait. There was a boy who—"

"Pine!" Selene was pointing to the entrance. What had once been a rectangle of pitch black was now suffused with a soft yellow light. "Torches. Someone's coming!"

"Mists!" he cursed. "Gather the children. We have to get them out of here."

But it was already too late. Two silhouettes in dark purple tabards slipped into the room, lanterns at their belts and crossbows in their hands. They were swiftly followed by two more, escorting a tall, gaunt figure wearing a high-necked leather coat and carrying a brass-topped cane. A pin shaped like a diamond shield gleamed on his left breast.

Thane.

TWENTY-THREE
AN ALLIANCE OF NECESSITY

"It is over. Despite all the time we have spent strapped into those accursed chairs. We have drained our bodies of tears, and it is still not enough. We cannot save ourselves. I cannot save my daughter. All we can do now is pass on what we know to those who will come after. Perhaps they will succeed where we have failed. At the very least, we will give them hope."

First Technologist Arniel Sin, The Time Before

"**B**ASTARD," PINE SPAT. "You heartless, self-serving, callous bastard."

Thane's steel eyes burned with anger as he surveyed the room, pausing to linger on the smashed remains of the pedestal and the corpse of the ichor-drenched warden.

"Perhaps. Yet, I am not the one to have single-handedly condemned the entirety of Keselgraad to a slow, painful death."

Pine almost leapt at him there and then, but the tiny kernel of logic in the back of his mind held him in check. A lone swordsman against four loaded crossbows. He would be riddled with bolts as soon as he began to charge; his breastplate useless at such close range. And if Selene followed his lead, she would die too, leaving the children to be strapped back into their chairs. He dropped his sword and raised his hands.

"Off you go, then," Thane said in disgust, gesturing to his honour guard to lower their crossbows. "Scurry back to the Mother and tell her what you have done. I'm sure you will be well rewarded."

Selene shared a confused glance with Pine. "What?"

"The destruction of the machine. She obviously doesn't trust me. Sending some of her puppets to make sure the job got done."

Pine let slip a disbelieving laugh. "The Mother? I've never even spoken to her. Mists, I've been locked in a prison cell for the last day and a half. How exactly do you think I could have managed to get to the Church?"

The fire in Thane's eyes dimmed. His gaze darted to Selene, who shook her head. "Then, why … how …"

"The paper. Spritt."

"You are down here because you are … investigating a murder?" Thane's mouth jerked, and Pine realised that he was seeing something extremely rare: the Keeper of the Peace was smiling.

"All my efforts. All my sacrifices. Undone by a pair of over-zealous watchmen. Watchmen whom I swore in myself. Fate has a twisted sense of humour."

He glanced over at the group of young children still sharing out the bag of food, and his smile fell, to be replaced by a hint of melancholy. "I took no pleasure in it," he said. "No pleasure at all. I had no choice."

Pine clenched his hands into fists. "That's not good enough, Thane. There is *always* a choice."

The Keeper of the Peace sighed. "So people keep telling

me." He turned to his honour guard. "Leave one of the lanterns here and wait for me in the tunnel."

"My Lord?"

"I am perfectly capable of defending myself against two tired watchmen. Make sure we are not disturbed. By anyone."

He waited until the four crossbowmen had left the room before continuing. "The Depths hold many secrets. There are things down here that you would not believe. Trapped in the dark. Waiting to be discovered. You might think that amethyst was our greatest discovery. It was not. It was what we found *beyond* that room. The laboratories. The archives. The amount of paper in those places would be enough to make me the richest man in Keselgraad. Yet, there was something even more valuable than the paper: its contents. *Knowledge*. Of what came before. And of how to prevent it coming again."

He spread his arms wide. "We are still in Keselgraad. A version of Keselgraad. Crushed under the weight of history. Abandoned. Its entire populace slaughtered by the Mists."

"You knew …" Selene murmured, half to herself. "All this time. All these years, you knew."

"At first, their written language appeared completely different from ours, but we soon found that wasn't the case. It was just … twisted, like looking at our own words through a pair of cracked glasses. Their records were fascinating. In a few short years, they had discovered the existence of the Mists and their ultimate purpose. A frenzied period of research followed; every mind in the entire city bent on finding a means of escaping their fate."

"And they succeeded," Pine said with a surreptitious

glance at the amethyst shard still glowing in the belly of the fallen warden. Behind the corpse, June, Roe, and another tall, gangly boy had finished their meal and were listening quietly.

"They did," Thane agreed. "Although, not quite in the way they had hoped. They found a substance capable of resisting the Mists. Better still, a substance seemingly present in all natural things. In water. In soil. In the very air. If they could harness that substance and concentrate it, they could form a protective shield."

"So, what was the problem?"

"The same one that puts a stop to so many dreams. *Time*. They couldn't find a way to harvest what they needed fast enough. The Mists would destroy them first. It was then that they made a decision." Thane leant forwards, his eyes gleaming. "They chose to keep working on the project. Not to save themselves, but to save *us*."

"The crystal."

"They activated it. And documented it. Described ways to maintain it. To repair it if it shattered. Failsafes. And then … they died. Leaving their greatest creation in the dark, draining the air and soil around it. Even the corpses of those torn apart by the Mists served a purpose, consumed as they rotted away. For a thousand years. Drop by drop. Until, at last, it was full." Thane gave another deep sigh. "If only we had left it here, in the Depths. Where it belonged. Rather than trying to remove it. Keselgraad would have been saved forever."

"Instead, you used the children of those killed by the Collapse to fuel this Mist-spawned contraption. What sort of heartless bastard sets up an orphanage like it's some sort of … slaughterhouse?"

Thane rapped the butt of his cane on the ground. "Don't be a fool! We had no idea that this room even existed when the tunnels collapsed! As patron of the expedition, I did what I thought was right and took it upon myself to provide for the progeny of those who perished in that awful tragedy. It was only later, once the shards started to dim, that we were forced to follow our predecessors' instructions on how to repair them."

He pointed to June and her violet irises. "When the amethyst shattered, it released its contents into the air. Tiny particles entered our lungs, our ears, our eyes."

Pine remembered lying there in the dirt of the tunnel, a fallen beam on his chest, the clouds of dust around him glittering like stars in the night sky.

"Then, why not me?" he asked angrily. "Why am I not strapped to one of the chairs? And why aren't *you*?"

Thane averted his gaze and stared down at his boots. "I tried. It didn't work. Whatever amount we had absorbed was too weak. We then wondered just how linked to our bodies this substance was. If, perhaps, it would grow and multiply as its host grew. As it … aged."

"Us," came a small voice. It was Roe, and Pine saw the indignation he felt mirrored in the young boy's taut expression. "You're talking about *us*."

"The owner of the orphanage was told to perform regular checks on the eyes of those in his care, whether they were survivors of the Collapse or not. If ever he saw flecks of amethyst, he was to inform us immediately."

"So that you could murder them."

"Murder? All those we took are still alive. I am not a monster, Pine, despite what you may think. They are cared for."

"Cared for? Most of them look like scarecrows. Sacks of flesh and bone."

Thane tightened his grip on his cane. "It has been … difficult for me to obtain supplies as of late. The Keepers Council have no knowledge of what is happening down here, which means I must resort to more *unofficial* means of procuring food and parts. Even worse, some of the criminals who I am forced to deal with often appropriate a percentage of the goods for themselves. Apples and the like that find their way into the Slums."

Pine was shaking his head. "Well, that's no longer your problem, is it, my Lord? There's not a hope in all the Mists that I'm letting you lay a hand on those children. I failed them once. I won't do so again. I owe it to their parents."

"I see." Thane's thin smile was now far from genuine. "It amuses me that you really believe you can stop me. I meant what I said earlier. I do not need my honour guard to cut you down." There was a soft click from the pommel of his cane as he drew forth the length of steel concealed in the wooden shaft. "The question you should be asking yourself is why I haven't done so already."

Pine faltered, realising he was right. He had been around Thane long enough to know that he was as unscrupulous as he was uncompromising. This was a man who hadn't hesitated to send his political rival to the cross – and his former Watch captain along with him. If he had considered Pine and Selene a threat, they would have been peppered with bolts and dumped in the corner next to Gamin. So, as he hadn't killed them, that could only mean …

"You need us."

Thane tutted. "Not quite. I need *her*." He pointed his blade at Selene, who had remained mostly silent throughout the exchange. Pine watched as her shoulders sagged.

"How did you find out?" she asked in a quiet voice.

"You should have chosen another Noble House to pretend to be a part of. Lady Hellington is from House Eckelston, and I make sure that I *thoroughly* study all those who sit on the Keepers Council. The Keeper of the Coin has many cousins. Only one has a daughter. Or had, rather. She died only a few months after childbirth. And you do not bear her name."

"What … what is he talking about, Selene?" Pine demanded.

"I'm saying that your fellow watchman is an imposter," Thane explained.

Selene was shaking her head. "I don't understand. If you knew this, why accept me into the Watch? Why swear me in?"

"You were a puzzle. One I needed to solve. Keeping you close at hand made that easier." He frowned. "Although, I do hate unresolved mysteries. Ever since your arrival six months ago, my informants have been scouring the city from top to bottom for clues. Do you know what they found?"

Selene was tugging hard at her necklace. "I can explain, I——"

"Nothing. They found nothing. When every possible logical hypothesis has been explored and discarded, then whatever remains, no matter how illogical, must be the truth. And so, despite it going against everything I believe, I can only conclude one thing."

She hung her head, defeated.

"You are not from Keselgraad," Thane said.

"No."

Pine stared at her, anger and incomprehension assaulting his tired mind like the voices of the damned. He had been to the highest levels of the city. He had stood and looked out over the Mists. It was an unending wasteland. There was nothing else there. Nothing. A sea of infinite white. She was lying. She had to be.

"There *is* another city," Thane breathed in wonder. "Fascinating. I suppose there is no reason why the Keselgraadians would be the only ones to find a way to escape their fate. How far away is it?"

"I'm not sure," Selene replied reluctantly. "We have maps, many maps, but they are not to scale. It took me two days to walk here."

"*Walk?*" Pine laughed incredulously. "Through the Mists? You must take us for fools."

She tugged at the necklace that she was always fiddling with, pulling it out from under her tunic. A small transparent crystal dangled from the end of the chain, twinkling in the lantern's light.

"Travel between our two cities was commonplace before the Mists. Our ancestors shared their knowledge. Instead of one large amethyst, we conceived a score of smaller ones. They protect us from the corruption. However, despite our best efforts, these too are failing. It was why I was sent here. To find another solution. And I have. It's *you*, Pine. You and all of those who inhaled parts of the shattered gemstone. I saw it when you were on the cross. The Mists couldn't touch you."

He remembered. The way those tendrils slipped softly over his skin. Almost like a caress. Feeling and probing. Tenderly. Warily.

"Then, I … I can leave," he realised. "I can escape this place."

Selene nodded. "We all can."

Thane cut the air with his blade. "You are failing to take into account our current predicament," he said with a touch of impatience. "The Mother wishes to hasten the demise of Keselgraad. She ordered me to destroy the machine so that the shards could no longer be repaired."

"The Mother?" Pine asked. "Why?"

"Because she fears us," Thane answered in a bitter tone. "Or rather, what we might become. The same substance that keeps the Mists at bay is also changing us. Making us stronger."

"Strong enough to challenge *her*."

"One day, yes. So, she condemns us. Without the contraption, the remaining amethysts will flicker and fade. And death with enter Keselgraad. I cannot allow that to happen. I need to stop her. And for that, I need allies."

Thane turned to Selene. "You must understand that once our city is destroyed, she will set her sights on yours. Help me destroy her before that happens. There has to be something your city can provide. Weapons. Men. Crystals. Anything."

"We … we are still weak. Still gathering our forces. Besides, we have no means to send supplies through the Mists unharmed."

"Yet, you managed it."

"With a single crystal. One of the last. Now depleted."

"Even so, you got inside the city."

"There are passageways. Dug by your ancestors. Most of them have collapsed, but a few still remain. They lead to the surface."

"Hmmm. Perhaps if you cannot reach us by going *over* ground, you could attempt to go *under*."

Selene blanched. "A tunnel linking our cities? There are miles upon miles of terrain to cover. It would take years."

"Nevertheless, unless you discover some miraculous alternative, I fear it is the only way." Thane picked up the hollow shaft of his cane and sheathed his rapier. "The Church spire still shines strongly and will continue to do so for some time yet. I will do what I can to impede the Mother's progress. I am the Keeper of the Peace, after all."

Pine frowned. "You are letting us go? What assurance do you have that we will return?"

"None. Only your good conscience. If you decide to leave Keselgraad and its inhabitants to be slaughtered, you will have to live with that."

Thane took a few steps back towards the entrance to the room and then stopped. "The warden. It still hasn't got back up."

"Probably due to the fact that I cut a hole in his belly," Pine remarked.

"No ... no, I've seen them suffer far more grievous wounds than that and shrug them off as if they were insect bites. It must be ..." He went over to the corpse and prodded at the shard still lodged deep in its flesh. "The amethyst. The wardens always refused to touch them. Whatever is contained within those gems must be anathema to them." Thane reached down and tore the crystal free with a soft squelching sound. "Perhaps I can find a way to use this."

He stood and allowed his gaze to roam the room, lingering on the half-starved, puffy-eyed children and Roe's scowling face.

"I ... I will not apologise for what I have done," he stated. "But I regret it. I deeply regret it. Like so many things that I have been forced to do for the city I love." He stowed the amethyst in a pocket of his greatcoat, under his diamond-shaped pin of office. "Maybe now, at least, you will find peace."

"Mother keep you," Pine said, wincing as he realised what he had just said.

Thane gave a wry smile. "I really hope not. For if she does, we are all well and truly lost."

TWENTY-FOUR
THE JOURNEY HOME

"What goes up must come down."

Motto of the Keselgraadian operator's guild

H IS MEN WERE waiting for him further up the passageway. Thane could feel their nervousness. The way their eyes jumped from shadow to shadow.

"Back to the surface," he ordered, handing his lantern to the nearest guard. "I'll inform the Mother that we have done what she asked."

And then I'll convene the Council, he thought. *I'll tell them everything. The amethyst, the machine, Jeckle. Everything that, in my hubris, I stupidly kept to myself.*

There was no time for petty power games now. No time for politics. Keselgraad was facing the greatest threat it had ever known, and he was the only one who could stop it.

Thane reached the pulley system at the bottom of the shaft and gave two sharp tugs on the rope to signal to the four men he had left up top. He stuck his cane into his belt, crossed his ankles, and allowed himself to be slowly pulled back to the surface as decades of earth and rock passed him by. There was still so much to discover. So much *knowledge*. They had barely scratched the surface. What else might be hiding down in this long-forgotten warren of corridors, waiting to be found? Weapons? Medicine? If his ancestors had known about the Mists, perhaps they had also surmised the Mother's role in all of this. Perhaps … they had even managed to create something that could stop her.

The guards at the top helped him off the rope, and Thane hurried back towards the entrance of the Mines without a word of thanks, the pounding of his boots echoing off the tunnel walls. He exploded out into the sunlight, startling the gaggle of rickshaw drivers lounging by their carts, and set his sights on the access to the central staircase.

Mud and detritus from the stinking streets spattered his greatcoat as he ran. He had always taken such care in his appearance. *Perception. Perception is key. If you appear to be in control, people will believe that you are. If you speak with authority, then they will listen. And they will follow. Unless, of course, there is something or someone even greater.*

The black queen.

The Mother.

Thane passed under the first-level archway and staggered to a halt before the lift operator. This particular guildsman had dry, flaky skin and wispy hair that swished and swayed when he moved like the tendrils of the Mists.

"The lift. Now," Thane snapped.

"Of course. Of course. I believe it is currently on level twelve. Let me just check your credentials are in order."

Thane reached past the old man and tugged on one of the ropes. Far above, a bell chimed.

"No time," he spat. His honour guard arrived just as the iron cage of the elevator clunked into place on the platform.

"Most irregular," the operator grumbled, running a wrinkled finger down the sheet of vellum. "Unauthorised use of the lift is punishable by death. The guild will hear of this."

"Shut up." Thane pulled the barred gate open and ushered his purple-clad soldiers inside. "Send us straight to the top. The Church of the Mother."

"Dear me. This really is most irregu—"

"NOW!"

The operator nodded meekly and selected another of the ropes. The elevator shuddered and groaned as if reluctant to move before rising ponderously with a creaking of pulleys.

"I will enter the Church alone," Thane told his men. "Do not wait for me. Find Hellington and Potsworn. Take them to my mansion and barricade the door. No one is to be allowed entry except me."

"What about the Keeper of the Faith?" one of the guards asked over the rumbling of the lift.

"No. She … she is lost."

Thane stared moodily through the bars, absently counting the levels as he passed each platform. The staircase was far from empty, the ancient stone steps worn smooth by carriers, messengers, and workers. Essential cogs in the machine that was Keselgraad, the stitches that held the tapestry of the city's economy together, travelling along their winding paths for hours on end. Most of them would spend an entire afternoon reaching their destination, whereas it would take Thane a couple of minutes.

And yet, he felt a sudden surge of envy. A simple,

monotonous life was becoming more and more appealing the deeper he became embroiled in Keselgraad's secrets. Those who climbed and descended the central stairs had only two things to worry about: where they were coming from, and where they were going. It must be … refreshing in its triviality.

The lift juddered to a sudden stop, throwing Thane against the bars and knocking two of his guard off their feet. He righted himself with a curse.

"Mist-spawned operators! Age is making them careless. Doddering old fools must have given me more bumps and bruises than my sparring instructor."

A dishevelled guard rearranged his tabard and gazed up into the darkness of the shaft. "What level are we on?"

Thane tapped his foot irritably against the metal floor. "Nowhere near the Church of the Mother, that much is certain." He looked outside. Eight feet away, the central staircase gleamed, its railing carefully polished and its gas lamps ready to be lit. Then, they must be close to the Noble Quarters. But where was the platform?

"We're stuck," he realised with a scowl. "In between two levels. You there!" he shouted to a passing carrier toiling up the steps. "Do you know who I am?"

"Y … yes, my Lord!" the man shouted back, bowing as far as his wicker basket would allow.

"How far up is the next platform?"

The carrier squinted. "Dunno, my Lord!"

"I need you to get up there as quickly as you can. Tell the operator that the Keeper of the Peace is stuck in his damned cage, and if he doesn't get it moving within the next five minutes, I'll gift him to the Mists myself!"

The man bobbed his head and increased his pace, bellowing at the other travellers to get out of his way.

Thane ground his teeth in frustration. It was as if the entire world was conspiring against him. More insufferable delays. The lift creaked mournfully as if sharing his pain.

"We could jump across to the stairs," a guard suggested, a slight tremble in his voice.

Eight feet. Tantalisingly close, but still too far. Thane would have had difficulty making such a distance in his prime, let alone now. And if he failed? A drop of several hundred feet, just enough time to go half-mad with horror before shattering every bone in his body. At this height, he would land with such force that they would have to scrape his remains off the ground.

"We wait," he said, his words undermined by another tortured squeal.

Mists! It shouldn't be taking this long!

A faint tremor made the lift thrum. Thane removed one of his gloves and placed his hand on the bars. He could sense the slightest of vibrations. Something wasn't right.

"Change of plan," he said, reaching through and unlatching the door from the other side. It swung open, giving Thane a perfect view of the shaft below, with its central staircase spiralling away hypnotically. Round and round. Like a worm, burrowing down into the darkness. It was a pit. A pitch-black, bottomless hole. A gullet of some enormous beast, waiting to swallow him whole.

Metal shrieked ominously. The vibrations increased in intensity.

"I can make it, my Lord," the guard insisted, judging the distance between the lift and the stairs where a small crowd was gathering; stocky carriers rubbing shoulders with traders and even a trio of lesser Nobles in sharply cut overcoats and conical felt hats.

Thane hesitated for a moment and then nodded. "What's your name?"

"Denton, my Lord."

"May the Mother keep you, Denton."

The guard slipped his tabard over his head and removed his weapon belt and leather breastplate. His eyes bounced between the metal plate he was standing on and the railing that protected the inner side of the stairwell. His lips moved in a silent prayer.

He jumped.

The lift rocked. For the briefest of moments, Thane thought that the guardsman would succeed. Denton arched across the gap, his arms extended. A round-faced carrier with hands the size of spades reached out over the railing to catch him. Their fingers brushed in a fleeting caress. Life and death decided by mere inches. Denton's expression of confidence shifted to one of abject terror as he realised that he wasn't going to make it.

The guardsman managed to cry out once before slamming into the rough stone of the shaft face first, shattering his nose and breaking his jaw. He was flipped onto his back, and his horror-filled gaze found Thane's; two white circles in a sea of red. Then, he fell.

Thane forced himself to watch as Denton's floundering body sank like a stone, his legs kicking the empty air, his screams twisted by the broken bones of his face.

Falling. Dwindling.

Until the darkness took him.

Mists!

The lift's metallic moan pulled Thane back to reality.

The rope, he thought with sickening certainty. *Someone is trying to sever the rope that is keeping us aloft.*

He could feel the men behind him begin to panic. One of them whimpered. Another was weeping silently, frightened tears cascading down his cheeks to wet his beard.

Inches, Thane fumed, tapping his cane against the floor in frustration. *Our salvation is inches away!*

He stopped suddenly and looked down at what he was holding. His father had left him many things. His title. His mansion. His seat on the Keepers Council. And a simple wooden cane, its pommel worn smooth by dozens of his ancestors. The elite of House Quellion.

Thane had never really questioned why gripping that brass sphere calmed his nerves and soothed his anger. Perhaps it was because the gesture reminded him who he was and where he came from. A dynasty of protectors. Of *leaders.* Men who never gave up, no matter how impossible the situation. He would not bring dishonour to House Quellion. He would not abandon hope.

Inches away.

Thane bunched his thigh muscles, breathed a silent prayer to the Mother, and leapt. Tortured metal wailed in his ears. It was as if the lift was voicing its disappointment as he escaped its trap. He arced across the space separating him from the stairwell, the wind from the shaft tugging at the lapels of his greatcoat. As he reached the pinnacle of his jump, one thing became clear.

He wasn't going to make it.

The darkness waited below, ready to swallow him.

Behind him, the rope holding the elevator finally snapped, sending his honour guard plummeting to their deaths with a cacophony of falling metal and desperate screams. Thane was gripping the pommel of his cane so tightly that his fingers felt like they were on fire.

His cane. A treasured heirloom. A weapon. A sign of his wealth and status. It represented so many things to him that he often forgot its simplest function.

A stick of wood.

A few inches long.

With a desperate cry, he thrust his cane out before him like a spear. The butt slammed against the iron railing of the stairwell, sending a fresh jolt of agony up the bones of his arm as it ricocheted off the bars. For a heart-stopping moment, Thane thought that the crowd lining the stairs would let him fall, but then the strong, calloused hands of a carrier latched on to the wood, and he found himself dangling from the other end, his booted feet scrabbling against the rough wall of the shaft.

"Pull me up!" he gasped. A horrific crash echoed up from below as the plunging lift finally hit ground level, sealing the honour guard into a grisly coffin of metal and bone.

Thane began to rise, his arms scraping against the stone. The bottom of the railing was the first thing to appear, followed by a pair of well-worn boots, and finally, the red-cheeked, sweaty face of the carrier, his broad features contorted with effort. One last heave and Thane was pulled over the top. He lay for a moment in an undignified mess on the steps, adrenaline crackling through his veins, his chest rising and falling as he took a series of long, calming gulps of air.

"What a terrible accident, my Lord," the carrier panted, wiping the perspiration from his brow and handing the cane back to Thane. "Praise the Mother that you managed to survive. Keselgraad would be lost without its Keeper of the Peace."

Praise the Mother? She just tried to kill me, Thane fumed as he attempted to compose himself. "May … she forever guide us," he replied aloud through gritted teeth.

Mists, where to now? The Council. Hellington and Potsworn. The Council is in danger.

"I must tell the other Keepers of what has happened here," he said to the carrier, reaching into his greatcoat for his money pouch. He withdrew a couple of coppers and rolled them around the palm of his gloved hand to make them jingle. "Will you carry a message for me?"

"Of course, my Lord."

"Please inform them that I require their presence at my mansion without delay. Insist on the urgency of the matter."

The carrier nodded and shouldered his way through the crowd of onlookers to begin his long journey up the stairs. Thane followed more slowly, supporting himself with his cane and attempting to refocus his frazzled mind.

It was obvious that the Mother had never intended him to return from the Depths alive. Going to the Church now would be suicide.

He approached the platform where the ropes had been cut, breathing a sigh of relief when he saw It was empty. The Mother was not infallible, then. She had not considered the possibility that Thane would survive. He needed to use that to his advantage; to go somewhere safe before she realised her mistake.

Home. He had to go home.
And prepare to face her wrath.

TWENTY-FIVE
THE BOARD FALLS

"The Mists have retreated. Those around me rejoice, but they do not understand. I can hear the tapping of nails on stone. I can taste the crackling of lightning on the tip of my tongue. She is coming. Coming to finish the deed herself. We are the last blasphemers whom she must eradicate before things can begin anew."

First Technologist Arniel Sin, The Time Before

THANE QUICKENED HIS pace, passing the remains of the frayed cable without a second glance, his gaze fixed resolutely on the winding staircase. Travellers called out his name or touched his clothes. He ignored them. His shoulder ached. His legs ached. The shard of amethyst felt like an iron bar in his pocket. After what felt like an age, the archway to his level came into view, its opening free of wardens.

A contingent of Thane's honour guard was standing to attention on the other side, their coned helms and curved halberds gleaming.

"My Lord?" their officer enquired, taking in Thane's dusty coat and dishevelled appearance.

"The wardens have betrayed us," he answered curtly. "They seek my death. We must prepare."

Two more purple-clad soldiers stood watch before the entrance of his fortified mansion. Thane waved them aside, pleased to see that a dozen crossbowmen now lined the crenellated wall that ringed the estate. His manservant was already waiting for him with a burnished silver breastplate and officer's sword. Thane shrugged off his greatcoat and accepted them gratefully, pausing for a moment to admire the coat of arms of House Quellion that had been etched into the armour's shining surface. He pulled it over his head and allowed his manservant to help him with the straps.

"How many men?"

"Eleven on the walls and twenty in the courtyard, my Lord. I have sent a runner to the Stables, but there's no reply as of yet."

And there never will be, Thane thought. *The City Watch belongs to the Mother now.*

"Barricade the gate," he ordered, smoothing down his grey hair. He felt better now that he was in his own domain. More in control. He left his cane and greatcoat with his manservant, instructing him to secure the amethyst shard in his office, then climbed the short set of marble steps leading to the battlements.

The men on the ramparts met him with a mixture of confusion and trepidation. Most of them had never loosed the crossbows they were holding at anything more than a bale of hay. Keselgraad had not known violence on this scale since the Uprising.

"They're coming," one of the guards grunted, and Thane followed his gaze. A black tide was descending the stairs from the Church of the Mother. Fifty wardens at least, near-identical in their dark leather apparel and ceramic masks. They marched in eerie silence, their booted feet rising and falling in unnatural unison. At their head strode Devrard, recognisable by his cracked eye-slit and the single tar-like tear that marred one cheek. He held a burlap sack in one hand and his stiletto in the other. The warden stopped just out of crossbow range and called up to Thane.

"Keeper of the Peace. The Mother requests your presence."

"I am afraid you must inform her that I am indisposed. There has been a terrible accident. The lift has collapsed. Several of my men are among the dead. The Keepers Council must convene immediately to discuss how best to respond to this awful tragedy."

Devrard cocked his head. "That will be impossible, I am afraid."

Thane felt a surge of anger. "This has always been our way. Ever since the Council's inception. Keselgraad before all else. The city before the Church. Even the Mother must abide by our traditions."

"I fear you have misunderstood me, my Lord. The Council will not be able to convene because it has been dissolved." He opened the burlap sack and tipped out its contents. The severed heads of Lord Potsworn and Lady Hellington hit the paving with a wet *thwack*. Potsworn's dark blue tongue protruded from his mouth like a dead slug, small amounts of blood still leaking from the ragged stump of his neck. Lady Hellington had been decapitated more efficiently; her wrinkled skin smoothly severed to form a near-perfect circle of red. The tight bun she had always used to style her hair had finally come undone and a gossamer veil of snowy white locks now mercifully hid her lifeless gaze.

"What … what have you done?" Thane asked, aghast. "The Council *is* Keselgraad. Without it, who will rule?"

Devrard spoke as if the answer was obvious. "The Mother, of course. As is her right. If you allow me to escort you to her, all will become clear."

"I … I cannot," Thane shouted back. "My ancestors gave their lives for the city. I have decided that I am ready to do the same."

"That is unfortunate," the warden admitted. He took five paces forwards and raised his hand. Metal blurred. The crossbowman next to Thane gave a surprised gurgle as a long, thin pommel seemed to appear as if by magic in his throat.

He threw his dagger, Thane thought in disbelief. Over fifty feet. He had always known that the wardens came back from the Mists changed. That whatever the Mater Sorores administered to them after their trial transformed them into something else. But he had never realised just how strong they had become. How … inhuman.

Devrard dropped his arm, and the wardens began moving once more towards the mansion. Slowly and calmly, the only sound the swish of their leather robes. To Thane, this was far, far worse than a frenetic charge. The crossbow-man lay dead at his feet, blood still pouring from the wound in his neck, the purple of his tabard stained black.

Thane snatched up the fallen crossbow, checked that the bolt was still loaded in the furrow, and raised it to his shoulder.

"LOOSE!" he yelled, aiming at Devrard and squeezing

hard on the trigger. The shaft whined through the air and thunked into the warden's shoulder.

Devrard barely slowed, pausing only to tug the iron tip free and toss it contemptuously to the ground.

More missiles rained down on the silent attackers, puncturing flesh and bone. A trio of wardens fell. Another, his right foot pinned in place, simply stopped moving and stared up at the ramparts.

"Reload. RELOAD!"

Thane set the crossbow vertically and ratcheted the string back into place. He rifled through the belt of the dead guard and found another bolt, slotting it into the furrow. The man to his left collapsed with a scream, a stiletto boring through the underside of his jaw up into his skull.

Mists!

Thane peered over the edge of the ramparts. The wardens had almost reached the doors. He ducked reflexively, feeling a puff of air as a dagger soared over his head.

Mists! Mists!

He rose and loosed blindly into the mass of bodies pushing against the barred entrance. Beyond, the three fallen wardens were already standing. One had lost his mask, revealing a diseased face covered with a mass of brown ichor-filled pustules that throbbed and pulsed.

Thane gazed at him fixedly for an instant until the resonant crack of splitting wood brought him back to the present.

They had broken through the front door.

"Keep throwing everything at them until you have nothing left," he ordered the nine remaining crossbowmen, dropping his own weapon and drawing his sword.

"What's the use?" the nearest guard moaned, his face speckled with the blood of one of his fallen comrades. "Our bolts might as well be raindrops for all the damage they're doing."

"You're slowing them down," Thane called back, already heading for the stairs. He reached the first-floor landing. The scene in the vestibule below was straight from one of his worst nightmares. The entrance had been breached. Wardens were spilling through the opening, slaughtering the remains of the honour guard who had mustered on the other side. Halberds were near-useless in such a confined space, and most of his men were frantically trying to draw their swords. Glittering stilettos darted left and right like snake tongues, biting into unprotected flesh. Hands. Necks. Faces.

Thane took a deep breath. "FOR KESELGRAAD!" he bellowed, punching his blade into the air. He raced down the last few steps and charged into the fray, yelling the name of House Quellion like a battle cry. A stiletto appeared out of nowhere and scratched a thin line across the silver of his breastplate. He retaliated instinctively, his return cut scything the warden's forearm from his body. He punched his wounded opponent hard in the face and watched with satisfaction as he collapsed.

Another dagger flashed out of the churning melee. Thane batted it away, flicked his sword over to his left hand, and decapitated the approaching warden with a smooth horizontal sweep. Two more stepped up to take his place. Thane felt his heart drop as he saw that one of them was missing his forearm.

Slowing them down is not enough, he thought. *There must be a way to end this. Permanently.*

Then he remembered. The Depths. The corpse of the warden lying in a pool of black ichor. The amethyst shard protruding from his belly.

The shard.

Thane blocked a stiletto with his sword and took another on his breastplate, shrieking in surprise as the pointed tip punched through the metal and entered his flesh. Pain flared.

Strong. They are too strong.

His counter opened a deep wound in the first warden's leg. He hammered the pommel of his sword into the mask of the second. Ceramic shattered. Thane spun on his heel and ran back up the stairs towards his office. The right side of his body was on fire. He slipped his fingers under his breastplate. They came back wet and sticky. Blood.

The door to his office was already open. Thane plunged inside. The chequered black and white board was still on his desk, its small carved pieces all perfectly placed, the tiny knights, towers, kings, and queens illuminated by the soft purple glow of the amethyst that his manservant had left for him.

Thane placed his fingers on the crystalline surface. It thrummed faintly. A way to defeat the wardens. A way to defeat the Mother.

"You are not an easy man to convince."

Devrard stood in the entrance. His mask was more red than white now as rivulets of gore dribbled down the cracked beak-like tip to drop onto the floor. He held his stiletto loosely in one hand.

"I remember you," Thane replied, his hand closing around the shard. "Before the Trials. Before you became … whatever you are now. When you were just a watchman."

Silence.

"A devout man. When the others left for a drink at the end of their shift, you left for the Church of the Mother."

"The Mother keeps us."

"She does. She keeps us from our freedom. She keeps us from evolving. She keeps us from living. You must see that."

"I—"

"You were not just a devout man, Devrard. You were a *good* man. And a good watchman. First into the fray. You followed the oath more than most. You protected this city."

"That is still my role. I am a warden."

"Then, help me protect it from *her*."

Devrard reached up and removed his mask. The skin underneath was puckered and burnt, as if his face had been thrust into a blazing fire. His eyebrows and lids were gone, the sockets filled with two black, glistening orbs of pure obsidian.

"It is too late," he whispered through mangled lips. "Far too late. This is who I am now. This is what she has made me."

"You can still refuse. You can still resist."

Devrard stepped closer and held out his hand. "Give me the shard."

"As you wish." Thane whipped his arm around, driving the sharp piece of amethyst as deeply as he could into the warden's chest. Devrard staggered backwards and fell to one knee. His shoulders shook. He vomited. A stream of black bile.

It's working, Thane thought, raising his blade high. "Keselgraad above all."

The sword came down in an arc of glittering steel.

Devrard's hand came up to meet it. There was a resonant crack as he caught the tip between a thumb and forefinger. The warden pulled, tugging the sword from Thane's grasp and throwing it aside. He rose, pausing for a moment to examine the amethyst lodged in his belly.

"A fine attempt. I feel a certain discomfort. However, I believe that the power of this particular shard is too diminished to pose a significant threat."

A powerful right hook cracked against Thane's jaw, and he was thrown through the air to crash against his desk, scattering the carved pieces.

Miniature knights and kings rained down onto the floor, pattering off the thick carpet of his office. All vanquished. All fallen.

All except one. Still upright.

Dominating the now empty board.

The black queen.

TWENTY-SIX
LOST AND FOUND

"This will be my final entry. I must tell you of one last act of defiance. Despite orders not to use our research for personal means, I have, in secret, constructed another crystal. Small enough to be worn as a necklace or amulet. It is glowing now, filled with my own tears. A gift for my daughter, along with this journal and archives of my discoveries. I will live on through her memories. I will live on through her love."

First Technologist Arniel Sin, The Time Before

"WHERE IS THE lady taking us?" June asked Roe. They had been following the two watchmen through a maze of different tunnels for what seemed like hours, with no sign of getting any closer to the surface. At some point, the girl's hand had managed to find its way into his.

"Mists if I know," Roe replied, resisting the urge to rub at his eyes. He had been blinking furiously almost non-stop since being freed from the horrible contraption that had harvested the tears from his body, and his sockets still itched.

"Stop doing that, you'll only clog them up with more dust," June remonstrated. "Besides, I like the new colour."

He growled an incoherent reply and looked up ahead

where Spider was deep in conversation with one of the watchmen. What was his name? Ah, yes, Pine, the scarred, grey-haired captain who claimed to have known Roe's parents.

Lies, probably. More lies to encourage the orphans to trust them. Well, Roe was not going to be tricked all over again. He would never trust anyone again. *Ever.*

And speaking of trust, how in all the Mists could they even be sure the woman was leading them somewhere safe? She claimed to be from another city. Which was about as likely as Roe being Keeper of the Peace. So where was she taking them?

"A copper for your thoughts," June said. Her amethyst-tinged eyes studied him from behind her mop of straw hair.

"I was beginning to wonder if we made the right choice, leaving the orphanage. Krabbon was a bastard, but at least he was our bastard. There were ways to avoid—"

"He *beat* you, Roe!"

"I deserved that. I should never have tried to steal the—"

"He cut your arms. Sent our friends to be strapped into those awful chairs. Freeing us from that man's terrible yoke was the best thing that ever happened to me."

They reached another fork in the tunnels. The woman called Selene hesitated for a moment, her eyes darting between the two near-identical pools of blackness, before selecting the passage on the right.

"At least we got to see the sun," Roe said with a shiver. Goosebumps prickled along his bare skin.

"You did, you mean," June retorted. "For the last year, it was the Mines for me. Always the Mines. Scrabbling around in the dark. Squeezing through gaps too small for a grown man. Sometimes they were so narrow I had to lie on my belly and wriggle like a worm. Scratches on my face. On my arms." She patted her head. "I used to have such nice hair. Before I started losing whole clumps of it down there, stolen by the spiteful rocks and roots. And the dirt … Mists. Krabbon never allowed me enough water to scrub it all out. Always itching. Like lice on my scalp."

Roe gave her hand a squeeze. "I'm sorry. I didn't know."

"Every day. Every. Single. Day. I begged him to send someone else. There were plenty of other orphans my size. He laughed and told me it wasn't because I was small that the miners wanted me. It was because I was lucky."

"Lucky?"

"They gave me a name. Little canary. I stumbled upon veins of ore even the best of their prospectors had missed." She smiled at Roe proudly. "There was a hewer who got lost once. Turned out he had fallen into a crevasse and become stuck. Nobody wanted me to join the search party. But I did. And *I* found him."

"That's … how?"

They were interrupted by a burst of raised voices from up ahead. Another fork in the tunnels. Pine and Selene were bickering. It ended in defeat for the Watch captain, who conceded with a litany of growling expletives.

"How did I know where he was?" June asked. "I'm not sure. It just seemed obvious to me. Like lacing up my tunic or cooking a stew."

"Those are things we learn."

She pulled her hand away. "You don't believe me."

Roe sighed. "I … I want to. We've seen a man take a dagger to the face and go on living. A woman who claims to come from another city and assures us we can survive the Mists. Things are changing. I think … I think I just need some time to adjust."

June bowed her head, and the two orphans trudged on, surrounded by the other victims of Thane's unhinged machinations. Roe recognised Scarab, one of the first to have disappeared, now more man than boy, his arms and chin covered with thick hair. Beside him walked Moth, her pretty face pale from exhaustion. It must have been terrible to have been imprisoned in the Depths for years; pulled from their cells and strapped into the chairs whenever a crystal needed to be repaired.

And they're still trapped, Roe thought morosely. *This Mist-spawned place is a labyrinth. We're going to die down here. Perhaps, in a hundred years, when the cycle begins anew, our successors will explore the Depths much like we did and discover our cracked bones.*

The path split into five indistinguishable passageways. Selene chose the central one. Roe heard a soft tut from his left. He frowned.

"June?"

"Yes?"

"Are we going the right way?"

"I'm not sure, I—"

"Just tell me."

Her eyes sparkled in the shadows. "No."

"You can feel it, can't you? Like a vein of copper or that lost miner. You can sense the path to the surface."

A barely perceptible nod.

"Mists, June! Why didn't you say anything?"

She wiped at her eyes. "To whom? Who's going to listen to a little girl with holes in her tunic and dirt in her hair?"

Roe took her hand again and placed it firmly in his. "I am."

He dragged her past a startled Scarab and tapped Spider on the back. The slender boy turned and raised an inquisitive eyebrow. "What?"

"Come with me."

Pine and Selene were not far ahead, walking abreast, each adapting their pace to the other in typical watchman fashion. Twin crimson cloaks rippled.

Roe cleared his throat. "Stop."

It came out as a croak. He tried again. "STOP!"

Pine turned, his furrowed brow tugging at the scars on his face. "I know you're tired," he said, not unkindly. "But Thane will have reached the exit to the Mines by now, and the chances are he'll betray us at the first possible opportunity. We have to keep moving."

"No, it's not that. It's …. This isn't the path to the surface."

Selene ran her fingers through her copper hair, producing more dust. "I'm fairly sure—"

"It's blocked," June interrupted, averting her gaze. "We have to go back. Take a left at the last junction."

"Have you ever been down here, little girl?"

"Um, no."

"Then, what makes you so sure?"

"I … I just know," June finished lamely.

Selene gave a dismissive chuckle. "Instinct honed from your many years working as a miner, I imagine."

Pine, however, was looking at June strangely, a faraway look in his eye. "Have we … have me met before?"

"I don't think so, Captain."

"Aldin or Pine will suffice. I am no longer a captain of anything or anyone." He squatted down with a wince, the scabbard of his sword scraping against the floor of the tunnel. "Your face is familiar, yet I can't quite place it."

"That's because you've seen it before," Spider said, his usual monotone tinged with bitterness. "You've seen all of our faces before. When you left us to die."

Pine blanched. "That's not fair! Lord Thane swore he would take care of you. I had no reason not to trust him. The orphanage …"

"You had *every* reason. You must have felt it. Even then. How he was *using* you."

Scarred hands clenched and unclenched. "You don't understand. I was reeling from the loss of my friends. They all—"

"Your friends … your *friends?* They were our PARENTS!"

Spider's voice echoed down the tunnel, causing the other orphans to stop and stare. Roe had never seen the older boy so emotional, his entire body shaking in an effort to contain his anger.

"You're just as bad as Thane. Worse, in fact. At least he never hid the fact that he was a callous, self-serving bastard. Someone only looking out for himself."

Two spots of crimson burst into life on Pine's cheeks. "Don't compare me to him. I am *nothing* like him. I care."

"Then, tell me my name."

Pine faltered. "What?"

"I hate the name Spider. *Hate* it. Every time I hear it,

I think of Krabbon. Calling us insects. It was his way of belittling us. Of controlling us. Of making us feel like we were nothing. In taking our names, he took our *identities*. He took our *lives*. If you truly cared for us back then. If you had one ounce of empathy or compassion, then you must remember who we were. Tell me my name."

Spider turned and pointed at Roe and then June. "Or his. Or hers. Mists, there are plenty of us here. Take your pick. One name."

Pine's gaze flickered from one orphan to the next in quick succession. Again and again, the amethyst specks in his irises glittering like stars. His lips moved, forming a single word.

"Sorry."

Spider gave a snort of disgust. "Don't be. You are only confirming who I already know you to be. An outsider. You both are. Untrustworthy. Whereas June is …" he trailed off, unable to finish.

"Family," Roe said, feeling warmth bloom in his chest as he realised it to be true. June, Spider, Ant, and the others. He had known them all his life. Through all his hardships. They were not just orphans. They were his siblings. They were his brothers and sisters.

"Aye," Scarab agreed in his deep rumble. "Family. Tell us where you want to go, Sister, and we will follow."

Roe felt her hand tighten around his as she summoned her courage.

"Back to the junction."

The older boy scratched at his beard and nodded, then stood aside to let her pass. "Lead on."

Pine opened his mouth to say something, but a scathing

look from Spider made him shut it again. Selene shrugged. "It appears we've been overruled, Aldin."

He took the torch from her and passed it to Roe. "You don't seem that upset."

"No." She patted him on the shoulder. "To be perfectly honest, I wasn't *entirely* sure we were going the right way."

⌘

Fresh air.

Roe was sure he could sense it, a slight breeze that tickled his eyelashes. They were getting closer to the surface. They had to be.

June plodded along silently at his side, an expression of grim determination on her round face. She paused every so often to place a hand on the wall of the tunnel or to cock her head to listen to something only she could hear. But she never faltered. Never hesitated.

Roe found himself thinking back to what Thane had said. *'The same substance that keeps the Mists at bay is also changing us. Making us stronger.'* It sounded like the ravings of a madman. Looking deep inside himself, Roe recognised the same emptiness that had always lurked there. He was no stronger. No braver. Just a broken life cut to shreds by bad luck and poor decisions.

And now they were heading straight towards that which terrified him the most – the Mists – their survival based purely on the flimsy assurances of a woman they had just met. If she was wrong, their fate would be the same as Ant's; the flesh torn from their skin inch by agonising inch.

He realised that June was no longer beside him. She had

wandered on ahead, her pale tunic shimmering like a ghost in the darkness of the tunnel. She turned suddenly, her lips pursed in confusion.

"I—" she began to say before a deep rumbling wall of sound rolled over them like a tidal wave. Roe clapped his hands over his ears as a multitude of painful vibrations wracked his tired bones.

Cracks appeared in the ceiling overhead, thin as straw, a network of tiny fractures that spread across the stone like lightning. Fractures became fissures. A chunk of rock the size of Roe's head smashed into the floor beside him, peppering his legs with shards. A second, smaller piece hit him on the shoulder. Somewhere behind him, he could hear Pine's voice, urging them to run.

Roe stumbled to his feet, narrowly avoiding another falling stone. Three short snaps, like the lashing of a whip, made him look up. A trio of crevices were snaking over the ceiling, shedding dust and grit, converging on a single point a dozen feet in front of him.

A flicker of pale blue.

"JUNE!" he yelled in panic, forcing his aching legs to move. He lurched towards her, his heart screaming in his chest. The serpentine fissures met above the girl's head and ruptured with a titanic resonance that exploded through the ringing in his ears.

I'm too late, he realised in terror. *Far too late.*

An avalanche of earth and stone cascaded from the collapsing ceiling, a deadly hailstorm of boulders and soil. Roe saw June raise her hands as if to ward off the incoming barrage, a tiny figure in the eye of the storm. The first rock brushed against the tips of her fingers.

A flash of purple light.

Everything *stopped.*

There was no other way to describe it. One moment, Roe was overwhelmed by a cacophony of sound, the next there was utter silence. He stared in amazement at a large shard, inches from his face, seemingly suspended in mid-air, vibrating ever so slightly as if fighting to break free from whatever held it in place.

From *whoever* held it in place.

June's trembling limbs were spread wide; sweat rolled down her forehead and neck, blood ran from her left nostril, her brow was furrowed in intense concentration.

And yet, somehow, she was smiling.

She lowered her arms, and the debris around her floated harmlessly earthwards to land on the floor of the tunnel with the faintest of clinks. Roe laughed in wonder.

"How … how did you do that?"

June shrugged, swaying on her feet. Roe caught her before she fell.

"The Mother keeps us," she murmured from his arms, resting her head against his chest. The amethyst glow in her eyes had dimmed to a glimmer, and Roe could see the original colour bleeding back through.

Thane was right, he thought. *We are becoming stronger. Strong enough to escape this place. Strong enough to escape the Mother.*

Unless she finds a way to stop us first.

TWENTY-SEVEN
BEYOND KESELGRAAD

"Isolationism was perhaps our greatest mistake. Like many of the poor decisions we made, it was driven by arrogance and egocentrism. Just imagine if all the cities of this world had come together to form a single, unified force. We would have been unstoppable."

Herina Sin, Daughter of the First Technologist, The Time Before

THE MISTS SQUIRMED and probed at the edge of the tunnel, held back by some invisible barrier. Even when strapped to the cross, Pine had never been this close. He found himself fixated by the random swirls in the fog, the tendrils contorting into mysterious abstract shapes.

"What now?" asked the boy named Roe, his cheeks as white as the Mists themselves, his gaze darting over the undulating veil as if trying to pierce its secrets. Pine could sense that the orphan was afraid, and he didn't blame him, it was an entirely logical reaction. So, why didn't he feel it himself? He searched his mind and found only apprehension and … curiosity.

"We must be cautious," Selene said, gnawing on her bottom lip. Throughout their trip through the tunnels, she had been constantly tying her hair back, yet it always managed to work its way free and now hung once more around her face.

Pine chuckled. "It's a bit late to start now. The way I see it, there are only two paths. One leads to freedom, the other to captivity."

"And if what happened to you on the cross was just a stroke of good luck? Or some sort of side effect of the Mother reappearing among us?"

"Mists, woman! A few hours ago, you were trying to talk me into this, and now you're trying to talk me out of it?"

Selene chewed harder, visibly flustered. "I … I know, it's just that I don't want to force you to do anything you're not—"

Run.

The whisper in Pine's mind was so real that for a minute, he thought it was Selene who had spoken. He removed his helm and pressed his bandaged hand against his forehead.

The dream. The woman at the font. Black liquid.

Run.

Pine blinked slowly. The voice faded.

Fate and fortune.

"I'm not going back," he said firmly. "There is nothing left for me in Keselgraad. This is my path. My *fate*. Besides, I think I've finally found some faith."

"Faith?" Selene's eyebrows shot up in surprise. "Faith in the Mother?"

"No. Faith in *myself*." Pine thrust his arm into the Mists. There was a brief instant of pain, then nothing. Tentacular strands writhed inches from his skin, repulsed by the same barrier that prevented them from entering the city of

Keselgraad. Pine swished his injured hand left and right, watching in fascination while the Mists fled his touch as if blown away by some unseen wind.

"Roe, you try," he said. The boy's face was ashen. He shook his head wordlessly.

"You were exposed to the same substance as me," Pine insisted. "At the same time."

"Ant died … you don't understand. His screams. I still hear his screams. I can't."

"He was not an orphan of the Collapse," Spider said from behind Selene. "He did not have whatever taints our blood. He had no hope of survival."

"I … I can't," Roe repeated, rooted to the spot. "I can't do it alone."

Spider brushed past Selene and held out his hand. "Then, we go together."

Roe took it, and together they left the safety of the tunnel entrance. The Mists churned. Pine could almost hear them whispering angrily, like petulant children denied their favourite food. The air around the two boys blurred, thick and greasy. Yet, not a single strand could break through.

It's working, he thought with excitement.

Spider turned to Scarab and beckoned. The larger boy was hesitant, inching his way forwards with his arms raised protectively. He let out a booming laugh when he realised that he was safe. Soon, the other orphans were running into the Mists, flapping their arms like wings, twirling, jumping, dancing. Pine couldn't help but laugh at the absurdity of it all. How quickly a monstrous, terrifying force had been reduced to a child's plaything.

"You'll have to keep me close," Selene said, her voice

muffled. She had torn off a strip of her guard's cloak and wrapped it around her head to protect her nose, mouth, and hair. More shredded fabric lay scattered at her feet.

Pine's good humour died. "You no longer have your crystal," he stated.

"No." She selected one of the larger pieces and began to cover up her left hand. "I'm hoping that whatever repellent you are all creating will be enough to keep me safe, too. If I fall—"

"That won't—"

"Listen, Aldin. If I fall, it will be up to you to take them the rest of the way. It won't be easy. There's no sun to follow. No stars or moon to guide your path. Keselgraad will be visible for a time, but even the city will soon be lost from sight. Make sure to keep it behind you as long as you can. In a day or two, you will reach a forest. Beyond the forest are the hills. The Mists normally become thinner higher up, so you should be able to see my home."

Selene pulled the crimson cloth tight and turned her attention to her other forearm. "Once you reach the gates, tell them who you are and where you have come from. They will let you in."

"You can tell them yourself," Pine promised. He cupped his hands around his mouth and called the orphans to him. "Time to leave," he said. His words were met with a series of enthusiastic whoops.

"Don't celebrate yet. We have a lot of ground to cover and barely any supplies. Slow and steady is how we will do it. We stay as close to each other as we can. And no leaving the group, under any circumstances. Is that understood?"

"Hah!" Scarab barked. "Do not fret, Watchman. The Mists cannot touch us."

"It's not the Mists that I'm worried about," Pine replied, staring into the gossamer veil. "It's what might be hiding inside them."

⌘

Several hours later, Pine was forced to concede that his fears appeared to be completely unfounded. Wet soil squelched under his boots. Blades of grass tickled his shins. The occasional tree coalesced from the depths of the fog, covered with autumn leaves the colour of Selene's hair. Soon after, they discovered a gurgling stream that swerved and foamed between smooth rocks. They halted there for a time to scrub the dirt from their skin and replenish their supply of fresh water.

"We are making good progress," Selene mumbled to him. She had insisted on wearing her makeshift mask and gloves at all times, despite the Mists never approaching closer than five or six feet.

"I don't know why, but I always imagined the land around the city to be some sort of blackened wilderness," Pine said, watching as Roe and Spider grabbed Scarab's legs and attempted to pull him off his feet. "Instead, it's … beautiful."

"The Mists were not conceived to destroy all forms of life. Only us. There's still wildlife out here, too. The last time I passed through the forest, I stumbled across a deer and her young."

"A *deer*?"

"Ah. Like, um, a horse? But smaller, with spindly legs and horns."

"Sounds absolutely horrifying."

She gave a stifled chortle. "It's not. Nothing here is. I wonder what will happen if the Mother dies. Do you think the Mists will disappear?"

"You're talking about killing a goddess."

"Stranger things have happened. Remember why she created all of this. To stop us from becoming strong enough to challenge her." Selene leant closer. "It's already beginning. June is awakening; the others will follow. And wait until you see my *home*, Aldin. Wait until you see what we have already achieved. It *can* be done."

Pine locked his gaze with hers. He was suddenly aware of how close they were sitting, his knee brushing against hers, their boots inches apart. He could detect a faint scent of crushed flowers mixed with tanned leather and the oil from her breastplate. Selene's emerald eyes sparkled. Pine reached out to take her covered hand.

A bestial roar followed by a colossal splash made him jerk away. Scarab had succumbed to the combined assault of the other orphans and tumbled head-first into the cold water. He emerged, sputtering and cursing, his long hair a sodden mess.

"That's the first bath you've had in months," Moth called happily from the shoreline. "Perhaps now, you won't smell like you've been dragged through a pile of pigshi—"

Scarab erupted from the stream with a vengeance and began chasing after her, shedding icy droplets in his wake.

Danger!

The voice exploded in Pine's mind once more, stronger than before. He cried out in pain.

"Aldin?" Selene asked in concern. "Are you all right? You're bleeding."

He touched his fingers to his nose and felt a wetness there. "We have to go," he muttered, lifting his helm to massage his temples.

"What?"

"There's something … someone …"

"Slow down, you're not making any sense!"

"I've been starting to hear things in my head. Voices. Warnings. I don't know. A woman. I can't …"

"Scarab!" Selene shouted. "Spider! Roe! Playtime's over. We're leaving."

"Too late," June whispered, pointing at something behind Pine. Figures in the Mists. Black on white. Curved beaks cutting through the wispy tendrils.

Wardens.

There were eighteen of them. Moving with purpose. Too many to fight.

One of the smaller girls let out a tiny shriek as three more wardens appeared on the other side of the stream, cutting off their escape route.

Pine stood and drew his sword. "I'll hold them for as long as I can," he said to Selene. "As soon as they focus on me, break through the circle and lead the children to safety."

"Not a chance," she replied, tugging her own blade free from its scabbard. "They are old enough to handle themselves."

"That's an order, Watchman."

She laughed. "What was it you said? I am no longer a captain of anything or anyone."

"Selene …"

"No. I've made my choice. What's the plan?"

Pine shrugged. "Don't have one. I was just going to charge at them yelling."

"Like you did with that one in the Depths."

His mouth jerked. "It worked well enough then."

"Yes, but he was—"

"Captain." The leader of the wardens spoke with a dry rasp that made it sound like his throat was being scraped raw. "It has been too long."

Pine narrowed his eyes. "Do I know you?"

"Of course, Captain. I am the one who was named Chroll. Before the Mother made me hers."

The image of a long-limbed watchman with burns on his face formed in Pine's mind. "Chroll? Aye, I remember. Are you here to return us to Keselgraad?"

The bird-like mask shuddered. "I am afraid not, Captain. Her holiness deems that the damage you have done to the city is irrevocable."

"Damage?"

"Treason. Conspiring to overthrow the ruling Council. Heresy. Usually, a man convicted of such crimes would be gifted to the Mists, but for someone of your … talents, I fear a more traditional approach will be necessary."

A dagger had appeared in Chroll's hand. Pine hadn't even seen the warden draw it from his scabbard.

By the Mother, he's fast.

"I will consent to my punishment," he said aloud. "I

only ask that the children be spared the sight of my execution. If we could move to another location?"

Chroll coughed loudly, like a razor blade drawn over stubble. "Apologies, but the Mother was quite specific. You are *all* enemies of Keselgraad." He motioned the other wardens forwards. "And you must all die."

Pine raised his blade.

Three enemies to the left. Four to the right. Perhaps if he—

A large rock sailed past his head and slammed into Chroll's mask, shattering the ceramic. Pine turned in amazement to see Scarab, breathing hard, already heaving another missile from the shore of the stream, his biceps taut with effort.

Damn children, he thought with a mixture of annoyance and pride. *I told you to run.*

Then the wardens were upon him.

Pine blocked two stilettos with his sword, took a third on the shoulder, and felt a fourth tear a hole in his cloak. He retaliated with a knee to the groin, which had no apparent effect. His follow-up elbow to the stomach was more successful, soliciting a groan that allowed him to retreat a few paces.

A twig cracked behind him, and he ducked instinctively, sensing a whoosh of displaced air. He reversed his grip on his weapon and stabbed blindly backwards. There was a brief resistance before Pine felt a spattering of blood on his cloak as the steel tip bit deep. The injured warden staggered away and was lost to the fog.

Three more rocks span across Pine's vision. To his right, Selene was squaring off against two silent opponents. She had lost her helmet and crimson mask; her hair streaming out behind her like the tail of a comet and her brow creased with concentration as she used the long reach of her officer's sword to keep them at bay.

Pine was about to move to help her when a willow-like form elbowed him aside, its chalk-white skin stark against black hair. Spider. He approached from behind with barely a sound. Metal gleamed in his hand. He aimed low. The heel. A scything cut that sliced through leather, skin, and tendon. A warden fell like a puppet without strings.

Spider danced away.

Who are these orphans? Pine thought in wonder. *These children who fight like men and dare to challenge the Mother herself. Whatever happened during the Collapse has made them different. Made them … more.*

Selene had used Spider's distraction to her advantage, impaling one of the wardens on her blade. She caught Pine looking at her and flashed a weary smile.

Perhaps it is not so hopeless after all. Perhaps we can—

A searing pain exploded in Pine's right shoulder. He screamed and dropped his sword. A second dagger entered his thigh just above the knee, causing another flare of agony. His remaining leg could no longer support his weight, and he collapsed awkwardly, his head crunching into the ground.

A warden stood over him, a dark tar-like substance leaking sluggishly from a hole in his belly. It was the man he had stabbed moments earlier. The man he thought he had killed. Pine felt the tiny spark of hope that had flickered to life in his chest sputter and die. How could they prevail against an immortal enemy?

A fresh wave of pain threatened to engulf him. He

pushed it away angrily and attempted to rise. A black boot pressed him back into the dirt.

"Watch," a grating voice rasped in his ear. "Just watch."

Selene lasted another minute, her blade flashing, until a warden managed to slip under her guard and hammer the pommel of his dagger into her skull. She dropped without a sound, her hair matted with blood.

"No," Pine whispered.

Scarab was being dragged from the stream, his bearded face battered and bruised, his eyes dull and unfocused. Spider was surrounded by a forest of blades. His own stiletto was torn from his hands. A harsh kick drove the boy to his knees.

"No ..."

"Who first, I wonder?" Chroll said. "The Mother was quite specific. You instigated all of this, Captain. You will be the last to die."

He left Pine to squirm and walked among the prisoners, tapping his stiletto against his cracked mask.

"I think .... Yes, I think this one."

And, turning on his heel, he rammed his dagger as deep as he could into Spider's chest.

TWENTY-EIGHT
THE STRENGTH OF A NAME

"A family is like a tree. It has many branches, all growing in different directions. Some are short, some are long. Some are covered with leaves and flowers. Some are bare and brittle. Yet, they all stem from the same seed. And their roots remain as one."

Anonymous

"NO!" PINE SCREAMED as Spider tumbled onto his back in a spray of blood.

A second cry of pain followed his own; a high-pitched shriek of grief.

June stood on the shore of the stream, her eyes crackling with such intensity that they appeared on fire. Her wild mass of corn-coloured hair twisted and turned in all directions like a nest of angry snakes.

"He was my friend," she snarled, her voice far louder than a child's. "He was my ... BROTHER!"

The earth rumbled with that final word. Pine, his head still pressed into the grass, could feel the soil tremble against his cheek. As if it were listening. Or *awakening*.

"Quiet, little girl," Chroll said. "You will soon be joining him." He flicked his fingers at a couple of nearby wardens who advanced, daggers drawn.

There was a buzzing sound. Pine blinked. When he opened his eyes again, one of the wardens was missing his head. A blackish substance pumped from the stump of the jagged neck like a grisly fountain. The decapitated body managed a half-step forwards before collapsing.

"What …"

June was surrounded by a maelstrom of rocks and pebbles from the stream. They circled her tiny body, spinning round and round like a swarm of wasps. Pine watched in fascination as some of the smaller shards shifted and melted, only to reform into bigger pieces.

Round and round. Faster and faster.

A hurricane.

Amethyst lightning forked. Wind rippled from its centre, flattening the grass, uprooting small trees and bushes, pulling more rocks free from the earth to add to the storm. White-foamed waves formed in the stream as the water became caught up in the tempest. The Mists were pushed back, fleeing the pandemonium like a retreating army.

Pine squinted his eyes against the gale. June's feet were no longer touching the ground. She hung, suspended in the air, her face a furious mask. A rage-fuelled shout escaped her lips.

"BROTHER!"

A rock left its orbit and bored a hole through a warden's chest before landing in the grass next to Pine with a gory wet *thunk*.

"Kill her," Chroll ordered in his abrasive monotone.

The remaining wardens attacked.

And were torn apart.

Dagger-like shards punctured eye-slits and burrowed into the flesh beneath. Boulders cracked bones and shredded limbs. The earth itself began to writhe. Fissures appeared, swallowing wardens whole. Stalagmites taller than a man erupted from around June in a ring of defensive spikes, impaling her enemies on their sharp tips. Black ichor spattered the grass and the water of the stream like rain.

BROTHER! The word was repeated in Pine's mind, magnified tenfold. He gritted his teeth against the noise.

She's losing control, he thought. *So much power and so much rage.*

"JUNE!" he screamed. His voice was lost to the growling storm of rocks and dirt.

If I can hear her, then perhaps … perhaps she can hear me.

Pine forced himself to concentrate. Grit whipped through the grass to sting his face.

He closed his eyes.

June.

He could still sense her, twenty feet away, a shimmering glow in the dark.

June.

Captain. Watch.

Pine looked up to see Chroll suspended overhead; one long, knotted branch wrapped around his ankle, another encircling his wrist. The warden struggled weakly as he fought against the inevitable. Pine saw leather begin to tear, revealing necrotic skin covered in pestilent sores. Then the branches twisted, and Chroll was ripped in half, his torso and lower body jerking and spasming in a macabre dance of death. Pine was drenched in a nauseating mix of decaying flesh and viscera. He retched uncontrollably.

I have freed you.

"No," he mumbled, wiping at his face, ignoring the way the gesture made his shoulder burn. "Not like this."

They must pay. They must all pay.

June.

He probed deeper and was immediately repelled by a rippling barrier of incandescent anger.

Let me in.

NO!

Pine tasted more blood in his mouth and realised that this time it was his own. Gritting his teeth, he pushed on through the tempest. Images flashed in his mind. June, suspended in a cloud of amethyst fire, her pale tunic stained red, tearing down the walls of Keselgraad. The steeple of the Church of the Mother collapsing in on itself. Children screaming. Men and women weeping. Chaos. Violence. Death.

Rock and stone and dirt and dust.

This is not the way, June, he pulsed. *Vengeance has consequences.*

They must pay. They MUST ALL PAY!

All? What of the people who are suffering just like you suffered? The orphans? The weak? The kind? Like Mrs Pattyworth and her husband? Do they deserve your wrath?

A flicker of hesitation. A moment of calm in the storm.

An opportunity.

Pine pushed his consciousness through the gap in her defences. Onwards. Deeper and deeper into her mind. The images change. He sees a woman with a crimson bandana and curly hair.

Bera.

She is watching a child, her tunic so grubby that it looks like she is clothed in dirt.

I know you.

The child tries to stand. Two tottering steps, then she falls, catching her elbow on a loose rock. She should be crying. She gurgles instead, her little round face split by a toothless grin.

Bera arrives. Worry lines crease her forehead. She is holding something. A doll. Made of mud and dirt.

She bends down. Presses the doll into her daughter's hand and pulls her close.

Whispers her name in her ear.

Shala.

Words hold power. A sharp retort can cut as deeply as any sword, compassion dull an aching pain, and encouragement lend strength to weary limbs. And of all the words in the world, the most powerful is the one we hear first, the one that defines who we are, and who we will become.

The shrieking wind became a playful breeze. Stalagmites shattered. Boulders tumbled from the sky to sink into the grass or thunk into the muddy shore. The stream gurgled and bubbled, happily resuming its course towards some distant ocean.

And in the middle of it all, a little girl, covered in the torn remains of a dirty tunic, her arms wrapped around her shivering frame, her face streaked with tears.

Pine took a half-dozen exhausted, shambling steps and pulled the trembling bundle close to his chest.

"It's over," he whispered. "It's over, Shala."

A convenient lie. It was far from over.

In fact, it had barely begun.

He sighed and held her while she cried. The Mists shimmered and shifted around them as if sharing their pain. The other orphans began to join them, nursing an impressive collection of bumps and bruises but otherwise miraculously unharmed. He counted them. Ten. One was still missing.

A duo of blurry figures staggered from the fog, leaning heavily on one another. Selene, her burnished hair wild and free, a bruise the size of an egg marking her temple.

And at her side, his tunic caked in blood, another miracle.

Spider.

⌘

The fire crackled and popped, sending glittering sparks high into the air of the forest clearing where they were lost within the Mists. Roe stared moodily into the flames, watching them dance. Yellow and orange flickered, twisting into familiar shapes. Ant's bloody face. A long, curved beak. A stiletto. Krabbon's leering smile as his hands squeezed tighter and tighter. Tall stalks of ripe corn. A crystal, intense and coruscant, gorging itself on his tears. Brighter and brighter until its radiance burned his eyes from their sockets.

"Can't sleep?"

Pine took a seat on the fallen log beside Roe and held out his hands to the warmth. He looked so much older and frailer without his breastplate and cloak, the light of the fire deepening his wrinkles and highlighting the grey in his beard. There was something else different about him, too.

"Your palm," Roe said softly. "It's healing."

Pine pulled down the shoulder of his tunic. The wound made by Chroll's dagger still glistened with blood but was already scabbing over.

"We are changing," he replied simply.

Roe thought of his own injuries. Krabbon's birch stick across his backside. The bruises on his neck. The cuts on his arms. At some point, they had just … not bothered him anymore. They had faded away.

"The crystal?" he asked. "The crystal is doing all of this?"

"Not directly. You heard Thane. Whatever was in that thing found its way inside our bodies during the Collapse. It latched itself onto us. Growing. Maturing."

"I saw that dagger enter Spider's chest. He should be dead."

"We *all* should be dead." Pine glanced behind him where June – no, *Shala* – was snuggled up next to Selene, a crimson cloak covering them both. "I still don't quite understand why we are not."

They sat in silence for a while, studying the flames.

"I could have saved him," Roe said eventually.

"Who?"

"Ant. He was my friend. Another orphan."

"From the Collapse?"

"No. Worse. He was … unwanted. Abandoned by his parents. Why would you do that to a child?"

"There are many reasons," Pine replied softly. "None of them good."

"If I had followed him over the edge of the wall, I could have shielded him from the Mists. I was a coward."

"It's not your fault. You couldn't have known."

Roe looked up; his eyes fierce. "I didn't even *try*."

"Aye," Pine breathed. "We all have regrets. Things we wished we could have done differently. You can't dwell on them or they'll eat you up inside. Trust me on this. There's not a day that goes by without me asking myself if I could have prevented the Collapse. Saved my friends."

Roe picked up a nearby log and added it to the blaze. Fresh plumes of smoke spiralled skywards. One of the slumbering orphans moaned in his sleep. "You and my parents were close?" he asked tentatively.

Pine gave a sad smile. "I … I can't tell you, lad. Not because I don't want to, but because I don't even know who your parents *were*."

"And yet, you were friends."

"Of a sort. In a misguided way. We saw each other nearly every day. Mined together. Ate together. Mists, when Thane offered us a place on one of his infamous expeditions to the Depths, we spent weeks in each other's company. Yet, there was always an unspoken boundary between work and family. One that was never crossed. And when our shift ended, we all went back to our other lives."

Roe shook his head in confusion. "But I heard you. *Shala*. You called June by her true name. Not the one that bastard Krabbon stuck her with. How is it that you can remember hers but not mine?"

"I … I didn't remember it. She did." Pine looked at his hands. At the scars on his palms.

"What in the Mother are you talking about?"

"Voices … in my head. I've been plagued with them for some time now. A woman's in particular. Strangely familiar, yet too distorted for me to identify. When Shala lost control, I could … I could hear hers, too. And by following it back to its source, I managed to—"

"Speak to her?"

"It was even deeper than that. I shared a part of myself with her, and she did the same in return. I found her name in one of her memories. One she had forgotten. Or was too young to remember."

Roe licked his lips. "Then, you could do the same for me."

"I'm not sure."

"*Try.*" Low and urgent. The old oaks on the edge of the clearing creaked and swayed in apprehension.

Pine could only nod. He gazed into Roe's eyes. A brown so dark it was almost black. Flecked with amethyst. "This might hurt a little—"

Pain exploded in Roe's mind, sharp and raw. He stifled a scream and gripped the log he was sitting on. Splinters pierced his palms.

Let me in, Pine's voice insisted.

Tendrils inside his skull. No, not tendrils. Worms. Slithering. Writhing. Burrowing. Roe pressed both hands against his forehead and moaned.

Shall I stop?

No, he pulsed back. *I have to know. I need to know.*

A fresh wave of prickling agony. Roe squeezed his eyes shut. Blurry images flashed through the darkness. A woman, her worn face haggard, flickering in and out of focus. Her dress had been torn and repaired so many times that it looked like a patchwork quilt. Roe could see her lips moving but couldn't make out the words. She began to fade.

Wait! he ordered.

I cannot delve any further, Pine cautioned. *The strain will kill you.*

Please!

The pain intensified, and this time Roe could not stop himself from crying out. Shala jolted awake and began to rise. Selene pulled her back.

The woman and her multicoloured dress returned, clearer now. Her unwashed hair, streaked with dirt, hung like string on either side of her face. Scabs covered her shins and feet, her toenails were chipped and broken. Yet, when she spoke, it was with a voice filled with wonder and joy. It flowed through Roe like a cooling cascade, quenching the conflagration that raged in his mind.

"It was so hard for me to name you," she said. "At first, whenever I looked at you, I could see only *him*. That same flat nose. Those piercing eyes. You were a constant reminder of what he did to me … of what he *took* from me. But you are not him. And you never will be."

The woman coughed into her left hand. It came away stained with blood.

"We found a room down here. There was paper. Real paper. Covered in drawings of places that we will never know. Wonderful places. Magical places. Where the earth ends and water begins. Larger than any lake, an expanse of glittering turquoise stretching as far as the horizon and beyond. No Mists. No cities. No noise. Only the kiss of sunlight and the whisper of the waves. They called it the *ocean*."

Roe remembered. He remembered who this woman was. And what she was going to say.

"There is a tiny thing that makes its home on those shores. Its insides are weak and soft so it encases its body within a thick shell. It protects itself from all those who would try to do it harm. This is what we must do, you and I. Clothe ourselves in armour to ward off all the world's pain. To make us strong. To make us safe. To help us protect others." Her smile fell for a moment, revealing the despair and anguish hiding inside. She coughed again. Blood trickled from her mouth. "I ... I asked Gamin to tell me what this creature was called."

She spoke a single word.

Roe let out a terrible sob as grief and happiness collided in his heart in an explosion of overwhelming emotions. He was no longer broken. He was whole once more.

"I will not disappoint you, Mother," he said aloud. "I will be worthy of this name that you have given me. I will spend the rest of my days fighting to help those who cannot help themselves. I will be their protector. Their shield. Their ... light against the dark. I swear it."

"What did she call you?" Pine asked softly, fire dancing in his eyes.

Roe smiled through his tears.

"Brachyura."

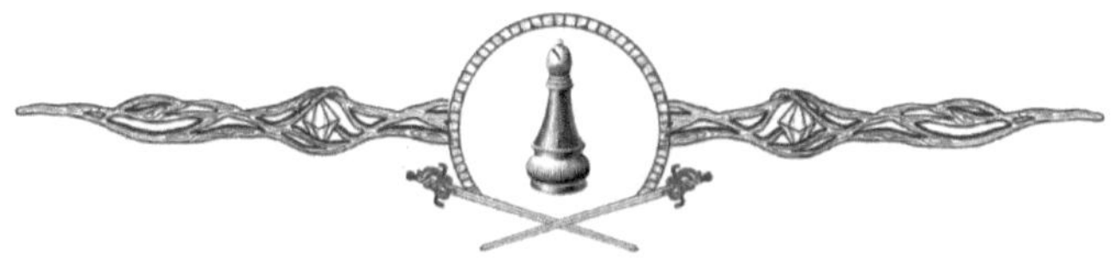

TWENTY-NINE
MATER LACHRYMARUM

"On the eighth day, the Mother loosens the bondage of death and receives the fallen from their graves."

From the scriptures of the Mother, date unknown

SISTER SUPERIOR NAYELLE watched the bees swarm over the Church's herb garden. Hundreds of mindless drones controlled by a single dominant Queen. By a single dominant *Mother*. Unequivocal obedience, without question or hesitation. Without ever asking themselves if they were truly doing the right thing.

Nayelle used to love the garden. It had been her refuge from the outside world, a haven of tranquillity that had allowed her to escape the constant prattling of the Keepers Council or the unending supplications of the faithful. But even that had been taken from her. For now, it was forever stained with the blood of an innocent man. A man she had murdered in the name of the Mother.

Her goddess had whispered three names in her ear, down under the altar of the Church, deep in the heart of that terrible blackness that threatened to consume her soul every time she plunged her hands into the icy liquid. The unfaithful.

Enemies of the Mother. Sowing lies and discord among her flock. And if their lies were not stopped, Keselgraad would descend into anarchy and chaos.

The swineherd and welder had been dealt with by her proxies. Members of the Mater Sorores who preached in the Slums. But for the last heretic, Spritt, the Mother had insisted that Nayelle intervene herself.

And so, she had obeyed.

Without question or hesitation.

She knew the herbs and plants of her garden well. Those that heal and those that harm. The precise amount that must be administered to send a man to his death. Foxglove is as deadly as it is beautiful, the smallest of doses can often suffice. Nayelle had laced a half-dozen wafers left over from a morning service and travelled to Spritt's home to offer him communion. She remembered his expression of pride when she had told him that the Mother had been touched by his devotion and wished to reward him.

The first symptoms had appeared within minutes. A dullness of the gaze. The cold sweats. The nausea. She had helped him to his bed and lit the candles she had brought, gently forcing more wafers into his mouth, watching as he retched and raved, as the vomit and urine stained his clothes. As his lips became red and raw. As he jerked and convulsed, his feet kicking so hard against the wall that she had to hold him down. Until the light finally left his eyes and he collapsed, slack-jawed, his last breath acrid and foul.

A tear dripped onto Nayelle's robes. She had obeyed.

Without question or hesitation.

She had believed herself to be a saviour. Instead, she had become a murderer. Spritt had been repairing the contraption that was being used to *maintain* the amethyst. He was protecting Keselgraad from the Mists. Without him, the machine would fail. The barrier would fall. And the city she loved so much would be devoured. By her fault. All in the name of the Mother.

Another tear splashed onto her blackened hands. She no longer attempted to scrub them clean. Since the goddess's return, she had been spending more and more time in the chamber under the altar, filling jars and jugs with that oily black liquid without ever managing to empty the font. The wardens used to ingest a small amount after being exposed to the Mists; now, they were consuming it every day.

A flicker in her mind. That was something else that had changed. She was beginning to hear things. Voices. Ghostly conversations, as if two people were standing a few feet behind her, hidden in the shadows. Most of the time they were inaudible, but occasionally, she could discern random words. Selene. The Mists. Roe. She had tried talking back, telling them to escape. To *run*. She had attempted to warn anyone listening that the Mists were dangerous. That the wardens were killers. That the Mother … that the Mother was a lie. It was like shouting into the void.

There was little else she could do. She was a prisoner of her own Church; her every move watched by the handful of wardens that now patrolled the cloister. There was no way out. No escape. Unless …

She fingered the triangular-shaped medallion that hung from her neck. The edges were sharp. Not sharp enough. Not yet. But perhaps if she found a suitable stone, she could file the metal to make it keen and biting.

"Sister Superior."

Devrard stood waiting patiently between two of the cloister's stone arches. His mask was partially hidden by the shadow cast by his hat, yet Nayelle could still see the traces of black ichor and dried blood that he hadn't washed off. Just like he hadn't bothered to repair the cracks in the ceramic. It wasn't that he had forgotten, it was just that he didn't seem to care anymore.

"Warden."

"The Mother requests your presence."

I could do it now, she thought. *Even without making it sharper. I could tear a hole in my throat. Just under my chin.*

Devrard's left finger moved ever so slightly. He knew. Nayelle would never make it in time. She sighed.

"Of course."

She followed the warden out of the garden, the humming of the bees ringing ominously in her ears.

⌘

The Mother was not alone. Lord Mattias Thane knelt in chains at her bare feet, his greatcoat in tatters, his jaw a bruised mass of yellowish-purple flesh. He looked up as Nayelle entered, and she saw the fear and despair that she was feeling reflected in his gaze.

"Keeper of the Faith."

"Keeper of the Peace."

His chuckle echoed eerily off the roof of the nave. "I appear to have failed at that particular task."

The Mother stirred. Sunlight from the stained-glass windows dappled her perfect golden hair. "Nonsense, Lord Thane. You have done the exact opposite."

He could not bring himself to look at her. "The Council is dead. My honour guard is slaughtered."

"Of course. And it was only thanks to your quick-thinking that the traitors didn't succeed in bringing their horrific plan to fruition."

"Their … plan?"

"Heresy. They were plotting an assassination attempt. Against me. Imagine if you hadn't been able to stop them. Without my guidance, Keselgraad would have been plunged into anarchy. And I know how much you hate anarchy, Lord Thane."

Her mouth twitched in a way that made Sister Nayelle want to scream. She managed a whimper instead.

The Mother leant forwards and placed a hand on Thane's head. Nayelle had never realised just how long and thin those pale fingers were. How *skeletal*.

"You are a child, Thane," the goddess said softly. "You are all my children. With your petty lusts and aspirations. Your minds are clear and open to me. A stream through which your thoughts wriggle like silver fish. You are as vain and predictable as your progenitors. It is *power* that you desire, Thane. And I will give it to you."

She tapped her middle finger on his scalp, making him flinch.

"Thanks to your destruction of that heretical contraption that you found down below, this city is now doomed to fall. Be it in ten years or twenty. I am content to wait. For I must not be seen as the instigator, do you understand? I must be loved and revered as their goddess, right until the very end, so that those who come after continue in their mindless adulation."

Without question or hesitation, Nayelle thought, and tittered.

"The void of leadership remaining after the despicable betrayal of the Council needs to be filled," the Mother continued with a thin smile. "The people must be fed. *Protected.* Crop yields must be studied. Forests pruned and planted. Tithes paid. Ore mined. A myriad of complicated logistical details that fail to interest me in any way whatsoever. The only things I care about are their *souls.*"

Another almost tender tap on Thane's head.

"I need a loyal, devout administrator. And who better than the man who saved Keselgraad? Rejoice, Lord Thane, for I am offering you what you have always wanted. You will *rule.*"

Nayelle could feel the weight of those words from where she was standing. A physical pressure, rooting her feet to the ground. For Thane, it must have been ten times worse, like being slowly crushed by a colossal boulder. She saw his shoulders shake. Then, with agonising slowness, inch by agonising inch, he raised his face to meet her gaze.

Something flashed in the depths of his granite eyes, there and gone again so quickly that Nayelle almost thought she had imagined it.

A flicker of amethyst.

Thane opened his bruised jaw wide enough to utter a single word.

"No."

The Mother's smile fell. "Ah. Resistance. Something I did not foresee. Interesting." She turned to study the stained-glass window shining brightly above her throne. "The location of Keselgraad was not chosen at random. The chamber beneath the Church is paramount to my existence here. It had to be built to my exact specifications."

She focused once more on Thane. "There are other rooms down there. Places that have been forgotten, hidden behind the walls. Dark, damp places that I reserve for those who have displeased me." She cocked her head, and Devrard appeared at her side.

"The Keeper of the Peace is in need of some time to meditate on his current situation," she said to the warden. "Place him in one of the cells and remove the little finger of his left hand."

Thane tried to move, but her touch was enough to hold him fast.

"Wait for three days, then feed it back to him. If he has not come to his senses by then, you may repeat the process. Let us see how many fingers his defiance is worth to him."

Devrard nodded and took a step forwards. Then shuddered to a halt.

Someone moaned. It took a moment for Nayelle to realise that it was the Mother; the cold arrogance of her expression was changing into another, more primal emotion.

Anger.

"What …" the goddess began. A drop of black liquid escaped one cerulean eye and trickled down her cheek. She touched her hand to her face and stared at the ichor. "What are they *doing*? They are killing my wardens. They are killing my *children*!"

Nayelle could feel it now; a whirling, rushing maelstrom of pain that thrummed up the central aisle of the Church and poured into her head to rebound off the inside of her skull. A single name, echoing over and over again until she thought her mind would burst.

Shala.

The Mother shrieked in a voice far too high-pitched to be confused with that of a human. Her skeletal fingers appeared to grow even longer to resemble claws. They closed over the armrests of the throne, cracking the stone as if it were dry wood.

"Fool," she hissed at Thane. "You were too late. Your thrice-accursed machine has expedited the metamorphosis. There is one among them who has begun to awaken." She hawked and spat. Two white teeth glistened among the sticky saliva and black ichor. "What do they hope to find out there in the Mists? There is nothing left. Nothing at all. Unless …"

She stood suddenly, dislodging a clump of hair from her scalp. Golden curls spiralled down like fallen leaves, revealing bare skin beneath.

"*You*," she snarled, taking a step towards Thane. Her feet clicked on the floor of the Church, and Nayelle could see that four long nails had sprouted from her toes. "You have some of that despicable essence inside you. It has helped you *hide* something from me." The goddess gripped his chin and tipped his head back so that she could hold his gaze. With a sickening pop of gelatinous fluid, her piercing blue eyes burst. Dark, sluggish liquid sloshed into the empty sockets, creating two reflective orbs of pure obsidian.

Show me.

Thane resisted for half a second before screaming as the goddess dug into his soul.

"This cannot be true," she murmured. "I would have

known. I would have seen." She released Thane, who slumped limply to the floor, shuddering.

"Another city. There is … another *city*. How did they manage to keep themselves from me? This changes everything. I can no longer remain complacent. I can no longer simply observe." She jerked her head at Devrard who slung the unresponsive body of Thane over one shoulder.

"Sister Superior," the Mother growled, spinning on her heel to stare at Nayelle, who flinched as those two shadowy pits reduced her thoughts to tatters. "Come."

The goddess stalked back towards the altar, shedding hair at every step, her limbs contorting and bending in unnatural ways. The pale, beautiful woman from the stained-glass window had almost completely gone, replaced by something else. Something far more sinister.

The Mother was forced to bend her head to enter the passageway below the altar. Whatever golden locks remained tumbled from her smooth scalp. Nayelle followed meekly, crunching over a half-dozen broken toenails. By the time she reached the chamber, the goddess was already positioned before the font, her arms plunged into the black liquid. Her face was changing, becoming more angular, her eyes expanding, the sockets lengthening. She glanced over at Nayelle and smiled, revealing two rows of triangular teeth.

"Witness," she ordered.

Ripples were breaking the tranquil surface of the dark substance that filled the font. Nayelle peered over the edge but could see nothing other than the Mother's reflection.

Wait.

Where was her own reflection? Or that of the walls and ceiling of the chamber. It wasn't a mirror image. It was a—

"Sister," the creature lisped. It spoke the word strangely, as if unused to human speech. "Lachrymarum. It has been a long time."

"It has," the goddess agreed.

"Why have you summoned me?"

"The Mists are no longer effective. There is a city. Another city."

Almond eyes studied the Mother from the depths of the font. "I told you they would not work, did I not?"

"You did, Tenebrarum. I should have listened."

"The humans are too resourceful. Too resilient. Too adaptable. Fear and fog will not contain them. They must be subjugated. With tooth and claw. *Culled*, like the beasts they are."

The Mother nodded. "I see that now. There is a risk, Tenebrarum. A risk that they might find the others. That they might find … the portals. A way to spread. I need allies. I need an *army*."

The creature grinned, wide and feral. She raised a multi-segmented arm and said something in a language that Nayelle didn't understand. Deep and guttural.

And behind her, the darkness *moved*.

Shadows appeared within shadows. Nightmarish forms took shape in the darkness, scores upon scores of hunched, greyish figures that cackled and chittered. Bulbous yellow eyes, too many to count, flickered into existence. There were claws, viciously hooked claws, that dangled from long, spindly limbs.

"If you wish for an army, my sister, then you shall have it."

The Mother was studying the host of shrieking monstrosities with something akin to rapt adoration.

"They are … beautiful. What … what are they?"

"They are my children. My followers. My servants. My legion. I do not name them, for they do not need to be named. Although … I have heard a word, whispered by the humans of my world as they cower in fear inside their wooden huts, afraid to venture out into the night. A word they scream as they are torn limb from limb. As everything they know and love is turned to blood and ash."

The creature known as Tenebrarum turned her withering gaze on Nayelle, and she despaired at the single-minded malice that swirled within.

"They call them … greylings."

END OF BOOK ONE

THANK YOU

ALDARIN. JELAÏA. PRAXIS. Reed. The fact that these names and the stories behind them are now known to so many people still blows my mind. Even now, two years after the release of *The Obsidian Eyes of Klief,* I still occasionally pinch myself to check that I'm not stuck in some sort of strange fever dream.

Any author will tell you that writing a book is great, but having people read it is even better. It has been amazing to scroll through all the ratings, reviews, and posts about the War of the Twelve series. Many of you thought it was good. And, much to my surprise, many of you wanted *more.*

That's where things become a bit tricky. I love those characters and that universe, but I don't want to be pigeon-holed into doing the same thing over and over again. One of the best aspects of writing is managing to surprise readers. I have a thousand stories that I want to tell. But they need to be new. They need to be *interesting.*

So, what if instead of going forwards, we go back? Back to how it all began. To another place. Different yet familiar. That is what this new story is all about. Before the Twelve became the indomitable legends that united the scattered human tribes and founded the nine Baronies.

And we are just getting started. I hope you will follow me down this new path. I will not lie, it will be a treacherous one, fraught with danger and loss. Nevertheless, these little beings must find the courage to follow it to its final destination, so that they may become the Twelve.

One last thing before you go. If this book has brought you joy, please consider leaving a rating or review on the platform of your choice. The more reviews a book has, the more Amazon and other retail sites make it visible to potential readers, so it really is the best way to help this story reach other fantasy lovers.

Until we meet again.

May the Twelve be with you.

Alex Robins

THE RUINED GODS TRILOGY

At the heart of every legend lies a truth. Twisted and reshaped by the currents of time.

For twenty years, strategos Dexios has led the phalanx of Thena against its enemies, pulled from one battleground to another in a relentless cycle of war and bloodshed. Now, finally, he has found the courage to leave that life behind. To relinquish his officer's sword and return to the verdant slopes of his vineyard with his wife and son.

Peace, however, is fragile and capricious. When Thena's northern allies bring word of an enormous tauran horde gathering on their borders, Dexios has no choice but to answer the call to arms one last time.

As humans and tauros collide, another evil wakes. Whispered rumours of a clawed creature that stalks the shadowy streets. Of violent murders committed in the name of deities long thought vanquished. To speak their names is heresy.

They are the Exiled.

The Banished.

The Ruined Gods.

The Complete Series is now available on Digital, Paperback, and free on Kindle Unlimited

* 9 7 8 2 9 5 8 8 4 5 0 3 2 *